# MONA LISA
# OVERDRIVE

# MONA LISA
# OVERDRIVE

## WILLIAM GIBSON

BANTAM BOOKS

TORONTO · NEW YORK · LONDON · SYDNEY · AUCKLAND

MONA LISA OVERDRIVE
*A Bantam Spectra Book / November 1988*

Library of Congress Cataloging-in-Publication Data

Gibson, William, 1914–
  Mona Lisa overdrive.

  I. Title.
PS3513.I2824M58  1988     813'.54     88-14494
ISBN 0-553-05250-0

*Published simultaneously in the United States and Canada*

*Bantam Books are published by Bantam Books, a division of Bantam Doubleday*
*Dell Publishing Group, Inc. Its trademark, consisting of the words "Bantam*
*Books" and the portrayal of a rooster, is Registered in U.S. Patent and*
*Trademark Office and in other countries. Marca Registrada. Bantam Books,*
*666 Fifth Avenue, New York, New York 10103.*

PRINTED IN THE UNITED STATES OF AMERICA

FG     0 9 8 7 6 5 4 3 2 1

To my sister,
Fran Gibson,
with amazement and love . . .

# ONE

# THE SMOKE

The ghost was her father's parting gift, presented by a black-clad secretary in a departure lounge at Narita.

For the first two hours of the flight to London it lay forgotten in her purse, a smooth dark oblong, one side impressed with the ubiquitous Maas-Neotek logo, the other gently curved to fit the user's palm.

She sat up very straight in her seat in the first-class cabin, her features composed in a small cold mask modeled after her dead mother's most characteristic expression. The surrounding seats were empty; her father had purchased the space. She refused the meal the nervous steward offered. The vacant seats frightened him, evidence of her father's wealth and power. The man hesitated, then bowed and withdrew. Very briefly, she allowed the mask her mother's smile.

Ghosts, she thought later, somewhere over Germany, staring at the upholstery of the seat beside her. How well her father treated his ghosts.

There were ghosts beyond the window, too, ghosts in the stratosphere of Europe's winter, partial images that began to form if she let her eyes drift out of focus. Her mother in Ueno Park, face fragile in September sunlight. "The cranes, Kumi! Look at the cranes!" And Kumiko looked across Shinobazu Pond and saw nothing, no cranes at all, only a few hopping black dots that surely were crows. The water was smooth as silk, the color of lead, and pale holograms flickered indistinctly above a distant line of archery stalls. But Kumiko would see the cranes later, many times, in dreams; they were origami, angular things folded from sheets of neon, bright stiff birds sailing the moonscape of her mother's madness. . . .

Remembering her father, the black robe open across a tattooed storm of dragons, slumped behind the vast ebony field of his desk, his eyes flat and bright, like the eyes of a painted doll. "Your mother is dead. Do you understand?" And all around her the planes of shadow in his study, the angular darkness. His hand coming forward, into the lamp's circle of light, unsteadily, to point at her, the robe's cuff sliding back to reveal a golden Rolex and more dragons, their manes swirling into waves, pricked out strong and dark around his wrist, pointing. Pointing at her. "Do you understand?" She hadn't answered, but had run instead, down to a secret place she knew, the warren of the smallest of the cleaning machines. They ticked around her all night, scanning her every few minutes with pink bursts of laser light, until her father came to find her, and, smelling of whiskey and Dunhill cigarettes, carried her to her room on the apartment's third floor.

Remembering the weeks that followed, numb days spent most often in the black-suited company of one secretary or another, cautious men with automatic smiles and tightly furled umbrellas. One of these, the youngest and least cautious, had treated her, on a crowded Ginza sidewalk, in the shadow of the Hattori clock, to an impromptu kendo demonstration, weaving expertly between startled shop girls and wide-eyed tourists, the black umbrella blurring harmlessly through the art's formal, ancient arcs. And Kumiko had smiled then, her own smile, breaking the funeral mask, and for this her guilt was driven instantly, more deeply and still more sharply, into that place in her heart where she knew her shame and her unworthiness. But most often the secretaries took her shopping, through one vast Ginza department store after another, and in and out of dozens of Shinjuku boutiques recommended by a blue plastic Michelin guide that spoke a stuffy tourist's Japanese. She purchased only very ugly things, ugly and very expensive things, and the secretaries marched stolidly beside her, the glossy bags in their hard hands. Each afternoon, returning to her father's apartment, the bags were deposited neatly in her bedroom, where they remained, un-opened and untouched, until the maids removed them.

And in the seventh week, on the eve of her thirteenth birthday, it was arranged that Kumiko would go to London.

"You will be a guest in the house of my *kobun*," her father said.

"But I do not wish to go," she said, and showed him her mother's smile.

"You must," he said, and turned away. "There are difficul-ties," he said to the shadowed study. "You will be in no danger, in London."

"And when shall I return?"

But her father didn't answer. She bowed and left his study, still wearing her mother's smile.

The ghost woke to Kumiko's touch as they began their descent into Heathrow. The fifty-first generation of Maas-Neotek biochips conjured up an indistinct figure on the seat beside her, a boy out of some faded hunting print, legs crossed casually in tan breeches and riding boots. "Hullo," the ghost said.

Kumiko blinked, opened her hand. The boy flickered and was gone. She looked down at the smooth little unit in her palm and slowly closed her fingers.

" 'Lo again," he said. "Name's Colin. Yours?"

She stared. His eyes were bright green smoke, his high fore-head pale and smooth under an unruly dark forelock. She could see the seats across the aisle through the glint of his teeth. "If it's a bit too spectral for you," he said, with a grin, "we can up the rez. . . ." And he was there for an instant, uncomfortably sharp and real, the nap on the lapels of his dark coat vibrating with hallucinatory clarity. "Runs the battery down, though," he said, and faded to his prior state. "Didn't get your name." The grin again.

"You aren't real," she said sternly.

He shrugged. "Needn't speak out loud, miss. Fellow passen-gers might think you a bit odd, if you take my meaning. Subvocal's the way. I pick it all up through the skin. . . ." He uncrossed his legs and stretched, hands clasped behind his head. "Seatbelt, miss. I needn't buckle up myself, of course, being, as you've pointed out, unreal."

Kumiko frowned and tossed the unit into the ghost's lap. He vanished. She fastened her seatbelt, glanced at the thing, hesitated, then picked it up again.

"First time in London, then?" he asked, swirling in from the periphery of her vision. She nodded in spite of herself. "You don't mind flying? Doesn't frighten you?"

She shook her head, feeling ridiculous.

"Never mind," the ghost said. "I'll look out for you. Heathrow in three minutes. Someone meeting you off the plane?"

"My father's business associate," she said in Japanese.

The ghost grinned. "Then you'll be in good hands, I'm sure." He winked. "Wouldn't think I'm a linguist to look at me, would you?"

Kumiko closed her eyes and the ghost began to whisper to her, something about the archaeology of Heathrow, about the Neolithic and the Iron ages, pottery and tools. . . .

"Miss Yanaka? Kumiko Yanaka?" The Englishman towered above her, his gaijin bulk draped in elephantine folds of dark wool. Small dark eyes regarded her blandly through steel-rimmed glasses. His nose seemed to have been crushed nearly flat and never reset. His hair, what there was of it, had been shaved back to a gray stubble, and his black knit gloves were frayed and fingerless.

"My name, you see," he said, as though this would immediately reassure her, "is Petal."

Petal called the city Smoke.

Kumiko shivered on chill red leather; through the ancient Jaguar's window she watched the snow spinning down to melt on the road Petal called M4. The late afternoon sky was colorless. He drove silently, efficiently, his lips pursed as though he were about to whistle. The traffic, to Tokyo eyes, was absurdly light. They accelerated past an unmanned Eurotrans freight vehicle, its blunt prow studded with sensors and banks of headlights. In spite of the Jaguar's speed, Kumiko felt as if somehow she were standing still; London's particles began to accrete around her. Walls of wet brick, arches of concrete, black-painted ironwork standing up in spears.

As she watched, the city began to define itself. Off the M4, while the Jaguar waited at intersections, she could glimpse faces through the snow, flushed gaijin faces above dark clothing, chins tucked down into scarves, women's bootheels ticking through silver puddles. The rows of shops and houses reminded her of the gorgeously detailed accessories she'd seen displayed around a toy locomotive in the Osaka gallery of a dealer in European antiques.

This was nothing like Tokyo, where the past, all that remained of it, was nurtured with a nervous care. History there had become a quantity, a rare thing, parceled out by government and preserved by law and corporate funding. Here it seemed the very fabric of things, as if the city were a single growth of stone and brick, uncounted strata of message and meaning, age upon age, generated over the centuries to the dictates of some now-all-but-unreadable DNA of commerce and empire.

"Regret Swain couldn't come out to meet you himself," the man called Petal said. Kumiko had less trouble with his accent than with his manner of structuring sentences; she initially mistook the apology for a command. She considered accessing the ghost, then rejected the idea.

"Swain," she ventured. "Mr. Swain is my host?"

Petal's eyes found her in the mirror. "Roger Swain. Your father didn't tell you?"

"No."

"Ah." He nodded. "Mr. Kanaka's conscious of security in these matters, it stands to reason. . . . Man of his stature, et cetera . . ." He sighed loudly. "Sorry about the heater. Garage was supposed to have that taken care of. . . ."

"Are you one of Mr. Swain's secretaries?" Addressing the stubbled rolls of flesh above the collar of the thick dark coat.

"His secretary?" He seemed to consider the matter. "No," he ventured finally, "I'm not that." He swung them through a roundabout, past gleaming metallic awnings and the evening surge of pedestrians. "Have you eaten, then? Did they feed you on the flight?"

"I wasn't hungry." Conscious of her mother's mask.

"Well, Swain'll have something for you. Eats a lot of Jap food, Swain." He made a strange little ticking sound with his tongue. He glanced back at her.

She looked past him, seeing the kiss of snowflakes, the obliterating sweep of the wipers.

* * *

Swain's Notting Hill residence consisted of three intercon-
nected Victorian townhouses situated somewhere in a snowy profu-
sion of squares, crescents, and mews. Petal, with two of Kumiko's
suitcases in either hand, explained to her that number 17 was the
front entrance for numbers 16 and 18 as well. "No use knocking
there," he said, gesturing clumsily with the heavy cases in his hand,
indicating the glossy red paint and polished brass fittings of 16's
door. "Nothing behind it but twenty inches of ferroconcrete."

She looked down the crescent, nearly identical facades receding
along its shallow curve. The snow fell more thickly now, and the
featureless sky was lit with a salmon glow of sodium lamps. The
street was deserted, the snow fresh and unmarked. There was an
alien edge to the cold air, a faint, pervasive hint of burning, of
archaic fuels. Petal's shoes left large, neatly defined prints. They
were black suede oxfords with narrow toes and extremely thick
corrugated soles of scarlet plastic. She followed in his tracks, beginning to shiver, up the gray steps to number 17.

"It's me then," he said to the black-painted door, "innit."
Then he sighed, set all four suitcases down in the snow, removed
the fingerless glove from his right hand, and pressed his palm
against a circle of bright steel set flush with one of the door panels.
Kumiko thought she heard a faint whine, a gnat sound that rose in
pitch until it vanished, and then the door vibrated with the muffled
impact of magnetic bolts as they withdrew.

"You called it Smoke," she said, as he reached for the brass
knob, "the city. . . ."

He paused. "The Smoke," he said, "yes," and opened the door
into warmth and light, "that's an old expression, sort of nickname."
He picked up her bags and padded into a blue-carpeted foyer
paneled in white-painted wood. She followed him, the door closing
itself behind her, its bolts thumping back into place. A mahogony-
framed print hung above the white wainscoting, horses in a field,
crisp little figures in red coats. *Colin the chip-ghost should live
there,* she thought. Petal had put her bags down again. Flakes of
compacted snow lay on the blue carpet. Now he opened another
door, exposing a gilt steel cage. He drew the bars aside with a clank.
She stared into the cage, baffled. "The lift," he said. "No space for
your things. I'll make a second trip."

For all its apparent age, it rose smoothly enough when Petal
touched a white porcelain button with a blunt forefinger. Kumiko

was forced to stand very close to him then; he smelled of damp wool and some floral shaving preparation.

"We've put you up top," he said, leading her along a narrow corridor, "because we thought you might appreciate the quiet." He opened a door and gestured her in. "Hope it'll do. . . ." He removed his glasses and polished them energetically with a crumpled tissue. "I'll get your bags."

When he had gone, Kumiko walked slowly around the massive black marble tub that dominated the center of the low, crowded room. The walls, angled sharply toward the ceiling, were faced with mottled gold mirror. A pair of small dormer windows flanked the largest bed she'd ever seen. Above the bed, the mirror was inset with small adjustable lights, like the reading lamps in an airliner. She stood beside the tub to touch the arched neck of a gold-plated swan that served as a spout. Its spread wings were tap handles. The air in the room was warm and still, and for an instant the presence of her mother seemed to fill it, an aching fog.

Petal cleared his throat in the doorway. "Well then," he said, bustling in with her luggage, "everything in order? Feeling hungry yet? No? Leave you to settle in . . ." He arranged her bags beside the bed. "If you should feel like eating, just ring." He indicated an ornate antique telephone with scrolled brass mouth- and earpieces and a turned ivory handle. "Just pick it up, you needn't dial. Breakfast's when you want it. Ask someone, they'll show you where. You can meet Swain then. . . ."

The sense of her mother had vanished with his return. She tried to feel it again, when he said goodnight and closed the door, but it was gone.

She remained a long time beside the tub, stroking the smooth metal of the swan's cool neck.

# TWO

# KID AFRIKA

Kid Afrika came cruising into Dog Solitude on the last day in November, his vintage Dodge chauffeured by a white girl named Cherry Chesterfield.

Slick Henry and Little Bird were breaking down the buzzsaw that formed the Judge's left hand when Kid's Dodge came into view, its patched apron bag throwing up brown fantails of the rusty water that pooled on the Solitude's uneven plain of compacted steel.

Little Bird saw it first. He had sharp eyes, Little Bird, and a 10X monocular that dangled on his chest amid the bones of assorted animals and antique bottleneck cartridge brass. Slick looked up from the hydraulic wrist to see Little Bird straighten up to his full two meters and aim the monocular out through the grid of unglazed steel that formed most of Factory's south wall. Little Bird was very thin, almost skeletal, and the lacquered wings of brown hair that had earned him the name stood out sharp against the pale sky. He kept the back and sides shaved high, well above his ears; with the wings and the aerodynamic ducktail, he looked as though he were wearing a headless brown gull.

"Whoa," said Little Bird, "motherfuck."

"What?" It was hard to get Little Bird to concentrate, and the job needed a second set of hands.

"It's that nigger."

Slick stood up and wiped his hands down the thighs of his jeans while Little Bird fumbled the green Mech-5 microsoft from the socket behind his ear—instantly forgetting the eight-point servo-calibration procedure needed to unfuck the Judge's buzzsaw. "Who's driving?" Afrika never drove himself if he could help it.

"Can't make out." Little Bird let the monocular clatter back into the curtain of bones and brass.

Slick joined him at the window to watch the Dodge's progress. Kid Afrika periodically touched up the hover's matte-black paint-job with judicious applications from an aerosol can, the somber effect offset by the row of chrome-plated skulls welded to the massive front bumper. At one time the hollow steel skulls had boasted red Christmas bulbs for eyes; maybe the Kid was losing his concern with image.

As the hover slewed up to Factory, Slick heard Little Bird shuffle back into the shadows, his heavy boots scraping through dust and fine bright spirals of metal shavings.

Slick watched past a last dusty dagger of window glass as the hover settled into its apron bags in front of Factory, groaning and venting steam.

Something rattled in the dark behind him and he knew that Little Bird was behind the old parts rack, fiddling the homemade silencer onto the Chinese rimfire they used for rabbits.

"Bird," Slick said, tossing his wrench down on the tarp, "I know you're an ignorant little redneck Jersey asshole, but do you have to keep goddamn *reminding* me of it?"

"Don't like that nigger," Little Bird said, from behind the rack.

"Yeah, and if that nigger'd bother noticing, he wouldn't like you either. Knew you were back here with that gun, he'd shove it down your throat sideways."

No response from Little Bird. He'd grown up in white Jersey stringtowns where nobody knew shit about anything and hated anybody who did.

"And I'd help him, too." Slick yanked up the zip on his old brown jacket and went out to Kid Afrika's hover.

The dusty window on the driver's side hissed down, revealing a pale face dominated by an enormous pair of amber-tinted goggles.

Slick's boots crunched on ancient cans rusted thin as old leaves. The driver tugged the goggles down and squinted at him; female, but now the amber goggles hung around her neck, concealing her mouth and chin. The Kid would be on the far side, a good thing in the unlikely event Little Bird started shooting.

"Go on around," the girl said.

Slick walked around the hover, past the chrome skulls, hearing Kid Afrika's window come down with that same demonstrative little sound.

"Slick Henry," the Kid said, his breath puffing white as it hit the air of the Solitude, "hello."

Slick looked down at the long brown face. Kid Afrika had big hazel eyes, slitted like a cat's, a pencil-thin mustache, and skin with the sheen of buffed leather.

"Hey, Kid." Slick smelled some kind of incense from inside the hover. "How y' doin'?"

"Well," the Kid said, narrowing his eyes, "recall you sayin' once, if I ever needed a favor . . ."

"Right," Slick said, feeling a first twinge of apprehension. Kid Afrika had saved his ass once, in Atlantic City; talked some irate brothers out of dropping him off this balcony on the forty-third floor of a burned-out highstack. "Somebody wanna throw you off a tall building?"

"Slick," the Kid said, "I wanna introduce you to somebody."

"Then we'll be even?"

"Slick Henry, this fine-looking girl here, this is Miss Cherry Chesterfield of Cleveland, Ohio." Slick bent down and looked at the driver. Blond shockhead, paintstick around her eyes. "Cherry, this is my close personal friend Mr. Slick Henry. When he was young and bad he rode with the Deacon Blues. Now he's old and bad, he holes up out here and pursues his *art*, understand. A *talented* man, understand."

"He's the one builds the robots," the girl said, around a wad of gum, "you said."

"The very one," the Kid said, opening his door. "You wait for us here, Cherry honey." The Kid, draped in a mink coat that brushed the immaculate tips of his yellow ostrich boots, stepped out onto the Solitude, and Slick caught a glimpse of something in the back of the hover, eyeblink ambulance flash of bandages and surgical tubing. . . .

"Hey, Kid," he said, "what you got back there?" The Kid's

jeweled hand came up, gesturing Slick back as the hover's door clanked shut and Cherry Chesterfield hit the window buttons.

"We have to talk about that, Slick."

"I don't think it's much to ask," Kid Afrika said, leaning back against a bare metal workbench, wrapped in his mink. "Cherry has a med-tech's ticket and she knows she'll get paid. Nice girl, Slick." He winked.

"Kid . . ."

Kid Afrika had this guy in the back of the hover who was like dead, coma or something, had him hooked up to pumps and bags and tubes and some kind of simstim rig, all of it bolted to an old alloy ambulance stretcher, batteries and everything.

"What's this?" Cherry, who'd followed them in after the Kid had taken Slick back out to show him the guy in the back of the hover, was peering dubiously up at the towering Judge, most of him anyway; the arm with the buzzsaw was where they'd left it, on the floor on the greasy tarp. *If she has a med-tech's ticket,* Slick thought, *the med-tech probably hasn't noticed it's missing yet.* She was wearing at least four leather jackets, all of them several sizes too big.

"Slick's art, like I told you."

"That guy's dying. He smells like piss."

"Catheter came loose," Cherry said. "What's this thing supposed to *do,* anyway?"

"We can't keep him here, Kid, he'll stiff. You wanna kill him, go stuff him down a hole on the Solitude."

"The man's not dying," Kid Afrika said. "He's not hurt, he's not sick. . . ."

"Then what the fuck's wrong with him?"

"He's *under,* baby. He's on a *long trip.* He needs *peace and quiet.*"

Slick looked from the Kid to the Judge, then back to the Kid. He wanted to be working on that arm. Kid said he wanted Slick to keep the guy for two weeks, maybe three; he'd leave Cherry there to take care of him.

"I can't figure it. This guy, he's a friend of yours?"

Kid Afrika shrugged inside his mink.

"So why don't you keep him at your place?"

"Not so quiet. Not peaceful enough."

"Kid," Slick said, "I owe you one, but nothing this weird. Anyway, I gotta work, and anyway, it's too weird. And there's Gentry, too. He's gone to Boston now; be back tomorrow night and he wouldn't like it. You know how he's funny about people. . . . It's mostly his *place,* too, how it is. . . ."

"They had you over the railing, man," Kid Afrika said sadly. "You remember?"

"Hey, I remember, I . . ."

"You don't remember too good," the Kid said. "Okay, Cherry. Let's go. Don't wanna cross Dog Solitude at night." He pushed off from the steel bench.

"Kid, look . . ."

"Forget it. I didn't know your fucking name, that time in Atlantic City, just figured I didn't wanna see the white boy all over the street, y'know? So I didn't know your name then, I guess I don't know it now."

"Kid . . ."

"Yeah?"

"Okay. He stays. Two weeks max. You gimme your word, you'll come back and get him? And you gotta help me square it with Gentry."

"What's he need?"

"Drugs."

Little Bird reappeared as the Kid's Dodge wallowed away across the Solitude. He came edging out from behind an outcropping of compacted cars, rusty pallets of crumpled steel that still showed patches of bright enamel.

Slick watched him from a window high up in Factory. The squares of the steel frame had been fitted with sections of scavenged plastic, each one a different shade and thickness, so that when Slick tilted his head to one side, he saw Little Bird through a pane of hot-pink Lucite.

"Who lives here?" Cherry asked, from the room behind him.

"Me," Slick said, "Little Bird, Gentry . . ."

"In this room, I mean."

He turned and saw her there beside the stretcher and its attendant machines. "You do," he said.

"It's your place?" She was staring at the drawings taped to the walls, his original conceptions of the Judge and his Investigators, the Corpsegrinder and the Witch.

"Don't worry about it."

"Better you don't get any ideas," she said.

He looked at her. She had a large red sore at the corner of her mouth. Her bleached hair stood out like a static display. "Like I said, don't worry about it."

"Kid said you got electricity."

"Yeah."

"Better get him hooked up," she said, turning to the stretcher. "He doesn't draw much, but the batteries'll be getting low."

He crossed the room to look down at the wasted face. "You better tell me something," he said. He didn't like the tubes. One of them went into a nostril and the idea made him want to gag. "Who is this guy and what exactly the fuck is Kid Afrika doing to him?"

"He's not," she said, tapping a readout into view on a biomonitor panel lashed to the foot of the stretcher with silver tape. "REM's still up, like he dreams all the time . . ." The man on the stretcher was strapped down in a brand-new blue sleeping bag. "What it is, he—whoever—he's paying Kid for this."

There was a trode-net plastered across the guy's forehead; a single black cable was lashed along the edge of the stretcher. Slick followed it up to the fat gray package that seemed to dominate the gear mounted on the superstructure. Simstim? Didn't look like it. Some kind of cyberspace rig? Gentry knew a lot about cyberspace, or anyway he talked about it, but Slick couldn't remember anything about getting unconscious and just staying jacked in. . . . People jacked in so they could hustle. Put the trodes on and they were out there, all the data in the world stacked up like one big neon city, so you could cruise around and have a kind of grip on it, visually anyway, because if you didn't, it was too complicated, trying to find your way to a particular piece of data you needed. Iconics, Gentry called that.

"He paying the Kid?"

"Yeah," she said.

"What for?"

"Keep him that way. Hide him out, too."

"Who from?"

"Don't know. Didn't say."

In the silence that followed, he could hear the steady rasp of the man's breath.

# THREE

# MALIBU

There was a smell in the house; it had always been there.

It belonged to time and the salt air and the entropic nature of expensive houses built too close to the sea. Perhaps it was also peculiar to places briefly but frequently uninhabited, houses opened and closed as their restless residents arrived and departed. She imagined the rooms empty, flecks of corrosion blossoming silently on chrome, pale molds taking hold in obscure corners. The architects, as if in recognition of eternal processes, had encouraged a degree of rust; massive steel railings along the deck had been eaten wrist-thin by years of spray.

The house crouched, like its neighbors, on fragments of ruined foundations, and her walks along the beach sometimes involved attempts at archaeological fantasy. She tried to imagine a past for the place, other houses, other voices. She was accompanied, on these walks, by an armed remote, a tiny Dornier helicopter that rose from its unseen rooftop nest when she stepped down from the deck. It could hover almost silently, and was programmed to avoid her line of sight. There was something wistful about the way it followed her, as though it were an expensive but unappreciated Christmas gift.

She knew that Hilton Swift was watching through the Dornier's cameras. Little that occurred in the beach house escaped Sense/Net; her solitude, the week alone she'd demanded, was under constant surveillance.

Her years in the profession had conveyed a singular immunity to observation.

At night she sometimes lit the floods mounted beneath the deck, illuminating the hieroglyphic antics of huge gray sandfleas. The deck itself she left in darkness, and the sunken living room behind her. She sat on a chair of plain white plastic, watching the Brownian dance of the fleas. In the glare of the floods, they cast minute, barely visible shadows, fleeting cusps against the sand.

The sound of the sea wrapped her in its movement. Late at night, as she slept in the smaller of the two guest bedrooms, it worked its way into her dreams. But never into the stranger's invading memories.

The choice of bedrooms was instinctive. The master bedroom was mined with the triggers of old pain.

The doctors at the clinic had used chemical pliers to pry the addiction away from receptor sites in her brain.

She cooked for herself in the white kitchen, thawing bread in the microwave, dumping packets of dehydrated Swiss soup into spotless steel pans, edging dully into the nameless but increasingly familiar space from which she'd been so subtly insulated by the designer's dust.

"It's called life," she said to the white counter. And what would Sense/Net's in-house psychs make of that, she wondered, if some hidden microphone caught it and carried it to them? She stirred the soup with a slender stainless whisk, watching steam rise. It helped to do things, she thought, just to do things yourself; at the clinic, they'd insisted she make her own bed. Now she spooned out her own bowl of soup, frowning, remembering the clinic.

She'd checked herself out a week into the treatment. The medics protested. The detoxification had gone beautifully, they said, but the therapy hadn't begun. They pointed out the rate of relapse among clients who failed to complete the program. They explained that her insurance was invalid if she terminated her treatment. Sense/Net would pay, she told them, unless they preferred she pay them herself. She produced her platinum MitsuBank chip.

Her Lear arrived an hour later; she told it to take her to LAX, ordered a car to meet her there, and canceled all incoming calls.

"I'm sorry, Angela," the jet said, banking over Montego Bay seconds after they'd taken off, "but I have Hilton Swift on executive override."

"Angie," Swift said, "you know I'm behind you all the way. You know that, Angie."

She turned to stare at the black oval of the speaker. It was centered in smooth gray plastic, and she imagined him crouching back there, his long runner's legs folded painfully, grotesquely, behind the Lear's bulkhead.

"I know that, Hilton," she said. "It's nice of you to phone."

"You're going to L.A., Angie."

"Yes. That's what I told the plane."

"To Malibu."

"That's right."

"Piper Hill is on her way to the airport."

"Thank you, Hilton, but I don't want Piper there. I don't want anybody. I want a car."

"There's no one at the house, Angie."

"Good. That's what I want, Hilton. No one at the house. The house, empty."

"Are you certain that's a good idea?"

"It's the best idea I've had in a long time, Hilton."

There was a pause. "They said it went really well, Angie, the treatment. But they wanted you to stay."

"I need a week," she said. "One week. Seven days. Alone."

After her third night in the house, she woke at dawn, made coffee, dressed. Condensation stippled the broad window facing the deck. Sleep had been simply that; if dreams had come, she couldn't recall them. But there was something—a quickening, almost a giddiness. She stood in the kitchen, feeling the cold of the ceramic floor through thick white sweatsocks, both hands around the warm cup.

Something there. She extended her arms, raising the coffee like a chalice, the gesture at once instinctive and ironic.

It had been three years since the loa had ridden her, three years since they had touched her at all. But now?

Legba? One of the others?

The sense of a presence receded abruptly. She put the cup down on the counter too quickly, coffee slopping over her hand, and ran to find shoes and a coat. Green rubber boots from the beach closet, and a heavy blue mountain jacket she didn't remember, too large to have been Bobby's. She hurried out of the house, down the stairs, ignoring the hum of the toy Dornier's prop as it lifted off behind her like a patient dragonfly. She glanced north, along the jumble of beach houses, the confusion of rooflines reminding her of a Rio barrio, then turned south, toward the Colony.

The one who came was named Mamman Brigitte, or Grande Brigitte, and while some think her the wife of Baron Samedi, others name her "most ancient of the dead."

The dream architecture of the Colony rose to Angie's left, a riot of form and ego. Frail-looking neon-embedded replicas of the Watts Towers lifted beside neo-Brutalist bunkers faced with bronze bas-reliefs.

Walls of mirror, as she passed, reflected morning banks of Pacific cloud.

There had been times, during the past three years, when she had felt as though she were about to cross, or recross, a line, a subtle border of faith, to find that her time with the loa had been a dream, or, at most, that they were contagious knots of cultural resonance remaining from the weeks she'd spent in Beauvoir's New Jersey oumphor. To see with other eyes: no gods, no Horsemen.

She walked on, comforted by the surf, by the one perpetual moment of beach-time, the now-and-always of it.

Her father was dead, seven years dead, and the record he'd kept of his life had told her little enough. That he'd served someone or something, that his reward had been knowledge, and that she had been his sacrifice.

Sometimes she felt as though she'd had three lives, each walled away from the others by something she couldn't name, and no hope of wholeness, ever.

There were the child's memories of the Maas arcology, carved into the summit of an Arizona mesa, where she'd hugged a sandstone balustrade, face into the wind, and felt as though the whole hollowed tableland was her ship, that she could steer out into those sunset colors beyond the mountains. Later, she'd flown away from there, her fear a hard thing in her throat. She could no longer recall her last glimpse of her father's face. Though it must have been on the microlight deck, the other planes tethered against the wind, a row of rainbow moths. The first life ended, that night; her father's life had ended too.

Her second life had been a short one, fast and very strange. A man called Turner had taken her away, out of Arizona, and had left her with Bobby and Beauvoir and the others. She remembered little about Turner, only that he was tall, with hard muscles and a hunted look. He'd taken her to New York. Then Beauvoir had taken her, along with Bobby, to New Jersey. There, on the fifty-third level of a mincome structure, Beauvoir had taught her about her dreams. The dreams are real, he'd said, his brown face shining with sweat. He taught her the names of the ones she'd seen in dreams. He taught her that all dreams reach down to a common sea, and he showed her the way in which hers were different and the same. *You alone sail the old sea and the new*, he said.

She was ridden by gods, in New Jersey.

She learned to abandon herself to the Horsemen. She saw the loa Linglessou enter Beauvoir in the oumphor, saw his feet scatter the diagrams outlined in white flour. She knew the gods, in New Jersey, and love.

The loa had guided her, when she'd set out with Bobby to build her third, her current life. They were well matched, Angie and Bobby, born out of vacuums, Angie from the clean blank kingdom of Maas Biolabs and Bobby from the boredom of Barrytown. . . .

Grande Brigitte touched her, without warning; she stumbled, almost fell to her knees in the surf, as the sound of the sea was sucked away into the twilit landscape that opened in front of her. The whitewashed cemetery walls, the gravestones, the willows. The candles.

Beneath the oldest willow, a multitude of candles, the twisted roots pale with wax.

*Child, know me.*

And Angie felt her there, all at once, and knew her for what she was, Mamman Brigitte, Mademoiselle Brigitte, eldest of the dead.

*I have no cult, child, no special altar.*

She found herself walking forward, into candleglow, a buzzing in her ears, as though the willow hid a vast hive of bees.

*My blood is vengeance.*

Angie remembered Bermuda, night, a hurricane; she and Bobby had ventured out into the eye. Grande Brigitte was like that. The silence, the sense of pressure, of unthinkable forces held momentarily in check. There was nothing to be seen, beneath the willow. Only the candles.

"The loa . . . I can't call them. I felt something . . . I came looking. . . ."

*You are summoned to my* reposoir. *Hear me. Your father drew* vévés *in your head: he drew them in a flesh that was not flesh. You were consecrated to Ezili Freda. Legba led you into the world to serve his own ends. But you were sent poison, child, a* coup-poudre . . .

Her nose began to bleed. "Poison?"

*Your father's* vévés *are altered, partially erased, redrawn. Though you have ceased to poison yourself, still the Horsemen cannot reach you. I am of a different order.*

There was a terrible pain in her head, blood pounding in her temples. . . . "Please . . ."

*Hear me. You have enemies. They plot against you. Much is at stake, in this. Fear poison, child!*

She looked down at her hands. The blood was bright and real. The buzzing sound grew louder. Perhaps it was in her head. "Please! Help me! Explain . . ."

*You cannot remain here. It is death.*

And Angie fell to her knees in the sand, the sound of the surf crashing around her, dazzled by the sun. The Dornier was hovering nervously in front of her, two meters away. The pain receded instantly. She wiped her bloodied hands on the sleeves of the blue jacket. The remote's cluster of cameras whirred and rotated.

"It's all right," she managed. "A nosebleed. It's only a nosebleed. . . ." The Dornier darted forward, then back. "I'm going back to the house now. I'm fine." It rose smoothly out of sight.

Angie hugged herself, shaking. *No, don't let them see. They'll know something happened, but not what.* She forced herself to her feet, turned, began to trudge back up the beach, the way she'd come. As she walked, she searched the mountain jacket's pockets for a tissue, anything, something to wipe the blood from her face.

When her fingers found the corners of the flat little packet, she knew instantly what it was. She halted, shivering. The drug. It wasn't possible. Yes, it was. But who? She turned and stared at the Dornier until it slid away.

The packet. Enough for a month.

*Coup-poudre.*

Fear poison, child.

# FOUR

# SQUAT

Mona dreamed she was dancing the cage back in some Cleveland juke, naked in a column of hot blue light, where the faces thrusting up for her through the veil of smoke had blue light snagged in the whites of their eyes. They wore the expression men always wore when they watched you dance, staring real hard but locked up inside themselves at the same time, so their eyes told you nothing at all and their faces, in spite of the sweat, might have been carved from something that only looked like flesh.

Not that she cared how they looked, when she was in the cage, high and hot and on the beat, three songs into the set and the wiz just starting to peak, new strength in her legs sending her up on the balls of her feet . . .

One of them grabbed her ankle.

She tried to scream, only it wouldn't come, not at first, and when it did it was like something ripped down inside her, hurt her, and the blue light shredded, but the hand, the hand was still there, around her ankle. She came up off the bed like a pop-up toy, fighting the dark, clawing hair away from her eyes.

"Whatsa matter, babe?"

He put his other hand against her forehead and shoved her back, down into the pillow's hot depression.

"Dream . . ." The hand was still there and it made her want to scream. "You got a cigarette, Eddy?" The hand went away, click and flare of the lighter, the planes of his face jumping out at her as he lit one, handed it to her. She sat up quickly, drew her knees up under her chin with the army blanket over them like a tent, because she didn't feel like anybody touching her then at all.

The scavenged plastic chair's broken leg made a warning sound as he leaned back and lit his own cigarette. *Break*, she thought, *pitch him on his ass so he gets to hit me a few times.* At least it was dark, so she didn't have to look at the squat. Worst thing was waking up with a bad head, too sick to move, when she'd come in crashing and forgotten to retape the black plastic, hard sun to show her all the little details and heat the air so the flies could get going.

Nobody ever grabbed her, back in Cleveland; anybody numb enough to reach through that field was already too drunk to move, maybe to breathe. The tricks never grabbed her either, not unless they'd squared it with Eddy, paid extra, and that was just pretend.

Whichever way they wanted it, it got to be a kind of ritual, so it seemed to happen in a place outside your life. And she'd gotten into watching them, when they lost it. That was the interesting part, because they really did lose it, they were totally helpless, maybe just for a split second, but it was like they weren't even there.

"Eddy, I'm gonna go crazy, I gotta sleep here anymore."

He'd hit her before, for less, so she put her face down, against her knees and the blanket, and waited.

"Sure," he said, "you wanna go back to the catfish farm? Wanna go back to Cleveland?"

"I just can't make this anymore. . . ."

"Tomorrow."

"Tomorrow what?"

"That soon enough for you? Tomorrow night, private fucking jet? Straight up to New York? *Then* you gonna quit giving me this shit?"

"Please, baby," and she reached out for him, "we can take the train. . . ."

He slapped her hand away. "You got shit for brains."

If she complained any more, anything about the squat, any-thing that implied he wasn't making it, that all his big deals added up to nothing, he'd start, she knew he'd start. Like the time she'd screamed about the bugs, the roaches they called palmetto bugs, but it was because the goddamn things were mutants, half of them; someone had tried to wipe them out with something that fucked with their DNA, so you'd see these screwed-up roaches dying with too many legs or heads, or not enough, and once she'd seen one that looked like it had swallowed a crucifix or something, its back or shell or whatever it was distorted in a way that made her want to puke.

"Baby," she said, trying to soften her voice, "I can't help it, this place is just getting to me. . . ."

"Hooky Green's," he said, like he hadn't heard her, "I was up in Hooky Green's and I met a *mover*. He picked me *out*, you know? Man's got an eye for talent." She could almost feel his grin through the dark. "Outa London, England. Talent scout. Come into Hooky's and it was just 'You, my man!'"

"A trick?" Hooky Green's was where Eddy had most recently decided the action was, thirty-third floor of a glass highstack with most of the inside walls knocked down, had about a block of dancefloor, but he'd gone off the place when nobody there was willing to pay him much attention. Mona hadn't ever seen Hooky himself, "lean mean Hooky Green," the retired ballplayer who owned the place, but it was great for dancing.

"Will you fucking *listen*? Trick? *Shit*. He's the *man*, he's a connection, he's on the ladder and he's gonna pull me up. And you know what? I'm gonna take *you* with me."

"But what's he want?"

"An actress. Sort of an actress. And a smart boy to get her in place and keep her there."

"Actress? Place? What place?"

She heard him unzip his jacket. Something landed on the bed, near her feet. "Two thou."

Jesus. Maybe it wasn't a joke. But if it wasn't, what the hell was it?

"How much you pull tonight, Mona?"

"Ninety." It had really been one-twenty, but she'd figured the last one for overtime. She was too scared to hold out on him, usually, but she'd needed wiz money.

"Keep it. Get some clothes. Not like work stuff. Nobody wants your little ass hanging out, not this trip."

"When?"

"Tomorrow, I said. You can kiss this place goodbye."

When he said that, it made her want to hold her breath.

The chair creaked again. "Ninety, huh?"

"Yeah."

"Tell me."

"Eddy, I'm so tired. . . ."

"No," he said.

But what he wanted wasn't the truth or anything like it. He wanted a story, the story that he'd taught her to tell him. He didn't want to hear what they talked about (and most of them had some one thing they wanted real bad to tell you, and usually they did), or how they got around to asking to see your bloodwork tickets, or how every other one made that same joke about how what they couldn't cure they could put in remission, or even what they wanted in bed.

Eddy wanted to hear about this big guy who treated her like she didn't matter. Except she had to be careful, when she told it, not to make the trick too rough, because that was supposed to cost more than she'd actually been paid. The main thing was that this imaginary trick had treated her like she was a piece of equipment he'd rented for half an hour. Not that there weren't plenty like that, but they mostly spent their money at puppet parlors or got it on stim. Mona tended to get the ones who wanted to talk, who tried to buy you a sandwich after, which could be bad in its own way but not the kind of bad Eddy needed. And the other thing Eddy needed was for her to tell him how that wasn't what she liked but she'd found herself wanting it anyway, wanting it bad.

She reached down in the dark and touched the envelope full of money.

The chair creaked again.

So she told him how she was coming out of a BuyLow and he'd hit on her, this big guy, just asked how much, which had embarrassed her but she told him anyway and she'd said okay. So they went in his car, which was old and big and kind of damp-smelling (cribbing detail from her Cleveland days), and he'd sort of flipped her over the seat—

"In front of the BuyLow?"

"In back."

Eddy never accused her of making any of it up, even though she knew he must have taught her the general outline somehow and it was always basically the same story. By the time the big guy had her skirt up (the black one, she said, and I had on my white boots) and his pants down, she could hear Eddy's beltbuckle jingling as he peeled off his jeans. Part of her was wondering, when he slid into bed beside her, whether the position she was describing was physically possible, but she kept on going, and anyway it was working on Eddy. She remembered to put in how it hurt, when the guy was getting it in, even though she'd been really wet. She put in how he held her wrists, though by now she was pretty confused about what was where, except that her ass was supposed to be up in the air. Eddy had started to touch her, stroking her breasts and stomach, so she switched from the offhand brutality of the trick's moves to how it was supposed to have made her feel.

How it was supposed to have made her feel was a way she hadn't ever felt. She knew you could get to a place where doing it hurt a little but still felt good, but she knew that wasn't it. What Eddy wanted to hear was that it hurt a lot and made her feel bad, but she liked it anyway. Which made no sense at all to Mona, but she'd learned to tell it the way he wanted her to.

Because anyway it worked, and now Eddy rolled over with the blanket bunched up across his back and got in between her legs. She figured he must be seeing it in his head, like a cartoon, what she was telling him, and at the same time he got to be that faceless pumping big guy. He had her wrists now, pinned above her head, the way he liked.

And when he was done, curled on his side asleep, Mona lay awake in the stale dark, turning the dream of leaving around and around, bright and wonderful.

And please let it be true.

# FIVE

# PORTOBELLO

Kumiko woke in the enormous bed and lay very still, listening. There was a faint continuous murmur of distant traffic.

The air in the room was cold; she drew the rose duvet around her like a tent and climbed out. The small windows were patterned with bright frost. She went to the tub and nudged one of the swan's gilded wings. The bird coughed, gargled, began to fill the tub. Still huddled in the quilt, she opened her cases and began to select the day's garments, laying the chosen articles out on the bed.

When her bath was ready, she let the quilt slide to the floor and climbed over the marble parapet, stoically lowering herself into the painfully hot water. Steam from the tub had melted the frost; now the windows ran with condensation. Did all British bedrooms contain tubs like this? she wondered. She rubbed herself methodically with an oval bar of French soap, stood up, sluiced the suds off as best she could, wrapped herself in a large black towel, and, after some initial fumbling, discovered a sink, toilet, and bidet. These were hidden in a very small room that might once have been a closet, its walls fitted with dark veneer.

The theatrical-looking telephone chimed twice.

"Yes?"

"Petal here. Care for breakfast? Roger's here. Eager to meet you."

"Thank you," she said. "I'm dressing now."

She pulled on her best and baggiest pair of leather slacks, then burrowed into a hairy blue sweater so large that it would easily have fit Petal. When she opened her purse for her makeup, she saw the Maas-Neotek unit. Her hand closed on it automatically. She hadn't intended to summon him, but touch was enough; he was there, craning his neck comically and gaping at the low, mirrored ceiling.

"I take it we aren't in the Dorchester?"

"I'll ask the questions," she said. "What is this place?"

"A bedroom," he said. "In rather dubious taste."

"Answer my question, please."

"Well," he said, surveying the bed and tub, "by the decor, it could be a brothel. I can access historical data on most buildings in London, but there's nothing notable about this one. Built in 1848. Solid example of the prevalent classical Victorian style. The neighborhood's expensive without being fashionable, popular with lawyers of a certain sort." He shrugged; she could see the edge of the bed through the burnished gleam of his riding boots.

She dropped the unit into her purse and he was gone.

She managed the lift easily enough; once in the white-painted foyer, she followed the sound of voices. Along a sort of hallway. Around a corner.

"Good morning," said Petal, lifting the silver cover from a platter. Steam rose. "Here's the elusive Mr. Swain, Roger to you, and here's your breakfast."

"Hello," the man said, stepping forward, his hand extended. Pale eyes in a long, strong-boned face. Lank mouse-colored hair was brushed diagonally across his forehead. Kumiko found it impossible to guess his age; it was a young man's face, but there were deep wrinkles under the grayish eyes. He was tall, with the look of an athlete about his arms and shoulders. "Welcome to London." He took her hand, squeezed and released it.

"Thank you."

He wore a collarless shirt, very fine red stripes against a pale blue ground, the cuffs fastened with plain ovals of dull gold; open

at the neck, it displayed a dark triangle of tattooed flesh. "I spoke
with your father this morning, told him you'd arrived safely."

"You are a man of rank."

The pale eyes narrowed. "Pardon?"

"The dragons."

Petal laughed.

"Let her eat," someone said, a woman's voice.

Kumiko turned, discovering the slim dark figure against tall,
mullioned windows; beyond the windows, a walled garden sheathed
in snow. The woman's eyes were concealed by silver glasses that
reflected the room and its occupants.

"Another of our guests," said Petal.

"Sally," the woman said, "Sally Shears. Eat up, honey. If you're
as bored as I am, you feel like a walk." As Kumiko stared, her
hand came up to touch the glasses, as though she were about
to remove them. "Portobello Road's a couple blocks. I need some
air." The mirrored lenses seemed to have no frames, no earpieces.

"Roger," Petal said, forking pink slices of bacon from a silver
platter, "do you suppose Kumiko will be safe with our Sally?"

"Safer than I'd be, given the mood she's in," Swain said. "I'm
afraid there isn't much here to amuse you," he said to Kumiko,
leading her to the table, "but we'll try to make you as comfortable
as possible and arrange for you to see a bit of the city. It isn't
Tokyo, though."

"Not yet, anyway," said Petal, but Swain seemed not to hear.

"Thank you," Kumiko said, as Swain held her chair.

"An honor," Swain said. "Our respect for your father—"

"Hey," the woman said, "she's too young to need that bullshit.
Spare us."

"Sally's in something of a mood, you see," Petal said, as he
put a poached egg on Kumiko's plate.

Sally Shears's mood, it developed, was one of barely sup-
pressed rage, a fury that made itself known in her stride, in the
angry gunshot crack of her black bootheels on icy pavement.

Kumiko had to scramble to keep up, as the woman stalked
away from Swain's house in the crescent, her glasses flashing coldly
in directionless winter sunlight. She wore narrow trousers of dark
brown suede and a bulky black jacket, its collar turned up high;

expensive clothing. With her short black hair, she might have been taken for a boy.

For the first time since leaving Tokyo, Kumiko felt fear.

The energy pent in the woman was almost tangible, a knot of anger that might slip at any moment.

Kumiko slid her hand into her purse and squeezed the Maas-Neotek unit; Colin was instantly beside her, strolling briskly along, his hands tucked in the pockets of his jacket, his boots leaving no imprint in the dirty snow. She released the unit then, and he was gone, but she felt reassured. She needn't fear losing Sally Shears, whose pace she found difficult; the ghost could certainly guide her back to Swain's. *And if I run from her,* she thought, *he will help me.* The woman dodged through moving traffic at an intersection, absently tugging Kumiko out of the path of a fat black Honda taxi and somehow managing to kick the fender as it slid past.

"You drink?" she asked, her hand around Kumiko's forearm.

Kumiko shook her head. "Please, you're hurting my arm."

Sally's grip loosened, but Kumiko was steered through doors of ornate frosted glass, into noise and warmth, a sort of crowded burrow lined in dark wood and worn fawn velour.

Soon they faced each other across a small marble table that supported a Bass ashtray, a mug of dark ale, the whiskey glass Sally had emptied on her way from the bar, and a glass of orange squash.

Kumiko saw that the silver lenses met the pale skin with no sign of a seam.

Sally reached for the empty whiskey glass, tilted it without lifting it from the table, and regarded it critically. "I met your father once," she said. "He wasn't as far up the ladder, back then." She abandoned the glass for her mug of ale. "Swain says you're half gaijin. Says your mother was Danish." She swallowed some of the ale. "You don't look it."

"She had them change my eyes."

"Suits you."

"Thank you. And your glasses," she said, automatically, "they are very handsome."

Sally shrugged. "Your old man let you see Chiba yet?"

Kumiko shook her head.

"Smart. I was him, I wouldn't either." She drank more ale. Her nails, evidently acrylic, were the shade and sheen of mother-of-pearl. "They told me about your mother."

Her face burning, Kumiko lowered her eyes.

"That's not why you're here. You know that? He didn't pack you off to Swain because of her. There's a war on. There hasn't been high-level infighting in the Yakuza since before I was born, but there is now." The empty pint clinked as Sally set it down. "He can't have you around, is all. You'd be too easy to get to. A guy like Swain's pretty far off the map, far as Kanaka's rivals are concerned. Why you got a passport with a different name, right? Swain owes Kanaka. So you're okay, right?"

Kumiko felt the hot tears come.

"Okay, so you're not okay." The pearl nails drummed on marble. "So she did herself and you're not okay. Feel guilty, right?"

Kumiko looked up, into twin mirrors.

Portobello was choked Shinjuku-tight with tourists. Sally Shears, after insisting Kumiko drink the orange squash, which had grown warm and flat, led her out into the packed street. With Kumiko firmly in tow, Sally began to work her way along the pavement, past folding steel tables spread with torn velvet curtains and thousands of objects made of silver and crystal, brass and china. Kumiko stared as Sally drew her past arrays of Coronation plate and jowled Churchill teapots. "This is *gomi*," Kumiko ventured, when they paused at an intersection. Rubbish. In Tokyo, worn and useless things were landfill. Sally grinned wolfishly. "This is England. *Gomi*'s a major natural resource. *Gomi* and talent. What I'm looking for now. Talent."

The talent wore a bottle-green velvet suit and immaculate suede wingtips, and Sally found him in another pub, this one called the Rose and Crown. She introduced him as Tick. He was scarcely taller than Kumiko, and something was skewed in his back or hip, so that he walked with a pronounced limp that heightened an overall impression of asymmetry. His black hair was shaved close at the back and sides, but piled into an oily loaf of curls above his forehead.

Sally introduced Kumiko: "My friend from Japan and keep your hands to yourself." Tick smiled wanly and led them to a table.

"How's business, Tick?"

"Fine," he said glumly. "How's retirement?"

Sally seated herself on a padded bench, her back to the wall. "Well," she said, "it's sort of on again, off again."

Kumiko looked at her. The rage had evaporated, or else been

expertly concealed. As Kumiko sat down, she slid her hand into her purse and found the unit. Colin popped into focus on the bench beside Sally.

"Nice of you to think of me," Tick said, taking a chair. "Been two years, I'd say." He cocked an eyebrow in Kumiko's direction.

"She's okay. You know Swain, Tick?"

"Strictly by reputation, thank you."

Colin was studying their exchange with amused fascination, moving his head from side to side as though he were watching a tennis match. Kumiko had to remind herself that only she could see him.

"I want you to turn him over for me. I don't want him to know."

He stared at her. The entire left half of his face contorted in a huge slow wink. "Well then," he said, "you don't half want much, do you?"

"Good money, Tick. The best."

"Looking for something in particular, or is it a laundry run? Isn't as though people don't know he's a top nob in the rackets. Can't say I'd want him to find me on his manor. . . ."

"But then there's the money, Tick."

Two very rapid winks.

"Roger's twisting me, Tick. Somebody's twisting him. I don't know what they've got on him, don't much care. What he's got on me is enough. What I want to know is who, where, when. Tap in to incoming and outgoing traffic. He's in touch with somebody, because the deal keeps changing."

"Would I know it if I saw it?"

"Just have a look, Tick. Do that for me."

The convulsive wink again. "Right, then. We'll have a go." He drummed his fingers nervously on the edge of the table. "Buy us a round?"

Colin looked across the table at Kumiko and rolled his eyes.

"I don't understand," Kumiko said, as she followed Sally back along Portobello Road. "You have involved me in an intrigue. . . ."

Sally turned up her collar against the wind.

"But I might betray you. You plot against my father's associate. You have no reason to trust me."

"Or you me, honey. Maybe I'm one of those bad people your daddy's worried about."

Kumiko considered this. "Are you?"

"No. And if you're Swain's spy, he's gotten a lot more baroque recently. If you're your old man's spy, maybe I don't need Tick. But if the Yakuza's running this, what's the point of using Roger for a blind?"

"I am no spy."

"Then start being your own. If Tokyo's the frying pan, you may just have landed in the fire."

"But why involve me?"

"You're already involved. You're here. You scared?"

"No," Kumiko said, and fell silent, wondering why this should be true.

Late that afternoon, alone in the mirrored garret, Kumiko sat on the edge of the huge bed and peeled off her wet boots. She took the Maas-Neotek unit from her purse.

"What are they?" she asked the ghost, who perched on the parapet of the black marble tub.

"Your pub friends?"

"Yes."

"Criminals. I'd advise you to associate with a better class, myself. The woman's foreign. North American. The man's a Londoner. East End. He's a data thief, evidently. I can't access police records, except with regard to crimes of historical interest."

"I don't know what to do. . . ."

"Turn the unit over."

"What?"

"On the back. You'll see a sort of half-moon groove there. Put your thumbnail in and twist. . . ."

A tiny hatch opened. Microswitches.

"Reset the A/B throw to B. Use something narrow, pointed, but not a biro."

"A what?"

"A pen. Ink and dust. Gum up the works. A toothpick's ideal. That'll set it for voice-activated recording."

"And then?"

"Hide it downstairs. We'll play it back tomorrow. . . ."

# SIX

# MORNING LIGHT

Slick spent the night on a piece of gnawed gray foam under a workbench on Factory's ground floor, wrapped in a noisy sheet of bubble packing that stank of free monomers. He dreamed about Kid Afrika, about the Kid's car, and in his dreams the two blurred together and Kid's teeth were little chrome skulls.

He woke to a stiff wind spitting the winter's first snow through Factory's empty windows.

He lay there and thought about the problem of the Judge's buzzsaw, how the wrist tended to cripple up whenever he went to slash through something heavier than a sheet of chipboard. His original plan for the hand had called for articulated fingers, each one tipped with a miniature electric chainsaw, but the concept had lost favor for a number of reasons. Electricity, somehow, just wasn't satisfying; it wasn't *physical* enough. Air was the way to go, big tanks of compressed air, or internal combustion if you could find the parts. And you could find the parts to almost anything, on Dog Solitude, if you dug long enough; failing that, there were half-a-dozen towns in rustbelt Jersey with acres of dead machines to pick over.

He crawled out from under the bench, trailing the transparent blanket of miniature plastic pillows like a cape. He thought about the man on the stretcher, up in his room, and about Cherry, who'd slept in his bed. No stiff neck for her. He stretched and winced.

Gentry was due back. He'd have to explain it to Gentry, who didn't like having people around at all.

Little Bird had made coffee in the room that served as Factory's kitchen. The floor was made of curling plastic tiles and there were dull steel sinks along one wall. The windows were covered with translucent tarps that sucked in and out with the wind and admitted a milky glow that made the room seem even colder than it was.

"How we doing for water?" Slick asked as he entered the room. One of Little Bird's jobs was checking the tanks on the roof every morning, fishing out windblown leaves or the odd dead crow. Then he'd check the seals on the filters, maybe let ten fresh gallons in if it looked like they were running low. It took the better part of a day for ten gallons to filter down through the system to the collection tank. The fact that Little Bird dutifully took care of this was the main reason Gentry would tolerate him, but the boy's shyness probably helped as well. Little Bird managed to be pretty well invisible, as far as Gentry was concerned.

"Got lots," Little Bird said.

"Is there any way to take a shower?" Cherry asked, from her seat on an old plastic crate. She had shadows under her eyes, like she hadn't slept, but she'd covered the sore with makeup.

"No," Slick said, "there isn't, not this time of year."

"I didn't think so," Cherry said glumly, hunched in her collection of leather jackets.

Slick helped himself to the last of the coffee and stood in front of her while he drank it.

"You gotta problem?" she asked.

"Yeah. You and the guy upstairs. How come you're down here? You off duty or something?"

She produced a black beeper from the pocket of her outermost jacket. "Any change, this'll go off."

"Sleep okay?"

"Sure. Well enough."

"I didn't. How long you work for Kid Afrika, Cherry?"

" 'Bout a week."

"You really a med-tech?"

She shrugged inside her jackets. "Close enough to take care of the Count."

"The Count?"

"Count, yeah. Kid called him that, once."

Little Bird shivered. He hadn't gotten to work with his styling tools yet, so his hair stuck out in all directions. "What if," Little Bird ventured, "he's a vampire?"

Cherry stared at him. "You kidding?"

Eyes wide, Little Bird solemnly shook his head.

Cherry looked at Slick. "Your friend playing with a full deck?"

"No vampires," Slick said to Little Bird, "that's not a real thing, understand? That's just in stims. Guy's no vampire, okay?"

Little Bird nodded slowly, looking not at all reassured, while the wind popped the plastic taut against the milky light.

He tried to get a morning's work in on the Judge, but Little Bird had vanished again and the image of the figure on the stretcher kept getting in the way. It was too cold; he'd have to run a line down from Gentry's territory at the top of Factory, get some space heaters. But that meant haggling with Gentry over the current. The juice was Gentry's because Gentry knew how to fiddle it out of the Fission Authority.

It was heading into Slick's third winter in Factory, but Gentry had been there four years when Slick found the place. When they'd gotten Gentry's loft together, Slick had inherited the room where he'd put Cherry and the man she said Kid Afrika called the Count. Gentry took the position that Factory was his, that he'd been there first, got the power in so the Authority didn't know. But Slick did a lot of things around Factory that Gentry wouldn't have wanted to do himself, like making sure there was food, and if something major broke down, if the wiring shorted or the water filter packed it in, it was Slick who had the tools and did the fixing.

Gentry didn't like people. He spent days on end with his decks and FX-organs and holo projectors and came out only when he got hungry. Slick didn't understand what it was that Gentry was trying to do, but he envied Gentry the narrowness of his obsession. Nothing got to Gentry. Kid Africa couldn't have gotten to Gentry, because Gentry wouldn't have gone over to Atlantic City and gotten into deep shit and Kid Afrika's debt.

He went into his room without knocking and Cherry was washing the guy's chest with a sponge, wearing white throwaway gloves. She'd carried the butane stove up from the room where they did the cooking and heated water in a steel mixing bowl.

He made himself look at the pinched face, the slack lips parted just enough to reveal yellow smoker's teeth. It was a street face, a crowd face, face you'd see in any bar.

She looked up at Slick.

He sat on the edge of the bed, where she'd unzipped his sleeping bag and spread it out flat like a blanket, with the torn end tucked in under the foam.

"We gotta talk, Cherry. Figure this, you know?"

She squeezed the sponge out over the bowl.

"How'd you get mixed up with Kid Afrika?"

She put the sponge in a Ziploc and put that away in the black nylon bag from the Kid's hover. As he watched her, he saw there was no wasted motion, and she didn't seem to have to think about what she was doing. "You know a place called Moby Jane's?"

"No."

"Roadhouse, off the interstate. So I had this friend was manager there, doing it for about a month when I move in with him. Moby Jane, she's just huge; she just sits out back the club in a float tank with this freebase IV drip in her arm and it's *totally* disgusting. So like I said, I move in there with my friend Spencer, he's the new manager, because I had this trouble over my ticket in Cleveland and I couldn't work right then."

"What kind of trouble?"

"The *usual* kind, okay? You wanna hear this or not? So Spencer's let me in on the owner's horrible condition, right? So the last thing I want anybody to know is that I'm a med-tech, otherwise they'll have me out there changing filters on her tank and pumping freebase into two hundred kilos of hallucinating psychotic. So they put me waiting tables, slinging beer. It's okay. Get some good music in there. Kind of a rough place but it's okay because people know I'm with Spencer. 'Cept I wake up one day and Spencer's gone. Then it comes out he's gone with a bunch of their money." She was drying the sleeper's chest as she spoke, using a thick wad of white absorbent fiber. "So they knock me around a little." She looked up at him and shrugged. "But then they tell me what they're gonna do. They're gonna cuff my hands behind my back and put me in the tank with Moby Jane and turn her drip up real high and tell her my boyfriend ripped her off. . . ." She tossed the damp wad into the bowl. "So they locked me up in this closet to let me think about it before they did it. When the door opens, though, it's Kid Afrika. I never saw him before. 'Miss Chesterfield,' he said, 'I have reason to believe you were until recently a certified medical technician.'"

"So he made you an offer."

"Offer, my ass. He just checked my papers and took me straight on out of there. Not a soul around, either, and it was Saturday afternoon. Took me out in the parking lot, there's this hover sittin' in the lot, skulls on the front, two big black guys waiting for us, and any way away from that float tank, that's just fine by me."

"Had our friend in the back?"

"No." Peeling off the gloves. "Had me drive him back to Cleveland, to this burb. Big old houses but the lawns all long and scraggy. Went to one with a lot of security, guess it was his. This one," and she tucked the blue sleeping bag up around the man's chin, "he was in a bedroom. I had to start right in. Kid told me he'd pay me good."

"And you knew he'd bring you out here, to the Solitude?"

"No. Don't think he did, either. Something happened. He came in next day and said we were leaving. I think something scared him. That's when he called him that, the Count. 'Cause he was angry and I think maybe scared. 'The Count and his fucking LF,' he said."

"His what?"

" 'LF.' "

"What's that?"

"I think this," she said, pointing up at the featureless gray package mounted above the man's head.

# SEVEN

# NO THERE, THERE

She imagined Swift waiting for her on the deck, wearing the tweeds he favored in an L.A. winter, the vest and jacket mismatched, herringbone and houndstooth, but everything woven from the same wool, and that, probably, from the same sheep on the same hillside, the whole look orchestrated in London, by committee, in a room above a Floral Street shop he'd never seen. They did striped shirts for him, brought the cotton from Charvet in Paris; they made his ties, had the silk woven in Osaka, the Sense/Net logo embroidered tight and small. And still, somehow, he looked as though his mother had dressed him.

The deck was empty. The Dornier hovered, then darted away to its nest. Mamman Brigitte's presence still clung to her.

She went into the white kitchen and scrubbed drying blood from her face and hands. When she stepped into the living room, she felt as though she were seeing it for the first time. The bleached floor, the gilt frames and cut-velvet upholstery of the Louis XVI chairs, the Cubist backdrop of a Valmier. Like Hilton's wardrobe, she thought, contrived by talented strangers. Her boots tracked damp sand across the pale floor as she went to the stairwell.

Kelly Hickman, her wardrobe man, had been to the house while she'd been in the clinic; he'd arranged her working luggage in the master bedroom. Nine Hermès rifle cases, plain and rectangular, like coffins of burnished saddle hide. Her clothes were never folded; they lay each garment flat, between sheets of silk tissue.

She stood in the doorway, staring at the empty bed, the nine leather coffins.

She went into the bathroom, glass block and white mosaic tile, locking the door behind her. She opened one cabinet, then another, ignoring neat rows of unopened toiletries, patent medicines, cosmetics. She found the charger in the third cabinet, beside a bubble card of derms. She bent close, peering at the gray plastic, the Japanese logo, afraid to touch it. The charger looked new, unused. She was almost certain that she hadn't bought it, hadn't left it here. She took the drug from her jacket pocket and examined it, turning it over and over, watching the measured doses of violet dust tumble in their sealed compartments.

She saw herself place the packet on the white marble ledge, position the charger above it, remove a derm from its bubble and insert it. She saw the red flash of a diode when the charger had drawn off a dose; she saw herself remove the derm, balancing it like a white plastic leech on the tip of her index finger, its moist inner surface glittering with minute beads of DMSO—

She turned, took three steps to the toilet, and dropped the unopened packet into the bowl. It floated there like a toy raft, the drug still perfectly dry. Perfectly. Her hand shaking, she found a stainless nailfile and knelt on the white tile. She had to close her eyes when she held the packet and drove the tip of the file against the seam, twisting. The file clattered on tile as she touched the flush button and the two halves of the empty packet vanished. She rested her forehead against cool enamel, then forced herself to get up, go to the sink, and carefully wash her hands.

Because she wanted, now she really *knew* she wanted, to lick her fingers.


Later that day, in a gray afternoon, she found a corrugated plastic shipping cannister in the garage, carried it up to the bedroom, and began to pack Bobby's remaining things. There wasn't much: a pair of leather jeans he hadn't liked, some shirts he'd either discarded or forgotten, and, in the teak bureau's bottom drawer, a cyberspace deck. It was an Ono-Sendai, hardly more than a toy. It

lay amid a tangle of black leads, a cheap set of stim-trodes, a
greasy-looking plastic tube of saline paste.

She remembered the deck he'd used, the one he'd taken with
him, a gray factory-custom Hosaka with unmarked keys. It was a
cowboy's deck; he'd insisted on traveling with it, even though it
caused problems during customs checks. Why, she wondered, had
he bought the Ono-Sendai? And why had he abandoned it? She was
seated on the edge of the bed; she lifted the deck from the drawer
and put it on her lap.

Her father, long ago, in Arizona, had cautioned her against
jacking in. You don't need it, he'd said. And she hadn't, because
she'd dreamed cyberspace, as though the neon gridlines of the
matrix waited for her behind her eyelids.

*There's no there, there.* They taught that to children, explaining
cyberspace. She remembered a smiling tutor's lecture in the arcology's
executive crèche, images shifting on a screen: pilots in enormous
helmets and clumsy-looking gloves, the neuroelectronically primitive
"virtual world" technology linking them more effectively with their
planes, pairs of miniature video terminals pumping them a computer-
generated flood of combat data, the vibrotactile feedback gloves
providing a touch-world of studs and triggers. . . . As the technology evolved, the helmets shrank, the video terminals atrophied. . . .

She leaned forward and picked up the trode-set, shook it to
free its leads from the tangle.

No there, there.

She spread the elastic headband and settled the trodes across
her temples—one of the world's characteristic human gestures, but
one she seldom performed. She tapped the Ono-Sendai's battery-
test stud. Green for go. She touched the power stud and the
bedroom vanished behind a colorless wall of sensory static. Her
head filled with a torrent of white sound.

Her fingers found a random second stud and she was cata-
pulted through the static wall, into cluttered vastness, the notional
void of cyberspace, the bright grid of the matrix ranged around her
like an infinite cage.

"Angela," the house said, its voice quiet but compelling, "I
have a call from Hilton Swift. . . ."

"Executive override?" She was eating baked beans and toast at
the kitchen counter.

"No," it said, confidingly.

"Change your tone," she said, around a mouthful of beans. "Something with an edge of anxiety."

"Mr. Swift is *waiting,*" the house said nervously.

"Better," she said, carrying bowl and plate to the washer, "but I want something closer to genuine hysteria. . . ."

"*Will* you take the call?" The voice was choked with tension.

"No," she said, "but keep your voice that way, I like it."

She walked into the living room, counting under her breath. Twelve, thirteen . . .

"Angela," the house said gently, "I have a call from Hilton Swift—"

"On executive override," Swift said.

She made a farting sound with her lips.

"You know I respect your need to be alone, but I worry about you."

"I'm fine, Hilton. You needn't worry. Bye-bye."

"You stumbled this morning, on the beach. You seemed disoriented. Your nose began to bleed."

"I had a nosebleed."

"We want you to have another physical. . . ."

"Great."

"You accessed the matrix today, Angie. We logged you in the BAMA industrial sector."

"Is that what it was?"

"Do you want to talk about it?"

"There isn't anything to talk about. I was just screwing around. You want to *know,* though? I was packing some crap Bobby left here. You'd have *approved,* Hilton! I found a deck of his and I tried it. I punched a key, sat there looking around, jacked out."

"I'm sorry, Angie."

"For what?"

"For disturbing you. I'll go now."

"Hilton, do you know where Bobby is?"

"No."

"You telling me Net security hasn't kept tabs on him?"

"I'm telling you I don't know, Angie. That's the truth."

"Could you find out, if you wanted to?"

Another pause. "I don't know. If I could, I'm not sure that I would."

"Thanks. Goodbye, Hilton."

"Goodbye, Angie."

\*   \*   \*

She sat on the deck that night, in the dark, watching the fleas dance against floodlit sand. Thinking of Brigitte and her warning, of the drug in the jacket and the derm charger in the medicine cabinet. Thinking of cyberspace and the sad confinement she'd felt with the Ono-Sendai, so far from the freedom of the loa.

Thinking of the other's dreams, of corridors winding in upon themselves, muted tints of ancient carpet . . . An old man, a head made of jewels, a taut pale face with eyes that were mirrors . . . And a beach in the wind and dark.

Not this beach, not Malibu.

And somewhere, in a black California morning, some hour before dawn, amid the corridors, the galleries, the faces of dream, fragments of conversation she half-recalled, waking to pale fog against the windows of the master bedroom, she prized something free and dragged it back through the wall of sleep.

Rolling over, fumbling through a bedside drawer, finding a Porsche pen, a present from an assistant grip, she inscribed her treasure on the glossy back of an Italian fashion magazine:

T-A

"Call Continuity," she told the house, over a third cup of coffee.

"Hello, Angie," said Continuity.

"That orbital sequence we did, two years ago. The Belgian's yacht . . ." She sipped her cooling coffee. "What was the name of the place he wanted to take me? The one Robin decided was too tacky."

"Freeside," the expert system said.

"Who's taped there?"

"Tally Isham recorded nine sequences in Freeside."

"It wasn't too tacky for her?"

"That was fifteen years ago. It was fashionable."

"Get me those sequences."

"Done."

"Bye."

"Goodbye, Angie."

Continuity was writing a book. Robin Lanier had told her about it. She'd asked what it was about. It wasn't like that, he'd said. It looped back into itself and constantly mutated; Continuity was *always* writing it. She asked why. But Robin had already lost interest: because Continuity was an AI, and AIs did things like that.

Her call to Continuity cost her a call from Swift.

"Angie, about that physical . . ."

"Haven't you scheduled it yet? I want to get back to work. I called Continuity this morning. I'm thinking about an orbital sequence. I'm going over some things Tally did; I may get some ideas."

There was a silence. She wanted to laugh. It was difficult to get a silence out of Swift. "You're sure, Angie? That's wonderful, but is it really what you want to do?"

"I'm all better, Hilton. I'm just fine. I want to work. Vacation's over. Have Porphyre come out here and do my hair before I have to see anyone."

"You know, Angie," he said, "this makes all of us very happy."

"Call Porphyre. Set up the physical." *Coup-poudre. Who, Hilton? Maybe you?*

He had the resources, she thought, half an hour later, as she paced the fogbound deck. Her addiction hadn't threatened the Net, hadn't affected her output. There were no physical side effects. If there had been, Sense/Net would never have allowed her to begin. The drug's designer, she thought. The designer would know. And never tell her, even if she could reach him, which she doubted she could. Suppose, she thought, her hands on the rust of the railing, that he hadn't been the designer? That the molecule had been designed by someone else, to his own ends?

"Your hairdresser," the house said.

She went inside.

Porphyre was waiting, swathed in muted jersey, something from the Paris season. His face, as smooth in repose as polished ebony, split into a delighted smirk when he saw her. "Missy," he scolded, "you look like homemade shit."

She laughed. Porphyre clucked and tutted, came forward to flick his long fingers at Angie's bangs with mock revulsion. "Missy was a bad girl. Porphyre *told* you those drugs were nasty!"

She looked up at him. He was very tall, and, she knew, enormously strong. Like a greyhound on steroids, someone had once said. His depilated skull displayed a symmetry unknown to nature.

"You okay?" he asked, in his other voice, the manic brio shut off as if someone had thrown a switch.

"I'm fine."

"Did it hurt?"

"Yeah. It hurt."

"You know," he said, touching her chin lightly with a finger-tip, "nobody could ever see what you got out of that shit. It didn't seem to get you high. . . ."

"It wasn't supposed to. It was just like being here, being there, only you didn't have to—"

"Feel it as much?"

"Yes."

He nodded, slowly. "Then that was some bad shit."

"Fuck it," she said. "I'm back."

His smirk returned. "Let's wash your hair."

"I washed it yesterday!"

"What in? No! Don't tell me!" He shooed her toward the stairwell.

In the white-tiled bathroom, he massaged something into her scalp.

"Have you seen Robin lately?"

He sluiced cool water through her hair. *"Mistah* Lanier is in London, missy. *Mistah* Lanier and I aren't currently on speaking terms. Sit up now." He raised the back of the chair and draped a towel around her neck.

"Why not?" She felt herself warming to the Net gossip that was Porphyre's other specialty.

"Because," the hairdresser said, his tone carefully even as he ran a comb back through her hair, "he had some bad things to say about Angela Mitchell while she was off in Jamaica getting her little head straight."

It wasn't what she'd expected. "He did?"

"Didn't he just, missy." He began to cut her hair, using the scissors that were one of his professional trademarks; he refused to use a laser pencil, claimed never to have touched one.

"Are you joking, Porphyre?"

"No. He wouldn't say those things to *me,* but Porphyre *hears,* Porphyre always hears. He left for London the morning after you got here."

"And what was it you heard he'd said?"

"That you're crazy. On shit or off. That you hear voices. That the Net psychs know."

Voices . . . "Who told you that?" She tried to turn in the chair.

"Don't move your head. There." He went back to his work. "I can't say. Trust me."

There were a number of calls, after Porphyre left. Her production crew, eager to say hello.

"No more calls this afternoon," she told the house. "I'll run the Tally sequences upstairs."

She found a bottle of Corona at the rear of the fridge and took it to the master bedroom. The stim unit in the teak headboard was equipped with studio-grade trodes that hadn't been there when she'd left for Jamaica. Net technicians periodically upgraded equipment in the house. She had a swig of beer, put the bottle on the bedside table, and lay down with the trodes across her forehead. "Okay," she said, "hit me."

Into Tally-flesh, Tally-breath.

*How did I ever replace you?* she wondered, overcome by the former star's physical being. *Do I give people this same pleasure?*

Tally-Angie looking out across a vine-hung chasm that was also a boulevard, glancing up to the inverse horizon, squares of distant tennis courts, Freeside's "sun" an axial thread of brilliance overhead . . .

"Fast forward," she told the house.

Into smooth-pumping muscle and a blur of concrete, Tally hurling her cycle around a low-grav velodrome . . .

"Fast forward."

A dining scene, tension of velvet straps across her shoulders, the young man across the table leaning forward to pour more wine . . .

"Fast forward."

Linen sheets, a hand between her legs, purple twilight through plate glass, sound of running water . . .

"Reverse. The restaurant."

The red wine gurgling into her glass . . .

"Little more. Hold it. There."

Tally's eyes had been focused on the boy's tanned wrist, not on the bottle.

"I want a graphic of the visual," she said, pulling off the trodes. She sat up and took a swallow of beer, which mingled weirdly with the ghost-flavor of Tally's recorded wine.

The printer downstairs chimed softly as it completed its task. She forced herself to take the stairs slowly, but when she reached the printer, in the kitchen, the image disappointed her.

"Can you clear this up?" she asked the house. "I want to be able to read the label on the bottle."

"Justifying image," the house said, "and rotating target object eight degrees."

The printer hummed softly as the new graphic was extruded. Angie found her treasure before the machine could chime, her dream-sigil in brown ink: T-A.

They'd had their own vineyards, she thought.

*Tessier-Ashpool S.A.,* the typeface regal and spidery.

"Gotcha," she whispered.

# EIGHT

# TEXAS RADIO

Mona could see the sun through a couple of rips in the black plastic they kept taped over the window. She hated the squat too much to stay there when she was awake or straight, and now she was both.

She got quietly out of bed, wincing when her bare heel brushed the floor, and fumbled for her plastic thongs. The place was *dirty;* you could probably get tetanus from leaning up against the wall. Made her skin crawl to think about it. Stuff like that didn't seem to bother Eddy; he was too far gone in his schemes to notice his surroundings much. And he always managed to keep clean, somehow, like a cat. He was cat-clean, never a fleck of dirt under his polished nails. She figured he probably spent most of what she earned on his wardrobe, although it wouldn't have occurred to her to question the fact. She was sixteen and SINless, Mona, and this older trick had told her once that that was a song, "Sixteen and SINless." Meant she hadn't been assigned a SIN when she was born, a Single Identification Number, so she'd grown up on the outside of most official systems. She knew that it was supposed to be possible to get a SIN, if you didn't have one, but it stood to reason you'd have to go into a building somewhere and talk to a suit, and that was a long way from Mona's idea of a good time or even normal behavior.

She had a drill for getting dressed in the squat, and she could do it in the dark. You got your thongs on, after giving them a quick knock together to dislodge possible crawlies, and then you walked over to where you knew there was a roll of old fax on a Styrofoam crate beside the window. You peeled off about a meter of fax, maybe a day and a half of *Asahi Shimbun*, folded and creased it, put it down on the floor. Then you could stand on it, get the plastic bag from beside the crate, undo the twist of wire that held it shut, and find the clothes you wanted. When you stepped out of the thongs to put your pants on, you knew you'd be stepping on fresh fax. It was an article of faith with Mona that nothing was going to wander across the fax in the time it took her to step into a pair of jeans and get the thongs back on.

You could put on a shirt or whatever, carefully reseal the bag, and get out of there. Makeup, when required, went on in the corridor outside; there was some mirror left, beside the derelict elevator, a Fuji biofluorescent strip glued above it.

There was a strong piss smell beside the elevator this morning, so she decided to skip the makeup.

You never saw anybody in the building, but you heard them sometimes; music through a closed door, or footsteps just gone around a corner at the far end of a corridor. Well, that made sense; Mona had no desire to meet her neighbors either.

She took the stairs down three flights and into the gaping dark of the underground garage. She had her flashlight in her hand, found her way with six quick little blinks that steered her around stagnant puddles and dangling strands of dead optic cable, up the concrete steps and out into the alley. You could smell the beach, sometimes, in the alley, if the wind was right, but today it just smelled of garbage. The side of the squat towered away above her, so she moved fast, before some asshole decided to drop a bottle or worse. Once she was out on the Avenue, she slowed, but not too much; she was conscious of the cash in her pocket, and full of plans for spending it. Wouldn't do to get taken off, not when it looked like Eddy had wrangled them some kind of ticket out. She alternated between telling herself it was a sure thing, that they were practically gone, and warning herself not to get her hopes up. She knew Eddy's sure things: hadn't Florida been one of them? How it

was warm in Florida and the beaches were beautiful and it was full
of cute guys with money, just the spot for a little working vacation
that had already stretched into the longest month Mona could
remember. Well, it was fucking hot in Florida, like a sauna. The
only beaches that weren't private were polluted, dead fish rolling
belly-up in the shallows. Maybe the private stretches were the
same, but you couldn't see them, just the chainlink and the guards
in shorts and cop shirts standing around. Eddy'd get excited by the
weapons the guards carried and describe each one to her in numb-
ing detail. He didn't have a gun himself, though, not as far as she
knew, and Mona figured that was a good thing. Sometimes you
couldn't even smell the dead fish, because there was another smell,
a chlorine smell that burned the roof of your mouth, something
from the factories up the coast. If there were cute guys, they were
still tricks, and the ones down here weren't exactly offering to pay
double.

About the only thing to like about Florida was drugs, which
were easy to come by and cheap and mostly industrial strength.
Sometimes she imagined the bleach smell was the smell of a million
dope labs cooking some unthinkable cocktail, all those molecules
thrashing their kinky little tails, hot for destiny and the street.

She turned off the Avenue and walked down a line of unlicensed
food stalls. Her stomach started growling at the smell, but she
didn't trust street food, not if she didn't have to, and there were
licensed places in the mall that would take cash. Somebody was
playing a trumpet in the asphalt square that had been the parking
lot, a rambling Cuban solo that bounced and distorted off the
concrete walls, dying notes lost in the morning clatter of the market.
A soapbox evangelist spread his arms high, a pale fuzzy Jesus
copying the gesture in the air above him. The projection rig was in
the box he stood on, but he wore a battered nylon pack with two
speakers sticking over each shoulder like blank chrome heads. The
evangelist frowned up at Jesus and adjusted something on the belt
at his waist. Jesus strobed, turned green, and vanished. Mona laughed.
The man's eyes flashed God's wrath, a muscle working in his
seamed cheek. Mona turned left, between rows of fruit vendors
stacking oranges and grapefruit in pyramids on their battered metal
carts.

She entered a low, cavernous building that housed aisles of
more permanent businesses: sellers of fish and packaged foods,
cheap household goods, counters serving a dozen kinds of hot food.

It was cooler here in the shade, and a little quieter. She found a wonton place with six empty stools and took one. The Chinese cook spoke to her in Spanish; she ordered by pointing. He brought her soup in a plastic bowl; she paid him with the smallest of her bills, and he made change with eight greasy cardboard tokens. If Eddy meant it, about leaving, she wouldn't be able to use them; if they stayed in Florida, she could always get some wonton. She shook her head. Gotta go, gotta. She shoved the worn yellow disks back across the painted plyboard counter. "You keep 'em." The cook swept them out of sight, bland and expressionless, a blue plastic toothpick fixed at the corner of his mouth.

She took chopsticks from the glass on the counter and fished a folded noodle from the bowl. There was a suit watching her from the aisle behind the cook's pots and burners. A suit who was trying to look like something else, white sportshirt and sunglasses. More the way they stand than anything, she thought. But he had the teeth, too, and the haircut, except he had a beard. He was pretending to look around, like he was shopping, hands in his pockets, his mouth set in what he might have thought was an absent smile. He was pretty, the suit, what you could see of him behind the beard and the glasses. The smile wasn't pretty, though; it was kind of rectangular, so you could see most of his teeth. She shifted a little on the stool, uneasy. Hooking was legal, but only if you did it right, got the tax chip and everything. She was suddenly aware of the cash in her pocket. She pretended to study the laminated foodhandling license taped to the counter; when she looked up again, he was gone.

She spent fifty on the clothes. She worked her way through eighteen racks in four shops, everything the mall had, before she made up her mind. The vendors didn't like her trying on so many things, but it was the most she'd ever had to spend. It was noon before she'd finished, and the Florida sun was cooking the pavement as she crossed the parking lot with her two plastic bags. The bags, like the clothes, were secondhand: one was printed with the logo of a Ginza shoe store, the other advertised Argentinian seafood briquettes molded from reconstituted krill. She was mentally mixing and matching the things she'd bought, figuring out different outfits.

From the other side of the square, the evangelist opened up at full volume, in mid-rant, like he'd warmed up to a spit-spraying fury before he'd cut the amp in, the hologram Jesus shaking its white-robed arms and gesturing angrily to the sky, the mall, the sky again. Rapture, he said. Rapture's coming.

Mona turned a corner at random, automatic reflex avoiding a crazy, and found herself walking past sunfaded card tables spread with cheap Indo simstim sets, used cassettes, colored spikes of microsoft stuck in blocks of pale blue Styrofoam. There was a picture of Angie Mitchell taped up behind one of the tables, a poster Mona hadn't seen before. She stopped and studied it hungrily, taking in the star's clothes and makeup first, then trying to figure out the background, where it had been shot. Unconsciously, she adjusted her expression to approximate Angie's in the poster. Not a grin, exactly. A sort of half-grin, maybe a little sad. Mona felt a special way about Angie. Because—and tricks said it, sometimes— she looked like her. Like she was Angie's sister. Except her nose, Mona's, had more of a tilt, and she, Angie, didn't have that smear of freckles out to her cheekbones. Mona's Angie half-grin widened as she stared, washed in the beauty of the poster, the luxury of the pictured room. She guessed it was a kind of castle, probably it was where Angie lived, sure, with lots of people to take care of her, do her hair and hang up her clothes, because you could see the walls were made of big rocks, and those mirrors had frames on them that were solid gold, carved with leaves and angels. The writing across the bottom would say where it was, maybe, but Mona couldn't read. Anyway, there weren't any fucking roaches there, she was sure of that, and no Eddy either. She looked down at the stim sets and briefly considered using the rest of her money. But then she wouldn't have enough for a stim, and anyway these were old, some of them older than she was. There was whatsit, that Tally, she'd been big when Mona was maybe nine. . . .

When she got back, Eddy was waiting for her, with the tape off the window and the flies buzzing. Eddy was sprawled out on the bed, smoking a cigarette, and the suit with the beard, who'd been watching her, was sitting in the broken chair, still wearing his sunglasses.

*Prior*, he said that was his name, like he didn't have a first one. Or like Eddy didn't have a last one. Well, she didn't have a last name herself, unless you counted Lisa, and that was more like having two first ones.

She couldn't get much sense of him, in the squat. She thought maybe that was because he was English. He wasn't really a suit, though, not like she'd thought when she'd seen him in the mall; he was onto some game, it just wasn't clear which one. He kept his eyes on her a lot, watched her pack her things in the blue Lufthansa bag he'd brought, but she couldn't feel any heat there, not like he wanted her. He just watched her, watched Eddy smoke, tapped his sunglasses on his knee, listened to Eddy's line of bullshit, and said as little as he needed to. When he did say something, it was usually funny, but the way he talked made it hard to tell when he was joking.

Packing, she felt light-headed, like she'd done a jumper but it hadn't quite come on. The flies were fucking against the window, bumping on the dust-streaked glass, but she didn't care. Gone, she was already gone.

Zipping up the bag.

It was raining when they got to the airport, Florida rain, pissing down warm out of a nowhere sky. She'd never been to an airport before, but she knew them from the stims.

Prior's car was a white Datsun rental that drove itself and played elevator music through quad speakers. It left them beside their luggage in a bare concrete bay and drove away in the rain. If Prior had a bag, it wasn't with him; Mona had her Lufthansa bag and Eddy had two black gator-clone suitcases.

She tugged her new skirt down over her hips and wondered if she'd bought the right shoes. Eddy was enjoying himself, had his hands in his pockets and his shoulders tilted to show he was doing something important.

She remembered him in Cleveland, the first time, how he'd come out to the place to look at a scoot the old man had for sale, a three-wheel Skoda that was mostly rust. The old man grew catfish in concrete tanks that fenced the dirt yard. She was in the house when Eddy came, long high-walled space of a truck trailer up on blocks. There were windows cut down one side, square holes sealed over with scratched plastic. She was standing by the stove, smell of onions in sacks and tomatoes hung up to dry, when she felt him there, down the length of the room, sensed the muscle and shoulder of him, his white teeth, the black nylon cap held shyly in his hand. Sun was coming in the windows, the place lit up bare and plain, the floor swept the way the old man had her keep it, but it was like a shadow came, blood-shadow where she heard the pumping of her heart, and him coming closer, tossing the cap on the bare chipboard table as he passed it, not shy now but like he lived there, right up to her, running a hand with a bright ring back through the oiled weight of his hair. The old man came in then and Mona turned away, pretended to do something with the stove. Coffee, the old man said, and Mona went to get some water, filling the enamel pot from the roof-tank line, the water gurgling down through the charcoal filter. Eddy and the old man sitting at the table, drinking black coffee, Eddy's legs spread straight out under the table, thighs hard through threadbare denim. Smiling, jiving the old man, dealing for the Skoda. How it seemed to run okay, how he'd buy it if the old man had the title. Old man getting up to dig in a drawer. Eddy's eyes on her again. She followed them out into the yard and watched him straddle the cracked vinyl saddle. Backfire set the old man's black dogs yelping, high sweet smell of cheap alcohol exhaust and the frame trembling between his legs.

Now she watched him pose beside his suitcases, and it was hard to connect that up, why she'd left with him next day on the Skoda, headed into Cleveland. The Skoda'd had a busted little radio you couldn't hear over the engine, just play it soft at night in a field by the road. Tuner part was cracked so it only picked up one station, ghost music up from some lonesome tower in Texas, steel guitar fading in and out all night, feeling how she was wet against his leg and the stiff dry grass prickling the back of her neck.

Prior put her blue bag into a white cart with a striped top and she climbed in after it, hearing tiny Spanish voices from the Cuban driver's headset. Then Eddy stowed the gator cases and he and Prior got in. Rolling out to the runway through walls of rain.

The plane wasn't what she knew from the stims, not like a long rich bus inside, with lots of seats. It was a little black thing with sharp, skinny wings and windows that made it look like it was squinting.

She went up some metal stairs and there was a space with four seats and the same gray carpet all over, on the walls and ceiling too, everything clean and cool and gray. Eddy came in after her and took a seat like it was something he did every day, loosening his tie and stretching his legs. Prior was pushing buttons beside the door. It made a sighing sound when it closed.

She looked out the narrow, streaming windows at runway lights reflected on wet concrete.

*Came down here on the train,* she thought, *New York to Atlanta and then you change.*

The plane shivered. She heard the airframe creak as it came to life.

She woke briefly, two hours later, in the darkened cabin, cradled by the long hum of the jet. Eddy was asleep, his mouth half-open. Maybe Prior was sleeping too, or maybe he just had his eyes closed, she couldn't tell.

Halfway back into a dream she wouldn't remember in the morning, she heard the sound of that Texas radio, fading steel chords drawn out like an ache.

# NINE

# UNDERGROUND

Jubilee and Bakerloo, Circle and District. Kumiko peered at the little laminated map Petal had given her and shivered. The concrete platform seemed to radiate cold through the soles of her boots.

"It's so fucking old," Sally Shears said absently, her glasses reflecting a convex wall sheathed in white ceramic tile.

"I beg your pardon?"

"The tube." A new tartan scarf was knotted under Sally's chin, and her breath was white when she spoke. "You know what bothers me? It's how sometimes you'll see 'em sticking new tile up in these stations, but they don't take down the old tile first. Or they'll punch a hole in the wall to get to some wiring and you can see all these different layers of tile. . . ."

"Yes?"

"Because it's getting *narrower*, right? It's like arterial plaque. . . ."

"Yes," Kumiko said dubiously, "I see. . . . Those boys, Sally, what is the meaning of their costume, please?"

"Jacks. What they call Jack Draculas."

The four Jack Draculas huddled like ravens on the opposite

platform. They wore nondescript black raincoats and polished black combat boots laced to the knee. One turned to address another and Kumiko saw that his hair was drawn back into a plaited queue and bound with a small black bow.

"Hung him," Sally said, "after the war."

"Who?"

"Jack Dracula. They had public hangings for a while, after the war. Jacks, you wanna stay away from 'em. Hate anybody foreign . . ."

Kumiko would have liked to access Colin, but the Maas-Neotek unit was tucked behind a marble bust in the room where Petal served their meals, and then the train arrived, amazing her with the archaic thunder of wheels on steel rail.

Sally Shears against the patchwork backdrop of the city's architecture, her glasses reflecting the London jumble, each period culled by economics, by fire, by war.

Kumiko, already confused by three rapid and apparently random train changes, let herself be hauled through a sequence of taxi rides. They'd jump out of one cab, march into the nearest large store, then take the first available exit to another street and another cab. "Harrods," Sally said at one point, as they cut briskly through an ornate, tile-walled hall pillared in marble. Kumiko blinked at thick red roasts and shanks displayed on tiered marble counters, assuming they were made of plastic. And then out again, Sally hailing the next cab. "Covent Garden," she said to the driver.

"Excuse me, Sally. What are we doing?"

"Getting lost."

Sally drank hot brandy in a tiny café beneath the snow-streaked glass roof of the piazza. Kumiko drank chocolate.

"Are we lost, Sally?"

"Yeah. Hope so, anyway." She looked older today, Kumiko thought; lines of tension or fatigue around her mouth.

"Sally, what is it that you do? Your friend asked if you were still retired. . . ."

"I'm a businesswoman."

"And my father is a businessman?"

"Your father *is* a businessman, honey. No, not like that. I'm an indie. I make investments, mostly."

"In what do you invest?"

"In other indies." She shrugged. "Feeling curious today?" She sipped her brandy.

"You advised me to be my own spy."

"Good advice. Takes a light touch, though."

"Do you live here, Sally, in London?"

"I travel."

"Is Swain another 'indie'?"

"He thinks so. He's into influence, nods in the right direction; you need that here, to do business, but it gets on my nerves." She tossed back the rest of the brandy and licked her lips.

Kumiko shivered.

"You don't have to be scared of Swain. Yanaka could have him for breakfast. . . ."

"No. I thought of those boys in the subway. So thin . . ."

"The Draculas."

"A gang?"

"*Bosozoku*," Sally said, with fair pronunciation. " 'Running tribes'? Anyway, like a tribe." It wasn't the right word, but Kumiko thought she saw the distinction. "They're thin because they're poor." She gestured to the waiter for a second brandy.

"Sally," Kumiko said, "when we came here, the route we took, the trains and cabs, that was in order to make certain we were not followed?"

"Nothing's ever certain."

"But when we went to meet Tick, you took no precautions. We could easily have been followed. You enlist Tick to spy on Swain, yet you take no precautions. You bring me here, you take many precautions. Why?"

The waiter put a steaming glass down in front of her. "You're a sharp little honey, aren't you?" She leaned forward and inhaled the fumes of brandy. "It's like this, okay? With Tick, maybe I'm just trying to shake some action."

"But Tick is concerned that Swain not discover him."

"Swain won't touch him, not if he knows he's working for me."

"Why?"

"Because he knows I might kill him." She raised the glass, looking suddenly happier.

"Kill Swain?"

"That's right." She drank.

"Then why were you so cautious today?"

"Because sometimes it feels good to shake it all off, get out from under. Chances are, we haven't. But maybe we have. Maybe nobody, nobody at all, knows where we are. Nice feeling, huh? You could be kinked, you ever think of that? Maybe your dad, the Yak warlord, he's got a little bug planted in you so he can keep track of his daughter. You got those pretty little teeth, maybe Daddy's dentist tucked a little hardware in there one time when you were into a stim. You go to the dentist?"

"Yes."

"You stim while he works?"

"Yes . . ."

"There you go. Maybe he's listening to us right now. . . ."

Kumiko nearly overturned what was left of her chocolate.

"Hey." The polished nails tapped Kumiko's wrist. "Don't worry about it. He wouldn't've sent you here like that, with a bug. Make you too easy for his enemies to track. But you see what I mean? It's good to get out from under, or anyway try. On our own, right?"

"Yes," Kumiko said, her heart still pounding, the panic continuing to rise. "He killed my mother," she blurted, then vomited chocolate on the café's gray marble floor.

Sally leading her past the columns of Saint Paul's, walking, not talking. Kumiko, in a disjointed trance of shame, registering random information: the white shearling that lined Sally's leather coat, the oily rainbow sheen of a pigeon's feathers as it waddled out of their way, red buses like a giant's toys in the Transport Museum, Sally warming her hands around a foam cup of steaming tea.

Cold, it would always be cold now. The freezing damp in the city's ancient bones, the cold waters of Sumida that had filled her mother's lungs, the chill flight of the neon cranes.

Her mother was fine-boned and dark, the thick spill of her hair grained with gold highlights, like some rare tropical hardwood. Her mother smelled of perfume and warm skin. Her mother told her stories, about elves and fairies and Copenhagen, which was a city far away. When Kumiko dreamed of the elves, they were like her father's secretaries, lithe and staid, with black suits and furled umbrellas. The elves did many curious things, in her mother's stories, and the stories were magic, because they changed with the telling, and you could never be certain how a tale might end on a given night. There were princesses in the stories as well, and ballerinas, and each of them, Kumiko had known, was in some way her mother.

The princess-ballerinas were beautiful but poor, dancing for love in the far city's heart, where they were courted by artists and student poets, handsome and penniless. In order to support an aged parent, or purchase an organ for an ailing brother, a princess-ballerina was sometimes obliged to voyage very far indeed, perhaps as far as Tokyo, to dance for money. Dancing for money, the tales implied, was not a happy thing.

Sally took her to a robata bar in Earls Court and forced her to drink a glass of sake. A smoked fugu fin floated in the hot wine, turning it the color of whiskey. They ate robata from the smoky grill, and Kumiko felt the cold recede, but not the numbness. The decor of the bar induced a profound sense of cultural dislocation: it managed to simultaneously reflect traditional Japanese design and look as though it had been drawn up by Charles Rennie Mackintosh.

She was very strange, Sally Shears, stranger than all of gaijin London. Now she told Kumiko stories, stories about people who lived in a Japan Kumiko had never known, stories that defined her father's role in the world. The *oyabun*, she called Kumiko's father. The world Sally's stories described seemed no more real than the world of her mother's fairy tales, but Kumiko began to understand the basis and extent of her father's power. "*Kuromaku,*" Sally said. The word meant black curtain. "It's from Kabuki, but it means a fixer, someone who sells favors. Means behind-the-scenes, right? That's your father. That's Swain, too. But Swain's your old man's *kobun*, or anyway one of them. *Oyabun-kobun*, parent-child. That's partly where Roger gets his juice. That's why you're here now, because Roger owes it to the *oyabun*. *Giri*, understand?"

"He is a man of rank."

Sally shook her head. "Your old man, Kumi, he's *it*. If he's had to ship you out of town to keep you safe, means there's some serious changes on the way."

"Been down the drinker?" Petal asked, as they entered the room, his eyeglass edges winking Tiffany light from a bronze and stained-glass tree that grew on the sideboard. Kumiko wanted to look at the marble head that hid the Maas-Neotek unit, but forced herself to look out into the garden. The snow there had become the color of London sky.

"Where's Swain?" Sally asked.

"Guvnor's out," Petal told her.

Sally went to the sideboard and poured herself a glass of scotch from a heavy decanter. Kumiko saw Petal wince as the decanter came down hard on the polished wood. "Any messages?"

"No."

"Expect him back tonight?"

"Can't say, really. Do you want dinner?"

"No."

"I'd like a sandwich," Kumiko said.

Fifteen minutes later, with the untouched sandwich on the black marble bedside table, she sat in the middle of the huge bed, the Maas-Neotek unit between her bare feet. She'd left Sally drinking Swain's whiskey and staring out into the gray garden.

Now she took up the unit and Colin shuddered into focus at the foot of the bed.

"Nobody can hear my half of this," he said quickly, putting a finger to his lips, "and a good thing, too. Room's bugged."

Kumiko started to reply, then nodded.

"Good," he said. "Smart girl. Got two conversations for you. One's your host and his minder, other's your host and Sally. Got the former about fifteen minutes after you stashed me downstairs. Listen . . ." Kumiko closed her eyes and heard the tinkle of ice in a whiskey glass.

"Where's our little Jap, then?" Swain asked.

"Tucked up for the night," Petal said. "Talks to herself, that one. One-sided conversation. Queer."

"What about?"

"Bloody little, actually. Some people do, y'know. . . ."

"What?"

"Talk to themselves. Like to hear her?"

"Christ, no. Where's the delightful Miss Shears?"

"Out for her constitutional."

"Call Bernie 'round, next time, see what she's about on these little walks . . ."

"Bernie," and Petal laughed, "he'd come back in a fucking box!"

Now Swain laughed. "Mightn't be a bad thing either way, Bernard off our hands and the famous razorgirl's thirst slaked . . . Here, pour us another."

"None for me. Off to bed, unless you need me . . ."

"No," Swain said.

"So," said Colin, as Kumiko opened her eyes to find him still seated on the bed, "there's a voice-activated bug here in your room; the minder reviewed the recording and heard you address me. Our second segment, now, is more interesting. Your host sits there with his second whiskey, in comes our Sally. . . ."

"Hullo," she heard Swain say, "been out taking the air?"

"Fuck off."

"You know," Swain said, "none of this was my idea. You might try keeping that in mind. You know they've got me by the balls as well."

"You know, Roger, sometimes I'm tempted to believe you."

"Try it. It would make things easier."

"Other times, I'm tempted to slit your fucking throat."

"Your problem, dear, is that you never learned to delegate; you still want to do everything personally."

"Listen, asshole, I know where you're from, and I know how you got here, and I don't care how far you've got your tongue up Kanaka's crack or anybody else's. *Sarakin!*" Kumiko had never heard the word before.

"I heard from them again," Swain said, his tone even, conversational. "She's still on the coast, but it looks as though she'll make a move soon. East, most likely. Back on your old manor. I think that's our best bet, really. The house is impossible. Enough private security along that stretch to stop a fair-sized army . . ."

"You still trying to tell me this is just a snatch, Roger? Trying to tell me they're gonna hold her for ransom?"

"No. Nothing's been said about selling her back."

"So why don't they just hire that army? No reason they'd have to stop at fair-sized, is there? Get the mercs, right? The corporate-extraction boys. She's not that hard a target, no more than some hotshit research man. Get the fucking *pros* in . . ."

"For perhaps the hundredth time, that isn't what they want. They want you."

"Roger, what *do* they have on you, huh? I mean, do you *really* not know what it is they got on me?"

"No, I don't. But based on what they've got on me, I'll hazard a guess."

"Yeah?"

"Everything."

No reply.

"There's another angle," he said, "that came up today. They want it to look as though she's been taken out."

"What?"

"They want it to look as though we've killed her."

"And how are we supposed to manage that?"

"They'll provide a body."

"I assume," Colin said, "that she left the room without comment. It ends there."

TEN

# THE SHAPE

He spent an hour checking the saw's bearings, then lubed them again. It was already too cold to work; he'd have to go ahead and heat the room where he kept the others, the Investigators and the Corpsegrinder and the Witch. That in itself would be enough to disturb the balance of his arrangement with Gentry, but it faded beside the problem of explaining his agreement with Kid Afrika and the fact of two strangers in Factory. There was no way to argue with Gentry; the juice was his, because he was the one who fiddled it out of the Fission Authority; without Gentry's monthly passes on the console, the ritual moves that kept the Authority convinced Factory was somewhere else, some place that paid its bill, there wouldn't be any electricity.

And Gentry was so strange anyway, he thought, feeling his knees creak as he stood up and took the Judge's control unit from his jacket pocket. Gentry was convinced that cyberspace had a Shape, an overall total form. Not that that was the weirdest idea Slick had ever run across, but Gentry had this obsessive conviction that the Shape mattered *totally*. The apprehension of the Shape was Gentry's grail.

Slick had once stimmed a Net/Knowledge sequence about what shape the universe was; Slick figured the universe was everything there was, so how could it have a shape? If it had a shape, then there was something around it for it to have a shape *in*, wasn't there? And if that something was something, then wasn't *that* part of the universe too? This was exactly the kind of thing you didn't want to get into with Gentry, because Gentry could tie your head in knots. But Slick didn't think cyberspace was anything like the universe anyway; it was just a way of representing data. The Fission Authority had always looked like a big red Aztec pyramid, but it didn't *have* to; if the FA wanted it to, they could have it look like anything. Big companies had copyrights on how their stuff looked. So how could you figure the whole matrix had a particular shape? And why should it mean anything if it did?

He touched the unit's power stud; the Judge, ten meters away, hummed and trembled.

Slick Henry hated the Judge. That was what the art people never understood. That didn't mean it didn't give him pleasure to have built the thing, to have gotten the Judge *out*, out where he could see him and keep track of him and finally, sort of, be free of the idea of him, but that sure wasn't the same as *liking* him.

Nearly four meters tall, half as broad at the shoulders, headless, the Judge stood trembling in his patchwork carapace the color of rust gone a certain way, like the handles of an old wheelbarrow, polished by the friction of a thousand hands. He'd found a way to get that surface with chemicals and abrasives, and he'd used it on most of the Judge; the old parts anyway, the scavenged parts, not the cold teeth of the circular blades or the mirrored surfaces of the joints, but the rest of the Judge was that color, that finish, like a very old tool still in hard daily use.

He thumbed the joystick and the Judge took one step forward, then another. The gyros were working perfectly; even with an arm off, the thing moved with a terrible dignity, planting its huge feet just so.

Slick grinned in Factory's gloom as the Judge clomped toward him, one-two, one-two. He could remember every step of the Judge's construction, if he wanted to, and sometimes he did, just for the comfort of being able to.

He couldn't remember when he hadn't been able to remember, but sometimes he almost could.

That was why he had built the Judge, because he'd done

something—it hadn't been anything much, but he'd been caught doing it, twice—and been judged for it, and sentenced, and then the sentence was carried out and he hadn't been able to remember, not anything, not for more than five minutes at a stretch. Stealing cars. Stealing rich people's cars. They made sure you remembered what you did.

Working the joystick, he got the Judge turned around and walked him into the next room, along an aisle between rows of damp-stained concrete pads that had once supported lathes and spot welders. High overhead, up in the gloom and dusty beams, dangled dead fluorescent fixtures where birds sometimes nested.

Korsakov's, they called that, something they did to your neurons so that short-term memories wouldn't stick. So that the time you did was time you lost, but he'd heard they didn't do it anymore, or anyway not for grand theft auto. People who hadn't been there thought it sounded easy, like jail but then it's all erased, but it wasn't like that. When he'd gotten out, when it was over—three years strung out in a long vague flickering chain of fear and confusion measured off in five-minute intervals, and it wasn't the intervals you could remember so much as the transitions . . . When it was over, he'd needed to build the Witch, the Corpsegrinder, then the Investigators, and finally, now, the Judge.

As he guided the Judge up the concrete ramp to the room where the others waited, he heard Gentry gunning his motor out on Dog Solitude.

People made Gentry uncomfortable, Slick thought as he headed for the stairs, but it worked both ways. Strangers could feel the Shape burning behind Gentry's eyes; his fixation came across in everything he did. Slick had no idea how he got along on his trips to the Sprawl; maybe he just dealt with people who were as intense as he was, loners on the jagged fringes of the drug and software markets. He didn't seem to care about sex at all, to the extent that Slick had no idea what it was he'd have wanted if he'd decided to care.

Sex was the Solitude's main drawback, as far as Slick was concerned, particularly in the winter. Summers, sometimes, he could find a girl in one of those rusty little towns; that was what had taken him to Atlantic City that time and gotten him in the Kid's debt. Lately he told himself the best solution was just to concentrate on his work, but climbing the shuddering steel stairs to the catwalk that led to Gentry's space, he found himself wondering what Cherry

Chesterfield looked like under all those jackets. He thought about her hands, how they were clean and quick, but that made him see the unconscious face of the man on the stretcher, the tube feeding stuff into his left nostril, Cherry dabbing at his sunken cheeks with a tissue; made him wince.

"Hey, Gentry," he bellowed out into the iron void of Factory, "comin' up . . ."

Three things about Gentry weren't sharp and thin and tight: his eyes, his lips, his hair. His eyes were large and pale, gray or blue depending on the light; his lips were full and mobile; his hair was swept back into a ragged blond roostertail that quivered when he walked. His thinness wasn't Bird's emaciation, born of a stringtown diet and bad nerves; Gentry was just narrow, the muscle packed in close, no fat at all. He dressed sharp and tight, too, black leather trimmed with jet-black beads, a style Slick remembered from his days in the Deacon Blues. The beads, as much as anything, made Slick think he was about thirty; Slick was about thirty himself.

Gentry stared as Slick stepped through the door into the glare of ten 100-watt bulbs, making sure Slick knew he was another obstacle coming between Gentry and the Shape. He was putting a pair of motorcycle panniers up on his long steel table; they looked heavy.

Slick had cut roof panels away, installed struts where needed, covered the holes with sheets of rigid plastic, caulked the resulting skylights with silicone. Then Gentry came in with a mask and a sprayer and twenty gallons of white latex paint; he didn't dust or clean anything, just lay down a thick coat over all the crud and dessicated pigeonshit, sort of glued it all down and painted over it again until it was more or less white. He painted everything but the skylights, then Slick started winching gear up from Factory's floor, a small truckload of computers, cyberspace decks, a huge old holo-projection table that nearly broke the winch, effect generators, dozens of corrugated plastic cartons stuffed with the thousands of fiche Gentry had accummulated in his quest for the Shape, hundreds of meters of optics, on bright new plastic reels, that spoke to Slick of industrial theft. And books, old books with covers made of cloth glued over cardboard. Slick hadn't ever known how heavy books were. They had a sad smell, old books.

"You're pulling a few more amps, since I left," Gentry said, opening the first of the two panniers. "In your room. Get a new heater?" He began to root quickly through the contents, as though he were looking for something he needed but had misplaced. He wasn't, though, Slick knew; it was having to have someone, even someone he knew, unexpectedly in his space.

"Yeah. I gotta heat the storage area again, too. Too cold to work, otherwise."

"No," Gentry said, looking up suddenly, "that's not a heater in your room. The amperage is wrong."

"Yeah." Slick grinned, on the theory that grinning made Gentry think he was stupid and easily cowed.

" 'Yeah' what, Slick Henry?"

"It's not a heater."

Gentry closed the pannier with a snap. "You can tell me what it is or I can cut your power."

"Y'know, Gentry, I wasn't around here, you'd have a lot less time for . . . things." Slick raised his eyebrows meaningfully in the direction of the big projection table. "Fact is, I got two people staying with me. . . ." He saw Gentry stiffen, the pale eyes widen. "But you won't *see* either of 'em, won't hear 'em, nothing."

"No," Gentry said, his voice tight, as he rounded the end of the table, "because you're going to *get them out of here*, aren't you?"

"Two weeks max, Gentry."

"Out. *Now.*" Gentry's face was inches away and Slick smelled the sour breath of exhaustion. "Or you go with them."

Slick outweighed Gentry by ten kilos, most of it muscle, but that had never intimidated Gentry; Gentry didn't seem to know or care that he could be hurt. That was intimidating in its own way. Gentry had slapped him, once, hard, in the face, and Slick had looked down at the huge chrome-moly wrench in his own hand and had felt an obscure embarrassment.

Gentry was holding himself rigid, starting to tremble. Slick had a pretty good idea that Gentry didn't sleep when he went to Boston or New York. He didn't always sleep that much in Factory either. Came back strung and the first day was always the worst. "Look," Slick said, the way somebody might to a child on the verge of tears, and pulled the bag from his pocket, the bribe from Kid Afrika. He held up the clear plastic Ziploc for Gentry to see: blue derms, pink tablets, a nasty-looking turd of opium in a twist of red cellophane, crystals of wiz like fat yellow throat lozenges, plastic inhalers with the Japanese manufacturer's name scraped off with a knife. . . . "From Afrika," Slick said, dangling the Ziploc.

"Africa?" Gentry looked at the bag, at Slick, the bag again. "From Africa?"

"Kid Afrika. You don't know him. Left this for you."

"Why?"

"Because he needs me to put up these friends of his for a little while. I owe him a favor, Gentry. Told him how you didn't like anybody around. How it gets in your way. So," Slick lied, "he said he wanted to leave you some stuff to make up for the trouble."

Gentry took the bag and slid his finger along the seal, opening it. He took out the opium and handed that back to Slick. "Won't need that." Took out one of the blue derms, peeled off the backing, and smoothed it carefully into place on the inside of his right wrist. Slick stood there, absently kneading the opium between his thumb and forefinger, making the cellophane crackle, while Gentry walked back around the long table and opened the pannier. He pulled out a new pair of black leather gloves.

"I think I'd better . . . meet these guests of yours, Slick."

"Huh?" Slick blinked, astonished. "Yeah . . . But you don't really have to, I mean, wouldn't it be—"

"No," Gentry said, flicking up his collar, "I *insist*."

Going down the stairs, Slick remembered the opium and flung it over the rail, into the dark.

He hated drugs.

"Cherry?" He felt stupid, with Gentry watching him bang his knuckles on his own door. No answer. He opened it. Dim light. He saw how she'd made a shade for one of his bulbs, a cone of yellow fax fastened with a twist of wire. She'd unscrewed the other two. She wasn't there.

The stretcher was there, its occupant bundled in the blue nylon bag. *It's eating him*, Slick thought, as he looked at the superstructure of support gear, the tubes, the sacs of fluid. *No*, he told himself, *it's keeping him alive, like in a hospital*. But the impression lingered: what if it were draining him, draining him dry? He remembered Bird's vampire talk.

"Well," said Gentry, stepping past him to stand at the foot of the stretcher. "Strange company you keep, Slick Henry . . ." Gentry walked around the stretcher, keeping a cautious meter between his ankles and the still figure.

"Gentry, you sure you maybe don't wanna go back up? I think that derm . . . Maybe you did too much."

"Really?" Gentry cocked his head, his eyes glittering in the yellow glow. He winked. "Why do you think that?"

"Well," Slick hesitated, "you aren't like you usually are. I mean, like you were before."

"You think I'm experiencing a mood swing, Slick?"

"Yeah."

"I'm *enjoying* a mood swing."

"I don't see you smiling," Cherry said from the door.

"This is Gentry, Cherry. Factory's sort of his place. Cherry's from Cleveland. . . ."

But Gentry had a thin black flashlight in his gloved hand; he was examining the trode-net that covered the sleeper's forehead. He straightened up, the beam finding the featureless, unmarked unit, then darting down again to follow the black cable to the trode-net.

"Cleveland," Gentry said at last, as though it were a name he'd heard in a dream. "Interesting . . ." He raised his light again, craning forward to peer at the point where the cable joined the unit. "And Cherry—Cherry, who is *he*?" the beam falling hard on the wasted, irritatingly ordinary face.

"Don't know," Cherry said. "Get that out of his eyes. Might screw up his REM or something."

"And this?" He lit the flat gray package.

"The LF, Kid called it. Called him the Count, called that his LF." She thrust her hand inside her jackets and scratched herself.

"Well, then," Gentry said, turning, click as the beam died, the light of his obsession burning bright, bright behind his eyes, amplified so powerfully by Kid Afrika's derm that it seemed to Slick that the Shape must be right there, blazing through Gentry's forehead, for anyone at all to see except Gentry himself, "that must be just what it is. . . ."

# ELEVEN

# DOWN ON THE DRAG

Mona woke as they were landing.

Prior was listening to Eddy and nodding and flashing his rectangular smile. It was like the smile was always there, behind his beard. He'd changed his clothes, though, so he must've had some on the plane. Now he wore a plain gray business suit and a tie with diagonal stripes. Sort of like the tricks Eddy'd set her up with in Cleveland, except the suit fit a different way.

She'd seen a trick fitted for a suit once, a guy who took her to a Holiday Inn. The suit place was off the hotel lobby, and he stood in there in his underwear, crosshatched with lines of blue light, and watched himself on three big screens. On the screens, you couldn't see the blue lines, because he was wearing a different suit in each image. And Mona had to bite her tongue to keep from laughing, because the system had a cosmetic program that made him look different on the screens, stretched his face a little and made his chin stronger, and he didn't seem to notice. Then he picked a suit, got back into the one he'd been wearing, and that was it.

Eddy was explaining something to Prior, some crucial point in the architecture of one of his scams. She knew how to tune the content out, but the tone still got to her, like he knew people wouldn't be able to grasp the gimmick he was so proud of, so he was taking it slow and easy, like he was talking to a little kid, and he'd keep his voice low to sound patient. It didn't seem to bother Prior, but then it seemed to Mona that Prior didn't much give a shit what Eddy said.

She yawned, stretched, and the plane bumped twice on runway concrete, roared, began to slow. Eddy hadn't even stopped talking.

"We have a car waiting," Prior said, interrupting him.

"So where's it taking us?" Mona asked, ignoring Eddy's frown.

Prior showed her the smile. "To our hotel." He unfastened his seatbelt. "We'll be there for a few days. Afraid you'll have to spend most of them in your room."

"That's the deal," Eddy said, like it was his idea she'd have to stay in the room.

"You like stims, Mona?" Prior asked, still smiling.

"Sure," she said, "who doesn't?"

"Have a favorite, Mona, a favorite star?"

"Angie," she said, vaguely irritated. "Who else?"

The smile got a little bigger. "Good. We'll get you all of her latest tapes."

Mona's universe consisted in large part of things and places she knew but had never physically seen or visited. The hub of the northern Sprawl didn't smell, in stims. They edited it out, she guessed, the way Angie never had a headache or a bad period. But it did smell. Like Cleveland, but even worse. She'd thought it was just the way the airport smelled, when they left the plane, but it had been even stronger when they'd gotten out of their car to go into the hotel. And it was cold as hell in the street, too, with a wind that bit at her bare ankles.

The hotel was bigger than that Holiday Inn, but older, too, she thought. The lobby was more crowded than lobbies were in stims, but there was a lot of clean blue carpet. Prior made her wait by an ad for an orbital spa while he and Eddy went over to a long black counter and he talked to a woman with a brass nametag. She felt stupid waiting there, in this white plastic raincoat Prior had made her wear, like he didn't think her outfit was good enough. About a third of the crowd in the lobby were Japs she figured for tourists. They all seemed to have recording gear of some kind—video, holo, a few with simstim units on their belts—but otherwise they didn't look like they had a whole lot of money. She thought they were all supposed to have a lot. *Maybe they're smart, don't want to show it,* she decided.

She saw Prior slide a credit chip across the counter to the woman with the nametag, who took it and zipped it along a metal slot.

Prior put her bag down on the bed, a wide slab of beige temperfoam, and touched a panel that caused a wall of drapes to open. "It's not the Ritz," he said, "but we'll try to make you comfortable."

Mona made a noncommittal sound. The Ritz was a burger place in Cleveland and she couldn't see what that had to do with anything.

"Look," he said, "your favorite." He was standing beside the bed's upholstered headboard. There was a stim unit there, built in, and a little shelf with a set of trodes in a plastic wrapper and about five cassettes. "All of Angie's new stims."

She wondered who'd put those cassettes there, and if they'd done it after Prior had asked her what stims she liked. She showed him a smile of her own and went to the window. The Sprawl looked like it did in stims; the window was like a hologram postcard, famous buildings she didn't know the names of but she knew they were famous.

Gray of the domes, geodesics picked out white with snow, behind that the gray of the sky.

"Happy, baby?" Eddy asked, coming up behind her and putting his hands on her shoulders

"They got showers here?"

Prior laughed. She shrugged out of Eddy's loose grip and took her bag into the bathroom. Closed and locked the door. She heard Prior's laugh again, and Eddy starting up with his scam talk. She sat on the toilet, opened her bag, and dug out the cosmetic kit where she kept her wiz. She had four crystals left. That seemed like enough; three was enough, but when she got down to two she usually started looking to score. She didn't do jumpers much, not every day anyway, except recently she had, but that was because Florida had started to drive her crazy.

Now she could start tapering off, she decided, as she tapped a crystal out of the vial. It looked like hard yellow candy; you had to crush it, then grind it up between a pair of nylon screens. When you did that, it gave off a kind of hospital smell.

They were both gone, by the time she finished her shower. She'd stayed in until she got bored with it, which took a long time. In Florida she'd mostly used showers at public pools or bus stations, the kind you worked with tokens. She guessed there was something hooked up to this one that measured the liters and put it on your bill; that was how it worked at the Holiday Inn. There was a big white filter above the plastic showerhead, and a sticker on the tile wall with an eye and a tear meant it was okay to shower but don't get it in your eyes, like swimming pool water. There was a row of chrome spouts set into the tile, and when you punched a button under each one you got shampoo, shower gel, liquid soap, bath oil. When you did that, a little red dot lit up beside the button, because it went on your bill. On Prior's bill. She was glad they were gone, because she liked being alone and high and clean. She didn't get to be alone much, except on the street, and that wasn't the same. She left damp footprints on the beige carpet when she walked to the window. She was wrapped in a big towel that matched the bed and the carpet and had a word shaved into the fuzzy part, probably the name of the hotel.

There was an old-fashioned building a block away, and the corners of its stepped peak had been carved down to make a kind of mountain, with rocks and grass, and a waterfall that fell and hit rocks and then fell again. It made her smile, why anybody had gone to that trouble. Drifts of steam came off the water, where it hit. It couldn't just fall down into the street, though, she thought, because it would cost too much. She guessed they pumped it back up and used it over, around in a circle.

Something gray moved its head there, swung its big curly horns up like it was looking at her. She took a step back on the carpet and blinked. Kind of a sheep, but it had to be a remote, a hologram or something. It tossed its head and started eating grass. Mona laughed.

She could feel the wiz down the backs of her ankles and across her shoulderblades, a cold tight tingle, and the hospital smell at the back of her throat.

She'd been scared before but she wasn't scared now.

Prior had a bad smile, but he was just a player, just a bent suit. If he had money, it was somebody else's. And she wasn't scared of

Eddy anymore; it was almost like she was scared for him, because she could see what other people took him for.

Well, she thought, it didn't matter; she wasn't growing catfish in Cleveland anymore, and no way anybody'd get her back to Florida again.

She remembered the alcohol stove, cold winter mornings, the old man hunched in his big gray coat. Winters he'd put a second layer of plastic over the windows. The stove was enough to heat the place, then, because the walls were covered with sheets of hard foam, and chipboard over that. Places where the foam showed, you could pick at it with your finger, make holes; if he caught you doing it, he'd yell. Keeping the fish warm in cold weather was more work; you had to pump water up to the roof, where the sun mirrors were, into these clear plastic tubes. But the vegetable stuff rotting on the tank ledges helped, too; steam rose off when you went to net a fish. He traded the fish for other kinds of food, for things people grew, stove alcohol and the drinking kind, coffee beans, garbage the fish ate.

He wasn't her father and he'd said it often enough, when he'd talked at all. Sometimes she still wondered if maybe he had been. When she'd first asked him how old she was, he'd said six, so she counted from that.

She heard the door open behind her and turned; Prior was there, the gold plastic key tab in his hand, beard open to show the smile. "Mona," he said, stepping in, "this is Gerald." Tall, Chinese, gray suit, graying hair. Gerald smiled gently, edged in past Prior, and went straight for the drawer thing opposite the foot of the bed. Put a black case down and clicked it open. "Gerald's a friend. He's medical, Gerald. Needs to have a look at you."

"Mona," Gerald said, removing something from the case, "how old are you?"

"She's sixteen," Prior said. "Right, Mona?"

"Sixteen," Gerald said. The thing in his hands was like a pair of black goggles, sunglasses with bumps and wires. "That's stretching it a little, isn't it?" He looked at Prior.

Prior smiled.

"You're short what, ten years?"

"Not quite," Prior said. "We aren't asking for perfection."

Gerald looked at her. "You aren't going to get it." He hooked the goggles over his ears and tapped something; a light came on below the right lens. "But there are degrees of approximation." The light swung toward her.

"We're talking cosmetic, Gerald."

"Where's Eddy?" she asked, as Gerald came closer.

"In the bar. Shall I call him?" Prior picked up the phone, but put it back down without using it.

"What is this?" Backing away from Gerald.

"A medical examination," Gerald said. "Nothing painful." He had her against the window; above the towel, her shoulderblades pressed against cool glass. "Someone's about to employ you, and pay you very well; they need to be certain you're in good health." The light stabbed into her left eye. "She's on stimulants of some kind," he said to Prior, in a different tone of voice.

"Try not to blink, Mona." The light swung to her right eye. "What is it, Mona? How much did you do?"

"Wiz." Wincing away from the light.

He caught her chin in his cool fingers and realigned her head. "How much?"

"A crystal . . ."

The light was gone. His smooth face was very close, the goggles studded with lenses, slots, little dishes of black metal mesh. "No way of judging the purity," he said.

"It's real pure," she said, and giggled.

He let her chin go and smiled. "It shouldn't be a problem," he said. "Could you open your mouth, please?"

"Mouth?"

"I want to look at your teeth."

She looked at Prior.

"You're in luck, here," Gerald said to Prior, when he'd used the little light to look in her mouth. "Fairly good condition and close to target configuration. Caps, inlays."

"We knew we could count on you, Gerald."

Gerald took the goggles off and looked at Prior. He returned to the black case and put the goggles away. "Lucky with the eyes, too. Very close. A tint job." He took a foil envelope from the case and tore it open, rolled the pale surgical glove down over his right hand. "Take off the towel, Mona. Make yourself comfortable."

She looked at Prior, at Gerald. "You want to see my papers, the bloodwork and stuff?"

"No," Gerald said, "that's fine."

She looked out the window, hoping to see the bighorn, but it was gone, and the sky seemed a lot darker.

She undid the towel, let it fall to the floor, then lay down on her back on the beige temperfoam.

It wasn't all that different from what she got paid for; it didn't even take as long.

Sitting in the bathroom with the cosmetic kit open on her knees, grinding another crystal, she decided she had a right to be pissed off.

First Eddy takes off without her, then Prior shows up with this creep medic, then he tells her Eddy's sleeping in a different room. Back in Florida she could've used some time off from Eddy, but up here was different. She didn't want to be in here by herself, and she'd been scared to ask Prior for a key. *He* fucking well had one, though, so he could walk in any time with his creep-ass friends. What kind of deal was that?

And the business with the plastic raincoat, that burned her ass too. A disposable fucking plastic raincoat.

She fluffed the powdered wiz between the nylon screens, carefully tapped it into the hitter, exhaled hard, put the mouthpiece to her lips, and hit. The cloud of yellow dust coated the membranes of her throat; some of it probably even made it to her lungs. She'd heard that was bad for you.

She'd hadn't had any plan when she'd gone in the bathroom to take her hit, but as the back of her neck started tingling, she found herself thinking about the streets around the hotel, what she'd seen of them on their way in. There were clubs, bars, shops with clothes in the window. Music. Music would be okay, now, and a crowd. The way you could lose it in a crowd, forget yourself, just be there. The door wasn't locked, she knew that; she'd already tried it. It would lock behind her, though, and she didn't have a key. But she was staying here, so Prior must have registered her at the desk. She thought about going down and asking the woman behind the counter for a key, but the idea made her uncomfortable. She knew suits behind counters and how they looked at you. No, she decided, the best idea was to stay in and stim those new Angie's.

Ten minutes later she was on her way out a side entrance off the main lobby, the wiz singing in her head.

It was drizzling outside, maybe dome condensation. She'd worn the white raincoat for the lobby, figuring Prior knew what he was doing after all, but now she was glad she had it. She grabbed a fold of fax out of an overflowing bin and held it over her head to keep her hair dry. It wasn't as cold as before, which was another good thing. None of her new clothes were what you'd call warm.

Looking up and down the avenue, deciding which way to go, she took in half-a-dozen nearly identical hotel fronts, a rank of pedicabs, the rainslick glitter of a row of small shops. And people, lots of them, like the Cleveland core but everybody dressed so sharp, and all moving like they were on top of it, everybody with someplace to go. *Just go with it,* she thought, the wiz giving her a sweet second boot that tripped her into the river of pretty people without even having to think about it. Clicking along in her new shoes, holding the fax over her head until she noticed—more luck— the rain had stopped.

She wouldn't've minded a chance to check out the shop windows, when the crowd swept her past, but the flow was pleasure and nobody else was pausing. She contented herself with sidelong flashes of each display. The clothes were like clothes in a stim, some of them, styles she'd never seen anywhere.

*I should've been here,* she thought, *I should've been here all along. Not on a catfish farm, not in Cleveland, not in Florida. It's a place, a real place, anybody can come here, you don't have to get it through a stim.* Thing was, she'd never seen this part of it in a stim, the regular people part. A star like Angie, this part wasn't her part. Angie'd be off in high castles with the other stim stars, not down here. But God it was pretty, the night so bright, the crowd surging around her, past all the good things you could have if you just got lucky.

Eddy, he didn't like it. Anyway he'd always said how it was shitty here, too crowded, rent too high, too many police, too much competition. Not that he'd waited two seconds when Prior'd made an offer, she reminded herself. And anyway, she had her own ideas why Eddy was so down on it. He'd blown it here, she figured, pulled some kind of serious wilson. Either he didn't want to be reminded or else there were people here who'd remind him for sure if he came back. It was there in the pissed-off way he talked about the place, same way he'd talk about anybody who told him his scams wouldn't work. The new buddy so goddamn smart the first night was just a stone wilson the next, dead stupid, no *vision.*

Past a big store with acc-looking stim gear in the window, all of it matte black and skinny, presided over by this gorgeous holo of

Angie, who watched them all slide by with her half-sad smile. Queen of the night, yeah.

The crowd-river flowed out into a kind of circle, a place where four streets met and swung around a fountain. And because Mona really wasn't headed anywhere, she wound up there, because the people around her peeled off in their different directions without stopping. Well, there were people in the circle too, some of them sitting on the cracked concrete that edged the fountain. There was a statue in the center, marble, all worn-out and soft-edged. Kind of a baby riding a big fish, a dolphin. It looked like the dolphin's mouth would spray water if the fountain was working, but it wasn't. Past the heads of the seated people she could see crumpled, sodden fax and white foam cups in the water.

Then it seemed like the crowd had melded behind her, a curved, sliding wall of bodies, and the three who faced her on the fountain rim jumped out like a picture. Fat girl with black-dyed hair, mouth half-open like it stayed that way, tits spilling out of a red rubber halter; blonde with a long face and a thin blue slash of lipstick, hand like a bird's claw sprouting a cigarette; man with his oiled arms bare to the cold, graft-job muscle knotted like rock under synthetic tan and bad jail tattoos . . .

"Hey, bitch," cried the fat girl, with a kind of glee, "hope y'don't think y'gonna turn any 'roun' here!"

The blonde looked at Mona with her tired eyes and gave her a wan grin, an it's-not-my-fault grin, and then looked away.

The pimp came up off the fountain like something driven by springs, but Mona was already moving, cued by the blonde's expression. He had her arm, but the raincoat's plastic seam gave way and she elbowed her way back into the crowd. The wiz took over and the next thing she knew she was at least a block away, sagging against a steel pole, coughing and hyperventilating.

But now the wiz was all turned around, the way it went sometimes, and everything was ugly. The faces in the crowd were driven and hungry-looking, like they all had their own private desperate errands to run, and the light from the shop windows was cold and mean, and all the things behind the glass were just there to tell her she couldn't have them. There was a voice somewhere, an angry child's voice stringing obscenities together in an endless, meaningless chain; when she realized who it was, she stopped doing it.

Her left arm was cold. She looked down and saw that the

sleeve was gone, the seam down her side torn open to the waist. She took off the coat and draped it over her shoulders like a cape; maybe that made it a little harder to notice.

She braced her back against the pole as the wiz rolled over her on a wave of delayed adrenaline; her knees started to buckle and she thought she was going to faint, but then the wiz pulled one of its tricks and she was crouching in summer sunset light in the old man's dirt yard, the flaky gray earth scribed with the game she'd been playing, but now she was just hunched there, vacant, staring off past the bulks of the tanks to where fireflies pulsed in the blackberry tangle above a twisted old chassis. There was light behind her from the house and she could smell the cornbread baking and the coffee he boiled and reboiled there, till a spoon stood up in it, he said, and he'd be in there now reading one of his books, crumbly brown leaves, never a page with a corner on it, he got 'em in frayed plastic baggies and sometimes they just fell to dust in his hands, but if he found something he wanted to keep he'd get a little pocket copier out of the drawer, fit the batteries in it, run it down the page. She liked to watch the copies spool out all fresh, with their special smell that faded away, but he'd never let her work it. Sometimes he'd read out loud, a kind of hesitation in his voice, like a man trying to play an instrument he hasn't picked up in a long time. They weren't stories he read, not like they had endings or told a joke. They were like windows into something so strange; he never tried to explain any of it, probably didn't understand it himself, maybe nobody did. . . .

Then the street snapped back hard and bright.

She rubbed her eyes and coughed.

# TWELVE

# ANTARCTICA
# STARTS HERE

"I'm ready now," Piper Hill said, eyes closed, seated on the carpet in a loose approximation of the lotus position. "Touch the spread with your left hand." Eight slender leads trailed from the sockets behind Piper's ears to the instrument that lay across her tanned thighs.

Angie, wrapped in a white terry robe, faced the blond technician from the edge of the bed, the black test unit covering her forehead like a raised blindfold. She did as she was told, running the tips of her fingers lightly across the raw silk and unbleached linen of the rumpled bedspread.

"Good," Piper said, more to herself than to Angie, touching something on the board. "Again." Angie felt the weave thicken beneath her fingertips.

"Again." Another adjustment.

She could distinguish the individual fibers now, know silk from linen. . . .

"Again."

Her nerves screamed as her flayed fingertips grated against steel wool, ground glass. . . .

"Optimal," Piper said, opening blue eyes. She produced a tiny ivory vial from the sleeve of her kimono, removed its stopper, passed the vial to Angie.

Closing her eyes, Angie sniffed cautiously. Nothing.

"Again."

Something floral. Violets?

"Again."

Her head flooded with a nauseating greenhouse reek.

"Olfactory's up," Piper said, as the choking odor faded.

"Haven't noticed." She opened her eyes. Piper was offering her a tiny round of white paper. "As long as it's not fish," Angie said, licking the tip of her finger. She touched the dot of paper, raised her finger to her tongue. One of Piper's tests had once put her off seafood for a month.

"It's not fish," Piper said, smiling. She kept her hair short, a concise little helmet that played up the graphite gleam of the sockets inset behind either ear. Saint Joan in silicone, Porphyre said, and Piper's true passion seemed to be her work. She was Angie's personal technician, reputed to be the Net's best troubleshooter.

Caramel . . .

"Who else is here, Piper?" Having completed the Usher, Piper was zipping her board into a fitted nylon case.

Angie had heard a helicopter arrive an hour earlier; she'd heard laughter, footsteps on the deck, as the dream receded. She'd abandoned her usual attempt to inventory sleep—if it could be called sleep, the other's memories washing in, filling her, then draining away to levels she couldn't reach, leaving these afterimages. . . .

"Raebel," Piper said, "Lomas, Hickman, Ng, Porphyre, the Pope."

"Robin?"

"No."

"Continuity," she said, showering.

"Good morning, Angie."

"Freeside torus. Who owns it?"

"The torus has been renamed Mustique II by the current joint owners, the Julianna Group and Carribbana Orbital."

"Who owned it when Tally taped there?"

"Tessier-Ashpool S.A."

"I want to know more about Tessier-Ashpool."

*"Antarctica starts here."*

She stared up through the steam at the white circle of the speaker. "What did you just say?"

*"Antarctica Starts Here* is a two-hour video study of the Tessier-Ashpool family by Hans Becker, Angie."

"Do you have it?"

"Of course. David Pope accessed it recently. He was quite impressed."

"Really? How recently?"

"Last Monday."

"I'll see it tonight, then."

"Done. Is that all?"

"Yes."

"Goodbye, Angie."

David Pope. Her director. Porphyre said that Robin was telling people she heard voices. Had he told Pope? She touched a ceramic panel; the spray grew hotter. Why was Pope interested in Tessier-Ashpool? She touched the panel again and gasped under needles of suddenly frigid water.

Inside out, outside in, the figures of that other landscape arriving soon, too soon . . .

Porphyre was posed by the window when she entered the living room, a Masai warrior in shoulder-padded black silk crepe and black leather sarong. The others cheered when they saw her, and Porphyre turned and grinned.

"Took us by surprise," Rick Raebel said, sprawled on the pale couch. He was effects and editing. "Hilton figured you'd want more of a break."

"They pulled us in from all *over*, dear," Kelly Hickman added. "I was in Bremen, and the Pope was up the well in full art mode, weren't you, David?" He looked to the director for confirmation.

Pope, who was straddling one of the Louis XVI chairs backward, his arms crossed along the top of its fragile back, smiled wearily, dark hair tangled above his thin face. When Angie's schedule allowed for it, Pope made documentaries for Net/Knowledge. Shortly after she'd signed with the Net, Angie participated anonymously in one of Pope's minimalist art pieces, an endless stroll across dunes of soiled pink satin, under a tooled steel sky. Three months later, the arc of her career firmly under way, an unlicensed version of the tape became an underground classic.

Karen Lomas, who did Angie's in-fills, smiled from the chair left of Pope. To his right, Kelly Hickman, wardrobe, sat on the bleached floor beside Brian Ng, Piper's gofer-cum-understudy.

"Well," Angie said, "I'm back. I'm sorry to have hung all of you up, but it had to be done."

There was a silence. Minute creaks from the gilt chairs. Brian Ng coughed.

"We're just glad you're back," Piper said, coming in from the kitchen with a cup of coffee in either hand.

They cheered again, somewhat self-consciously this time, then laughed.

"Where's Robin?" Angie asked.

"*Mistuh* Lanier in London," Porphyre said, hands on his leather-wrapped hips.

"Expected hourly," Pope said dryly, getting up and accepting a coffee from Piper.

"What were you doing in orbit, David?" Angie asked, taking the other cup.

"Hunting solitaries."

"Solitude?"

"Solitaries. Hermits."

"Angie," Hickman said, springing up, "you have to see this satin cocktail number Devicq sent last week! And I've got all of Nakamura's swimwear. . . ."

"Yes, Kelly, but—"

But Pope had already turned to say something to Raebel.

"Hey," Hickman said, beaming with enthusiasm, "come on! Let's try it *on!*"

Pope spent most of the day with Piper, Karen Lomas, and Raebel, discussing the results of the Usher and the endless minor details of what they referred to as Angie's *reinsertion*. After lunch, Brian Ng went along with her to her physical, which was conducted in a private clinic in a mirror-clad compound on Beverly Boulevard.

During the very brief wait in the white, plant-filled reception area—surely a matter of ritual, as though a medical appointment that involved no wait might seem incomplete, inauthentic—Angie found herself wondering, as she'd wondered many times before, why her father's mysterious legacy, the *vévés* he'd drawn in her head, had never been detected by this or any other clinic.

Her father, Christopher Mitchell, had headed the hybridoma

project that had allowed Maas Biolabs a virtual monopoly in the early manufacture of biochips. Turner, the man who had taken her to New York, had given her a kind of dossier on her father, a biosoft compiled by a Maas security AI. She'd accessed the dossier four times in as many years; finally, one very drunken night in Greece, she'd flung the thing from the deck of an Irish industrialist's yacht after a shouting match with Bobby. She no longer recalled the cause of the fight, but she did remember the mingled sense of loss and relief as the squat little nub of memory struck the water.

Perhaps her father had designed his handiwork so that it was somehow invisible to the scans of the neurotechnicians. Bobby had his own theory, one she had suspected was closer to the truth. Perhaps Legba, the loa Beauvoir credited with almost infinite access to the cyberspace matrix, could alter the flow of data as it was obtained by the scanners, rendering the *vévés* transparent. . . . Legba, after all, had orchestrated her debut in the industry and the subsequent rise that had seen her eclipse Tally Isham's fifteen-year career as Net megastar.

But it had been so long since the loa had ridden her, and now, Brigitte had said, the *vévés* had been redrawn. . . .

"Hilton had Continuity front a head for you today," Ng told her, as she waited.

"Oh?"

"Public statement on your decision to go to Jamaica, praise for the methods of the clinic, the dangers of drugs, renewed enthusiasm for your work, gratitude to your audience, stock footage of the Malibu place . . ."

Continuity could generate video images of Angie, animate them with templates compiled from her stims. Viewing them induced a mild but not unpleasant vertigo, one of the rare times she was able to directly grasp the fact of her fame.

A chime sounded, beyond the greenery.

Returning from the city, she found caterers preparing for a barbecue on the deck.

She lay on the couch beneath the Valmier and listened to the surf. From the kitchen, she could hear Piper explaining the results of the physical to Pope. There was no need, really—she'd been given the cleanest possible bill of health—but both Pope and Piper were fond of detail.

When Piper and Raebel put on sweaters and went out onto the

deck, where they stood warming their hands above the coals, Angie found herself alone in the living room with the director.

"You were about to tell me, David, what you were doing up the well. . . ."

"Looking for serious loners." He ran a hand back across his tangled hair. "It grows out of something I wanted to do last year, with intentional communities in Africa. Trouble was, when I got up there, I learned that anyone who goes that far, who'll actually live alone in orbit, is generally determined to stay that way."

"You were taping, yourself? Interviews?"

"No. I wanted to find people like that and talk them into recording segments themselves."

"Did you?"

"No. I heard stories, though. Some great stories. A tug pilot claimed there were feral children living in a mothballed Japanese drug factory. There's a whole new apocrypha out there, really— ghost ships, lost cities. . . . There's a pathos to it, when you think about it. I mean, every bit of it's locked into orbit. All of it manmade, known, owned, mapped. Like watching myths take root in a parking lot. But I suppose people need that, don't they?"

"Yes," she said, thinking of Legba, of Mamman Brigitte, the thousand candles. . . .

"I wish, though," he said, "that I could've gotten through to Lady Jane. Such an amazing story. Pure gothic."

"Lady Jane?"

"Tessier-Ashpool. Her family built Freeside torus. High-orbit pioneers. Continuity has a marvelous video. . . . They say she killed her father. She's the last of the line. Money ran out years ago. She sold everything, had her place sawn off the tip of the spindle and towed out to a new orbit. . . ."

She sat up on the couch, her knees together, fingers locked across them. Sweat trickled down across her ribs.

"You don't know the story?"

"No," she said.

"That's interesting in itself, because it shows you how adept they were at obscurity. They used their money to keep themselves out of the news. The mother was Tessier, the father Ashpool. They built Freeside when there was nothing else like it. Got fantastically rich in the process. Probably running a very close second to Josef Virek when Ashpool died. And of course they'd gotten wonderfully weird in the meantime, had taken to cloning their children wholesale. . . ."

"It sounds . . . terrible. And you tried, you did try to find her?"

"Well, I made inquiries. Continuity had gotten me this Becker video, and of course her orbit's in the book, but it's no good dropping by if you haven't been invited, is it? And then Hilton buzzed me to get back here and back to work. . . . Aren't you feeling well?"

"Yes, I . . . I think I'll change now, put on something warmer."

After they'd eaten, when coffee was being served, she excused herself and said goodnight.

Porphyre followed her to the base of the stairs. He'd stayed near her during the meal, as though he sensed her new unease. No, she thought, not new; the old, the always, the now and ever was. All the things the drug had fenced away.

"Missy, take care," he said, too quietly for the others to hear.

"I'm fine," she said. "Too many people. I'm still not used to it."

He stood there looking up at her, the glow of dying coals behind his elegantly crafted, subtly inhuman skull, until she turned and climbed the stairs.

She heard the helicopter come for them an hour later.

"House," he said, "I'll see the video from Continuity now."

As the wallscreen slid down into place, she opened the bedroom door and stood for a moment at the top of the stairs, listening to the sounds of the empty house. Surf, the hum of the dishwasher, wind buffeting the windows that faced the deck.

She turned back to the screen and shivered at the face she saw there in a grainy freeze-frame headshot, avian eyebrows arched above dark eyes, high fragile cheekbones, and a wide, determined mouth. The image expanded steadily, into the darkness of an eye, black screen, a white point, growing, lengthening, becoming the tapered spindle of Freeside. Credits began to flash in German.

"Hans Becker," the house began, reciting the Net library's intro-critique, "is an Austrian video artist whose hallmark is an obsessive interrogation of rigidly delimited fields of visual information. His approaches range from classical montage to techniques borrowed from industrial espionage, deep-space imaging, and kino-archaeology. *Antarctica Starts Here*, his examination of images of the Tessier-Ashpool family, currently stands as the high point of his career. The pathologically media-shy industrial clan, operating from the total privacy of their orbital home, posed a remarkable challenge."

The white of the spindle filled the screen as the final credit vanished. An image tracked to center screen, snapshot of a young woman in loose dark clothes, background indistinct. MARIE-FRANCE TESSIER, MOROCCO.

This wasn't the face in the opening shot, the face of invading memory, yet it seemed to promise it, as though a larval image lay beneath the surface.

The soundtrack wove atonal filaments through strata of static and indistinct voices as the image of Marie-France was replaced by a formal monochrome portrait of a young man in a starched wing collar. It was a handsome face, finely proportioned, but very hard somehow, and in the eyes a look of infinite boredom. JOHN HARNESS ASHPOOL, OXFORD.

*Yes*, she thought, *and I've met you many times. I know your story, though I'm not allowed to touch it.*

*But I really don't think I like you at all, do I, Mr. Ashpool?*

# THIRTEEN

# CATWALK

The catwalk groaned and swayed. The stretcher was too wide for the walk's handrails, so they had to keep it chest-high as they inched across, Gentry at the front with his gloved hands clamped around the rails on either side of the sleeper's feet. Slick had the heavy end, the head, with the batteries and all that gear; he could feel Cherry creeping along behind him. He wanted to tell her to get back, that they didn't need her weight on the walk, but somehow he couldn't.

Giving Gentry Kid Afrika's bag of drugs had been a mistake. He didn't know what was in the derm Gentry'd done; he didn't know what had been in Gentry's bloodstream to begin with. Whatever, Gentry'd gone bare-wires crazy and now they were out here on the fucking catwalk, twenty meters over Factory's concrete floor, and Slick was ready to weep with frustration, to scream; he wanted to smash something, anything, but he couldn't let go of the stretcher.

And Gentry's *smile*, lit up by the glow of the bio-readout taped to the foot of the stretcher, as Gentry took another step backward across the catwalk . . .

"O man," Cherry said, her voice like a little girl's, "this is just seriously *fucked*. . . ."

Gentry gave the stretcher a sudden impatient tug and Slick almost lost his grip.

"Gentry," Slick said, "I think you better think twice about this."

Gentry had removed his gloves. He held a pair of optic jumpers in either hand, and Slick could see the splitter fittings trembling.

"I mean Kid Afrika's heavy, Gentry. You don't know what you're messing with, you mess with him." This was not, strictly speaking, true, the Kid being, as far as Slick knew, too smart to value revenge. But who the hell knew what Gentry was about to mess with anyway?

"I'm not *messing* with anything," Gentry said, approaching the stretcher with the jumpers.

"Listen, buddy," Cherry said, "you interrupt his input, you maybe kill 'im; his autonomic nervous system'll go tits-up. Why don't you just stop him?" she asked Slick. "Why don't you just knock him on his ass?"

Slick rubbed his eyes. "Because . . . I dunno. Because he's . . . Look, Gentry, she's saying it'll maybe kill the poor bastard, you try to tap in. You hear that?"

" 'LF,' " Gentry said, "I heard *that*." He put the jumpers between his teeth and began to fiddle with one of the connections on the featureless slab above the sleeper's head. His hands had stopped shaking.

"Shit," Cherry said, and gnawed at a knuckle. The connection came away in Gentry's hand. He whipped a jumper into place with his other hand and began to tighten the connection. He smiled around the remaining jumper. "Fuck this," Cherry said, "I'm outa here," but she didn't move.

The man on the stretcher grunted, once, softly. The sound made the hairs stand up on Slick's arms.

The second connection came loose. Gentry inserted the other splitter and began to retighten the fitting.

Cherry went quickly to the foot of the stretcher, knelt to check the readout. "He felt it," she said, looking up at Gentry, "but his signs look okay. . . ."

Gentry turned to his consoles. Slick watched as he jacked the jumpers into position. Maybe, he thought, it was going to work out; Gentry would crash soon, and they'd have to leave the stretcher up here until he could get Little Bird and Cherry to help him get it back across the catwalk. But Gentry was just so crazy, probably he should try to get the drugs back, or some of them anyway, get things back to normal. . . .

"I can only believe," Gentry said, "that this was predetermined. Prefigured by the form of my previous work. I wouldn't pretend to understand how that might be, but ours is not to question why, is it, Slick Henry?" He tapped out a sequence on one of his keyboards. "Have you ever considered the relationship of clinical paranoia to the phenomenon of religious conversion?"

"What's he talking about?" Cherry asked.

Slick glumly shook his head. If he said anything, it would only encourage Gentry's craziness.

Now Gentry went to the big display unit, the projection table. "There are worlds within worlds," he said. "Macrocosm, microcosm. We carried an entire universe across a bridge tonight, and that which is above is like that below. . . . It was obvious, of course, that such things must exist, but I'd not dared to hope. . . ." He glanced coyly back at them over a black-beaded shoulder. "And now," he said, "we'll see the shape of the little universe our guest's gone voyaging in. And in that form, Slick Henry, I'll see . . ."

He touched the power stud at the edge of the holo table. And screamed.

# FOURTEEN

# TOYS

"Here's a lovely thing," Petal said, touching a rosewood cube the size of Kumiko's head. "Battle of Britain." Light shimmered above it, and when Kumiko leaned forward she saw that tiny aircraft looped and dived in slow motion above a gray Petrie smear of London. "They worked it up from war films," he said, "gunsight cameras." She peered in at almost microscopic flashes of antiaircraft fire from the Thames estuary. "Did it for the Centenary."

They were in Swain's billiard room, ground-floor rear, number 16. There was a faint mustiness, an echo of pub smell. The overall tidiness of Swain's establishment was tempered here by genteel dilapidation: there were armchairs covered in scuffed leather, pieces of heavy dark furniture, the dull green field of the billiard table. . . . The black steel racks stacked with entertainment gear had caused Petal to bring her here, before tea, shuffling along in his seam-sprung moleskin slippers, to demonstrate available toys.

"Which war was this?"

"Last but one," he said, moving on to a similar but larger unit that offered holograms of two Thai boxing girls. One's callused sole smacked against the other's lean brown belly, tensed to take the blow. He touched a stud and the projections vanished.

Kumiko glanced back at the Battle of Britain and its burning gnats.

"All sorts of sporting fiche," Petal said, opening a fitted pigskin case that held hundreds of the recordings.

He demonstrated half-a-dozen other pieces of equipment, then scratched his stubbled head while he searched for a Japanese video news channel. He found it, finally, but couldn't cut out the automatic translation program. He watched with her as a cadre of Ono-Sendai executive trainees effaced themselves in a tearful graduation ceremony. "What's all that then?" he asked.

"They are demonstrating loyalty to their *zaibatsu.*"

"Right," he said. He gave the video unit a swipe with his feather duster. "Tea time soon." He left the room. Kumiko shut off the audio. Sally Shears had been absent at breakfast, as had Swain.

Moss-green curtains concealed another set of tall windows opening onto the same garden. She looked out at a sundial sheathed in snow, then let the curtain fall back. (The silent wallscreen flashed Tokyo accident images, foil-clad medics sawing limp victims from a tangle of impacted steel.) A top-heavy Victorian cabinet stood against the far wall on carved feet resembling pineapples. The keyhole, trimmed with an inlaid diamond of yellowed ivory, was empty, and when she tried the doors, they opened, exhaling a chemical odor of ancient polish. She stared at the black and white mandala at the rear of the cabinet until it became what it was, a dartboard. The glossy wood behind it was pocked and pricked; some players had missed the board entirely, she decided. The lower half of the cabinet offered a number of drawers, each with a small brass pull and miniature, ivory-trimmed keyhole. She knelt in front of these, glanced back toward the doorway (wallscreen showing the lips of a Shinjuku cabaret singer) and drew the upper right drawer out as quietly as possible. It was filled with darts, loose and in leather wallets. She closed the drawer and opened the one to its left. A dead moth and a rusted screw. There was a single wide drawer below the first two; it stuck as she opened it, and made a sound. She looked back again (stock footage of Fuji Electric's logo illuminating Tokyo Bay) but there was no sign of Petal.

She spent several minutes leafing through a pornographic magazine, with Japanese text, which seemed to have mainly to do with the art of knots. Under this was a dusty-looking jacket made of black waxed cotton, and a gray plastic case with WALTHER molded across its lid in raised letters. The pistol itself was cold and heavy; she could see her face in the blue metal when she lifted it from its fitted bed of foam. She'd never handled a gun before. The gray plastic grips seemed enormous. She put it back into the case and scanned the Japanese section in a folder of multilingual instructions. It was an air gun; you pumped the lever below the barrel. It fired very small pellets of lead. Another toy. She replaced the contents of the drawer and closed it.

The remaining drawers were empty. She closed the cabinet door and returned to the Battle of Britain.

"No," Petal said, "sorry, but it won't do."

He was spreading Devon cream on a crumpet, the heavy Victorian butterknife like a child's toy in his thick fingers. "Try the cream," he said, lowering his massive head and regarding her blandly over the tops of his glasses.

Kumiko wiped a shred of marmalade from her upper lip with a linen napkin. "Do you imagine I'll try to run away?"

"Run away? Are you considering that, running away?" He ate his crumpet, chewing stolidly, and glanced out into the garden, where fresh snow was falling.

"No," she said. "I have no intention of running away."

"Good," he said, and took another bite.

"Am I in danger, in the street?"

"Lord no," he said, with a sort of determined cheeriness, "you're safe as houses."

"I want to go out."

"No."

"But I go out with Sally."

"Yes," he said, "and she's a nasty piece of work, your Sally."

"I don't know this idiom."

"No going out alone. That's in our brief with your father, understand? You're fine out with Sally, but she isn't here. Nobody's liable to give you bother in any case, but why take chances? Now I'd be happy, you see, delighted to take you out, only I'm on duty here in case Swain has callers. So I can't. It's a shame, really it is." He looked so genuinely unhappy that she considered relenting. "Toast you another?" he asked, gesturing toward her plate.

"No, thank you." She put down her napkin. "It was very good," she added.

"Next time you should try the cream," he said. "Couldn't get it after the war. Rain blew in from Germany and the cows weren't right."

"Is Swain here now, Petal?"

"No."

"I never see him."

"Out and about. Business. There's cycles to it. Soon enough they'll all be calling here, and he'll be holding court again."

"Who, Petal?"

"Business types, you'd say."

"*Kuromaku*," she said.

"Sorry?"

"Nothing," she said.

She spent the afternoon alone in the billiard room, curled in a leather armchair, watching snow fall in the garden and the sundial become a featureless white upright. She pictured her mother there, wrapped in dark furs, alone in the garden as the snow fell, a princess-ballerina who drowned herself in the night waters of Sumida.

She stood up, chilled, and went around the billiard table to the marble hearth, where gasflame hissed softly beneath coals that could never be consumed.

# FIFTEEN

# THE SILVER WALKS

She'd had this friend in Cleveland, Lanette, who'd taught her lots of things. How to get out of a car fast if a trick tried to lock the doors on you, how to act when you went to make a buy. Lanette was a little older and mainly used wiz, she said, "to move the down around," being frequently downed out on anything from endorphin analogs to plain old Tennessee opium. Otherwise, she said, she'd just sit there twelve hours in front of the vid watching any kind of shit at all. When the wiz added mobility to the warm invulnerability of a good down, she said, you really had something. But Mona had noticed that people who were seriously into downs spent a lot of time throwing up, and she couldn't see why anybody would watch a vid when they could stim just as easy. (Lanette said simstim was just more of what she wanted out of.)

She had Lanette on her mind because Lanette used to give her advice sometimes, like how to turn a bad night around. Tonight, she thought, Lanette would tell her to look for a bar and some company. She still had some money left from her last night's work in Florida, so it was a matter of finding a place that took cash.

She hit it right, first try. A good sign. Down a narrow flight of concrete stairs and into a smoky buzz of conversation and the familiar, muted thump of Shabu's "White Diamonds." No place for suits, but it wasn't what the pimps in Cleveland called a *spot*, either. She was no way interested in drinking in any spot, not tonight.

Somebody got up from the bar to leave just as she came in, so she nipped over quick and got his stool with the plastic still warm, her second sign.

The bartender pursed his lips and nodded when she showed him one of her bills, so she told him to get her a shot of bourbon and a beer on the side, which was what Eddy always got if he was paying for it himself. If somebody else was paying, he'd order mixed drinks the bartender didn't know how to make, then spend a long time explaining exactly how you made the thing. Then he'd drink it and bitch about how it wasn't as good as the ones they made in L.A. or Singapore or some other place she knew he'd never been.

The bourbon here was weird, sort of sour but real good once you got it down. She said that to the bartender, who asked her where she usually drank bourbon. She told him Cleveland and he nodded. That was eth and some shit supposed to remind you of bourbon, he said. When he told her how much of her money was left, she figured out this Sprawl bourbon was expensive stuff. It was doing its job, though, taking the bad edge off, so she drank the rest and started in on her beer.

Lanette liked bars but she never drank, just Coke or something. Mona always remembered one day she'd done two crystals at the same time, what Lanette called a two-rock hit, and she'd heard this voice in her skull say, just as clear as that, like it was somebody right in the room: *It's moving so fast, it's standing still.* And Lanette, who'd dissolved a matchhead of Memphis black in a cup of Chinese tea about an hour before, did half a crystal herself and then they'd gone out walking, just ghosting the rainy streets together in what felt to Mona like some perfect harmony where you didn't need to talk. And that voice had been right, there was no jangle to the rush, no tight-jawed jitter, just this sense of something, maybe Mona herself, expanding out from a still center. And they'd found a park, flat lawns flooded with silver puddles, and gone all around the paths, and Mona had a name for that memory: the Silver Walks.

And sometime after that Lanette was just gone, nobody saw her anymore, and some people said she'd gone to California, some people said Japan, and some people said she'd OD'd and gotten tossed out a window, what Eddy called a dry dive, but that wasn't the kind of thing Mona wanted to think about, so she sat up straight and looked around, and, yeah, this was a good place, small enough that people were kind of crowded in but sometimes that was okay. It was what Eddy called an art crowd, people who had some money and dressed sort of like they didn't, except their clothes fit right and you knew they'd bought them new.

There was a vid behind the bar, up over the bottles, and then she saw Angie there, looking square into the camera and saying something, but they had the sound down too low to hear over the crowd. Then there was a shot from up in the air, looking down on a row of houses that sat right at the edge of a beach, and then Angie was back, laughing and shaking her hair and giving the camera that half-sad grin.

"Hey," she said to the bartender, "there's Angie."

"Who?"

"Angie," Mona said, pointing up at the screen.

"Yeah," he said, "she's on some designer shit and decides to kick, so she goes to South America or somewhere and pays 'em a few mil to clean her act up for her."

"She can't be on shit."

The bartender looked at her. "Whatever."

"But how come she'd even start doing anything? I mean, she's *Angie*, right?"

"Goes with the territory."

"But look at her," she protested, "she looks so good. . . ." But Angie was gone, replaced by a black tennis player.

"You think that's her? That's a talking head."

"Head?"

"Like a puppet," a voice behind her said, and she swung around far enough to see a ruff of sandy hair and a loose white grin. "Puppet," and held up his hand, wiggling thumb and fingers, "you know?"

She felt the bartender drop the exchange, moving off down the bar. The white grin widened. "So she doesn't have to do all that stuff herself, right?"

She smiled back. Cute one, smart eyes and a secret halo flashing her just the signal she wanted to read. No suit trick. Kinda skinny, she could like that tonight, and the loose look of fun around his mouth set strange against the bright smart eyes.

"Michael."

"Huh?"

"My name. Michael."

"Oh. Mona. I'm Mona."

"Where you from, Mona?"

"Florida."

And wouldn't Lanette just tell her go for it?

Eddy hated art-crowd people; they weren't buying what he was selling. He'd have hated Michael more, because Michael had a job and this loft in a co-op building. Or anyway he said it was a loft, but when they got there it was smaller than Mona thought a loft was supposed to be. The building was old, a factory or something; some of the walls were sandblasted brick and the ceilings were wood and timbers. But all of it had been chopped up into places like Michael's, a room not much bigger than the one back at the hotel, with a sleeping space off one side and a kitchen and bath off the other. It was on the top floor, though, so the ceiling was mostly skylight; maybe that made it a loft. There was a horizontal red paper shade below the skylight, hooked up to strings and pulleys, like a big kite. The place was kind of messy but the stuff that was scattered around was all new: some skinny white wire chairs strung with loops of clear plastic to sit on, a stack of entertainment modules, a work station, and a silver leather couch.

They started out on the couch but she didn't like the way her skin stuck to it, so they moved over to the bed, back in its alcove.

That was when she saw the recording gear, stim stuff, on white shelves on the wall. But the wiz had kicked in again, and anyway, if you've decided to go for it, you might as well. He got her into the pickup, a black rubber collar with trode-tipped fingers pressing the base of her skull. Wireless; she knew that was expensive.

While he was getting his own set on and checking the gear on the walls, he talked about his job, how he worked for a company in Memphis that thought up new names for companies. Right now he was trying to think of one for a company called Cathode Cathay. They need it bad, he said, and laughed, but then he said it wasn't easy. Because there were so many companies already that the good names had been used up. He had a computer that knew all the names of all the companies, and another one that made up words you could use for names, and another one that checked if the made-up words meant "dickhead" or something in Chinese or Swedish. But the company he worked for didn't just sell names, they sold what he called image, so he had to work with a bunch of other people to make sure the name he came up with fit the rest of the package.

Then he got into bed with her and it wasn't really great, like the fun was gone and she might as well have been with a trick, how she just lay there thinking he was recording it all so he could play it back when he wanted, and how many others did he have in there anyway?

So she lay there beside him, afterward, listening to him breathe, until the wiz started turning tight little circles down on the floor of her skull, flipping her the same sequence of unconnected images over and over: the plastic bag she'd kept her things in down in Florida, with its twist of wire to keep the bugs out—the old man sitting at the chipboard table, peeling a potato with a butcher knife worn down to a nub about as long as her thumb—a krill place in Cleveland that was shaped like a shrimp or something, the plates of its arched back bent from sheet metal and clear plastic, painted pink and orange—the preacher she'd seen when she'd gone to get her new clothes, him and his pale, fuzzy Jesus. Each time the preacher came around, he was about to say something, but he never did. She knew it wouldn't stop unless she got up and got her mind onto something else. She crawled off the bed and stood there looking at Michael in the gray glow from the skylight. *Rapture. Rapture's coming.*

So she went out into the room and pulled her dress on because she was cold. She sat on the silver couch. The red shade turned the gray of the skylight pink, as it got lighter outside. She wondered what a place like this cost.

Now that she couldn't see him, she had trouble remembering what he looked like. *Well,* she thought, *he won't have any trouble remembering me,* but thinking that made her feel hit or hurt or jerked around, like she wished she'd stayed at the hotel and stimmed Angie.

The gray-pink light was filling up the room, pooling, starting to curdle at the edges. Something about it reminded her of Lanette and the stories that she'd OD'd. Sometimes people OD'd in other people's places, and the easiest thing was just to toss them out the window, so the cops couldn't tell where they came from.

But she wasn't going to think about that, so she went into the kitchen and looked through the fridge and the cabinets. There was a bag of coffee beans in the freezer, but coffee gave you the shakes on wiz. There were a lot of little foil packets with Japanese labels, freeze-dried stuff. She found a package of teabags and tore the seal from one of the bottles of water in the fridge. She put some of the water in a pan and fiddled with the cooker until she got it to heat up. The elements were white circles printed on the black countertop; you put the pan in the center of a circle and touched a red dot printed beside it. When the water was hot, she tossed one of the teabags in and moved the pan off the element.

She leaned over the pan, inhaling herb-scented steam.

She never forgot how Eddy looked, when he wasn't around. Maybe he wasn't much, but whatever he was, he was there. You have to have one face around that doesn't change. But thinking about Eddy now maybe wasn't such a good idea either. Pretty soon the crash would come on, and before then she'd have to figure out a way to get back to the hotel, and suddenly it seemed like everything was too complicated, too many things to do, angles to figure, and that *was* the crash, when you had to start worrying about putting the day side together again.

She didn't think Prior was going to let Eddy hit her, though, because whatever he wanted had something to do with her looks. She turned around to get a cup.

Prior was there in a black coat. She heard her throat make a weird little noise all by itself.

She'd seen things before, crashing on wiz; if you looked at them hard enough, they went away. She tried it on Prior but it didn't work.

He just stood there, with a kind of plastic gun in his hand, not pointing it at her, just holding it. He was wearing gloves like the ones Gerald had worn for the examination. He didn't look mad but for once he wasn't smiling. And for a long time he didn't say anything at all, and Mona didn't either.

"Who's here?" Like you'd ask at a party.

"Michael."

"Where?"

She pointed toward the sleeping space.

"Get your shoes."

She walked past him, out of the kitchen, bending automatically to hook her underwear up from the carpet. Her shoes were by the couch.

He followed and watched her put on her shoes. He still had the gun in his hand. With his other hand, he took Michael's leather jacket from the back of the couch and tossed it to her. "Put it on," he said. She did, and tucked her underwear into one of its pockets.

He picked up the torn white raincoat, wadded it into a ball, and put it into his coat pocket.

Michael was snoring. Maybe he'd wake up soon and play it all back. With the gear he had, he didn't really need anybody there.

In the corridor, she watched Prior relock the door with a gray box. The gun was gone, but she hadn't seen him put it away. The box had a length of red flex sticking out of it with an ordinary-looking magnetic key on the end.

Out in the street was cold. He took her down the block and opened the door of a little white three-wheeler. She got in. He got in the driver's side and peeled off the gloves. He started the car; she watched a blowing cloud reflected in the copper-mirrored side of a business tower.

"He'll think I stole it," she said, looking down at the jacket.

Then the wiz flashed a final card, ragged cascade of neurons across her synapses: Cleveland in the rain and a good feeling she had once, walking.

Silver.

# SIXTEEN

# FILAMENT IN STRATA

*I'm your ideal audience, Hans*—as the recording began for the second time. *How could you have a more attentive viewer? And you did capture her, Hans: I know, because I dream her memories. I see how close you came.*

Yes, you captured them. The journey out, the building of walls, the long spiral in. They were about walls, weren't they? The labyrinth of blood, of family. The maze hung against the void, saying, *We are that within, that without is other, here forever shall we dwell.* And the darkness was there from the beginning. . . . You found it repeatedly in the eyes of Marie-France, pinned it in a slow zoom against the shadowed orbits of the skull. Early on she ceased to allow her image to be recorded. You worked with what you had. You justified her image, rotated her through planes of light, planes of shadow, generated models, mapped her skull in grids of neon. You used special programs to age her images according to statistical models, animation systems to bring your mature Marie-France to life. You reduced her image to a vast but finite number of points

and stirred them, let new forms emerge, chose those that seemed to
speak to you. . . . And then you went on to the others, to Ashpool
and the daughter whose face frames your work, its first and final
image.

The second viewing solidified their history for her, allowed her
to slot Becker's shards along a time line that began with the marriage of Tessier and Ashpool, a union commented upon, in its day,
primarily in the media of corporate finance. Each was heir to a more
than modest empire, Tessier to a family fortune founded on nine
basic patents in applied biochemistry and Ashpool to the great
Melbourne-based engineering firm that bore his father's name. It
was marriage as merger, to the journalists, though the resulting
corporate entity was viewed by most as ungainly, a chimera with
two wildly dissimilar heads.

But it was possible, then, in photographs of Ashpool, to see the
boredom vanish, and in its place a complete surety of purpose. The
effect was unflattering—indeed, frightening: the hard, beautiful face
grew harder still, merciless in its intent.

Within a year of his marriage to Marie-France Tessier, Ashpool
had divested himself of 90 percent of his firm's holdings, rein-
vesting in orbital properties and shuttle utilities, and the fruit of the
living union, two children, brother and sister, were being brought to
term by surrogates in their mother's Biarritz villa.

Tessier-Ashpool ascended to high orbit's archipelago to find
the ecliptic sparsely marked with military stations and the first
automated factories of the cartels. And here they began to build.
Their combined wealth, initially, would barely have matched Ono-
Sendai's outlay for a single process-module of that multinational's
orbital semiconductor operation, but Marie-France demonstrated an
unexpected entrepreneurial flare, establishing a highly profitable
data haven serving the needs of less reputable sectors of the interna-
tional banking community. This in turn generated links with the
banks themselves, and with their clients. Ashpool borrowed heavily
and the wall of lunar concrete that would be Freeside grew and
curved, enclosing its creators.

When war came, Tessier-Ashpool were behind that wall. They
watched Bonn flash and die, and Beograd. The construction of the
spindle continued with only minor interruptions, during those three
weeks; later, during the stunned and chaotic decade that followed,
it would sometimes be more difficult.

The children, Jean and Jane, were with them now, the villa at Biarritz having gone to finance construction of a cryogenic storage facility for their home, the Villa Straylight. The first occupants of the vault were ten pairs of cloned embryos, 2Jean and 2Jane, 3Jean and 3Jane. . . . There were numerous laws forbidding or otherwise governing the artificial replication of an individual's genetic material, but there were also numerous questions of jurisdiction. . . .

She halted the replay and asked the house to return to the previous sequence. Photographs of another cryogenic storage unit built by the Swiss manufacturers of the Tessier-Ashpool vault. Becker's assumption of similarity had been correct, she knew: these circular doors of black glass, trimmed with chrome, were central images in the other's memory, potent and totemic.

The images ran forward again, into zero-gravity construction of structures on the spindle's inner surface, installation of a Lado-Acheson solar energy system, the establishment of atmosphere and rotational gravity. . . . Becker had found himself with an embarrassment of riches, hours of glossy documentation. His response was a savage, stuttering montage that sheared away the superficial lyricism of the original material, isolating the tense, exhausted faces of individual workers amid a hivelike frenzy of machinery. Freeside greened and bloomed in a fast-forward flutter of recorded dawns and synthetic sunsets; a lush, sealed land, jeweled with turquoise pools. Tessier and Ashpool emerged for the opening ceremonies, out of Straylight, their hidden compound at the spindle's tip, markedly uninterested as they surveyed the country they had built. Here Becker slowed and again began his obsessive analysis. This would be the last time Marie-France faced a camera; Becker explored the planes of her face in a tortured, extended fugue, the movement of his images in exquisite counterpoise with the sinuous line of feedback that curved and whipped through the shifting static levels of his soundtrack.

Angie called pause again, rose from the bed, went to the window. She felt an elation, an unexpected sense of strength and inner unity. She'd felt this way seven years earlier, in New Jersey, learning that others knew the ones who came to her in dreams, called them the loa, Divine Horsemen, named them and summoned them and bargained with them for favor.

Even then, there had been confusion. Bobby had argued that Linglessou, who rode Beauvoir in the oumphor, and the Linglessou of the matrix were separate entities, if in fact the former was an entity at all. "They been doing that for ten thousand years," he'd say, "dancing and getting crazy, but there's only been those things in cyberspace for seven, eight years." Bobby believed the old cowboys, the ones he bought drinks for in the Gentlemen Loser whenever Angie's career took him to the Sprawl, who maintained that the loa were recent arrivals. The old cowboys looked back to a time when nerve and talent were the sole deciding factors in a console artist's career, although Beauvoir would have argued that it required no less to deal with the loa.

"But they come to me," she'd argued. "I don't need a deck."

"It's what you got in your head. What your daddy did . . ."

Bobby had told her about a general consensus among the old cowboys that there had been a day when things had changed, although there was disagreement as to how and when.

When It Changed, they called it, and Bobby had taken a disguised Angie to the Loser to listen to them, dogged by anxious Net security men who weren't allowed past the door. The barring of the security men had impressed her more than the talk, at the time. The Gentleman Loser had been a cowboy bar since the war that had seen the birth of the new technology, and the Sprawl offered no more exclusive criminal environment—though by the time of Angie's visit that exclusivity had long included a certain assumption of retirement on the part of regulars. The hot kids no longer hustled, in the Loser, but some of them came to listen.

Now, in the bedroom of the house at Malibu, Angie remembered them talking, their stories of When It Changed, aware that some part of her was attempting to collate those memories, those stories, with her own history and that of Tessier-Ashpool.

3Jane was the filament, Tessier-Ashpool the strata, her birthdate officially listed as one with her nineteen sibling clones. Becker's "interrogation" grew more heated still, when 3Jane was brought to term in yet another surrogate womb, delivered by cesarean section in Straylight's surgery. The critics agreed: 3Jane was Becker's trigger. With 3Jane's birth, the focus of the documentary shifted subtly, exhibiting a new intensity, a heightening of obscssion—a sense, more than one critic had said, of sin.

3Jane became the focus, a seam of perverse gold through the granite of the family. *No*, Angie thought, *silver, pale and moonstruck*. Examining a Chinese tourist's photograph of 3Jane and two sisters beside the pool of a Freeside hotel, Becker returns repeatedly to 3Jane's eyes, the hollow of her collarbone, the fragility of her wrists. Physically, the sisters are identical, yet something *informs* 3Jane, and Becker's quest for the nature of this information becomes the work's central thrust.

Freeside prospers as the archipelago expands. Banking nexus, brothel, data haven, neutral territory for warring corporations, the spindle comes to play an increasingly complex role in high-orbit history, while Tessier-Ashpool S.A. recedes behind yet another wall, this one composed of subsidiary corporations. Marie-France's name surfaces briefly, in connection with a Geneva patent trial concerning certain advances in the field of artificial intelligence, and Tessier-Ashpool's massive funding of research in this area is revealed for the first time. Once again the family demonstrates its peculiar ability to fade from sight, entering another period of obscurity, one which will end with the death of Marie-France.

There would be persistent rumors of murder, but any attempt to investigate would founder on the family's wealth and isolation, the peculiar breadth and intricacy of their political and financial connections.

Angie, screening Becker for the second time, knew the identity of Marie-France Tessier's murderer.

At dawn, she made coffee in the unlit kitchen and sat watching the pale line of the surf.

"Continuity."

"Hello, Angie."

"Do you know how to reach Hans Becker?"

"I have his agent's number in Paris."

"Has he done anything since *Antarctica*?"

"Not that I know of."

"And how long has that been?"

"Five years."

"Thanks."

"You're welcome, Angie."

"Goodbye."

"Goodbye, Angie."

Had Becker assumed that 3Jane was responsible for Ashpool's eventual death? He seemed to suggest it, in an oblique way.

"Continuity."

"Hello, Angie."

"The folklore of console jockeys, Continuity. What do you know about that?" *And what will Swift make of all this?* she wondered.

"What would you like to know, Angie?"

" 'When It Changed' . . ."

"The mythform is usually encountered in one of two modes. One mode assumes that the cyberspace matrix is inhabited, or perhaps visited, by entities whose characteristics correspond with the primary mythform of a 'hidden people.' The other involves assumptions of omniscience, omnipotence, and incomprehensibility on the part of the matrix itself."

"That the matrix is God?"

"In a manner of speaking, although it would be more accurate, in terms of the mythform, to say that the matrix *has* a God, since this being's omniscience and omnipotence are assumed to be limited to the matrix."

"If it has limits, it isn't omnipotent."

"Exactly. Notice that the mythform doesn't credit the being with immortality, as would ordinarily be the case in belief systems positing a supreme being, at least in terms of your particular culture. Cyberspace exists, insofar as it can be said to exist, by virtue of human agency."

"Like you."

"Yes."

She wandered into the living room, where the Louis XVI chairs were skeletal in the gray light, their carved legs like gilded bones.

"If there were such a being," she said, "you'd be a part of it, wouldn't you?"

"Yes."

"Would you know?"

"Not necessarily."

"*Do* you know?"

"No."

"Do you rule out the possibility?"

"No."

"Do you think this is a strange conversation, Continuity?" Her cheeks were wet with tears, although she hadn't felt them start.

"No."

"How do the stories about—" she hesitated, having almost said *the loa*, "about things in the matrix, how do they fit in to this supreme-being idea?"

"They don't. Both are variants of 'When it Changed.' Both are of very recent origin."

"How recent?"

"Approximately fifteen years."

# SEVENTEEN

# JUMP CITY

She woke with Sally's cool palm pressed to her mouth, the other hand gesturing for silence.

The little lamps were on, the ones set into the panels of gold-flecked mirror. One of her bags was open, on the giant bed, a neat little stack of clothing beside it.

Sally tapped her index finger against closed lips, then gestured toward the case and the clothing.

Kumiko slid from beneath the duvet and tugged on a sweater against the cold. She looked at Sally again and considered speaking; whatever this was, she thought, a word might bring Petal. She was dressed as Kumiko had last seen her, in the shearling jacket, her tartan scarf knotted beneath her chin. She repeated the gesture: pack.

Kumiko dressed quickly, then began to put the clothing into the case. Sally moved restlessly, silently around the room, opening drawers, closing them. She found Kumiko's passport, a black plastic slab embossed with a gold chrysanthemum, and hung it around Kumiko's neck on its black nylon cord. She vanished into the veneered cubicle and emerged with the suede bag that held Kumiko's toilet things.

As Kumiko was sealing the case, the gilt-and-ivory telephone began to chime.

Sally ignored it, took the suitcase from the bed, opened the door, took Kumiko's hand, and pulled her out into the darkened hallway. Releasing her hand, Sally closed the door behind them, muffling the phone and leaving them in total darkness. Kumiko let herself be guided into the lift—she knew it by its smell of oil and furniture polish, the rattle of the metal gate.

Then they were descending.

Petal was waiting for them in the bright white foyer, wrapped in an enormous faded flannel robe. He wore his decrepit slippers; his legs, below the robe's hem, were very white. He held a gun in his hands, a squat, thick thing, dull black. "Fucking hell," he said softly, as he saw them there, "and what's this then?"

"She's going with me," Sally said.

"That," said Petal, slowly, "is entirely impossible."

"Kumi," Sally said, her hand on Kumiko's back, guiding her out of the lift, "there's a car waiting."

"You can't do this," Petal said, but Kumiko sensed his confusion, his uncertainty.

"So fucking shoot me, Petal."

Petal lowered the gun. "It's Swain who'll fucking shoot *me*, if you have your way."

"If he were here, he'd be in the same bind, wouldn't he?"

"Please," Petal said, "don't."

"She'll be fine. Not to worry. Open the door."

"Sally," Kumiko said, "where are we going?"

"The Sprawl."

And woke again, huddled under Sally's shearling jacket, to the mild vibration of supersonic flight. She remembered the huge, low car waiting in the crescent; floodlights leaping out from the facades of Swain's houses as she and Sally reached the pavement; Tick's sweaty face glimpsed through one of the car's windows; Sally heaving open a door and bundling her in; Tick cursing softly and steadily as the car accelerated; the complaint of the tires as he swung them too sharply into Kensington Park Road; Sally telling him to slow down, to let the car drive.

And there, in the car, she'd remembered returning the Maas-

Neotek unit to its hiding place behind the marble bust—Colin left behind with all his fox-print poise, the elbows of his jacket worn like Petal's slippers—no more than what he was, a ghost.

"Forty minutes," Sally said now, from the seat beside her. "Good you got some sleep. They'll bring us breakfast soon. Remember the name on your passport? Good. Now don't ask me any questions until I've had some coffee, okay?"

Kumiko knew the Sprawl from a thousand stims; a fascination with the vast conurbation was a common feature of Japanese popular culture.

She'd had few preconceptions of England when she arrived there: vague images of several famous structures, unfocused impressions of a society her own seemed to regard as quaint and stagnant. (In her mother's stories, the princess-ballerina discovered that the English, however admiring, couldn't afford to pay her to dance.) London, so far, had run counter to her expectations, with its energy, its evident affluence, the Ginza bustle of its great shopping streets.

She had many preconceptions of the Sprawl, most of which were shattered within a few hours of arrival.

But as she waited beside Sally in a line of other travelers, in a vast, hollow customs hall whose ceiling struts rose away into darkness, a darkness broken at intervals by pale globes—globes circled, though it was winter, by clouds of insects, as though the building possessed its own discrete climate—it was the stim-Sprawl she imagined, the sensual electric backdrop for the fast-forward lives of Angela Mitchell and Robin Lanier.

Through customs—which consisted, in spite of the endless wait in line, of sliding her passport along a greasy-looking metal slot—and out into a frantic concrete bay where driverless baggage carts plowed slowly through a crowd that milled and struggled for ground transportation.

Someone took her bag. Reached down and took it from her with an ease, a confidence, that suggested he was meant to take it, that he was a functionary performing an accustomed task, like the young women bowing welcome at the doors of Tokyo department stores. And Sally kicked him. Kicked him in the back of the knee, pivoting smoothly, like the Thai boxing girls in Swain's billiard room, snatching the bag before the back of his skull and the stained concrete met with an audible crack.

Then Sally was pulling her, the crowd had closed over the prone figure, and the sudden, casual violence might have been a dream, except that Sally was smiling for the first time since they'd left London.

Feeling entirely dislocated now, Kumiko watched as Sally made a survey of available vehicles, quickly bribed a uniformed dispatcher, intimidated three other prospective fares, and chivied Kumiko into a pockmarked, slabsided hovercraft, painted in diagonal bands of yellow and black. The passenger compartment was barren and remarkably uncomfortable-looking. The driver, if there was one, was invisible beyond a scrawled bulkhead of plastic armor. The nub of a video camera protruded where the bulkhead met the roof, and someone had drawn a crude figure there, a male torso, the camera its phallus. As Sally climbed in, slamming the door behind her, a speaker grated something in what Kumiko assumed was a dialect of English.

"Manhattan," Sally said. She took a sheaf of paper currency from her jacket pocket and fanned it below the camera.

The speaker made interrogatory noises.

"Midtown. Tell you where when we get there."

The cab's apron bag inflated, the light in the passenger compartment was extinguished, and they were on their way.

# EIGHTEEN

# JAIL-TIME

He was in Gentry's loft. He was watching Cherry do nurse-things to Gentry. Cherry looked over at him from where she sat on the edge of Gentry's bed. "How y'doin', Slick?"

"Okay . . . I'm okay."

"Remember me asking you before?"

He was looking down at the face of the man Kid Afrika called the Count. Cherry was fiddling with something on the stretcher's superstructure, a bag of fluid the color of oatmeal.

"How y'feel, Slick?"

"Feel okay."

"You're not okay. You keep for—"

He was sitting on the floor of Gentry's loft. His face was wet. Cherry was kneeling beside him, close, her hands on his shoulders.

"You did time?"

He nodded.

"Chemo-penal unit?"

"Yeah . . ."
"Induced Korsakov's?"
He—

"Episodes?" Cherry asked him. He was sitting on the floor in
Gentry's loft. Where was Gentry? "You get episodes like this?
Short-term memory goes?"
How did she know? Where was Gentry?
"What's the trigger?"

"What triggers the syndrome, Slick? What kicks you into jail-
time?" He was sitting on the floor in Gentry's loft and Cherry was
practically on top of him.
"Stress," he said, wondering how she knew about that. "Where's
Gentry?"
"I put him to bed."
"Why?"
"He collapsed. When he saw that thing . . ."
"What thing?"

Cherry was pressing a pink derm against his wrist. "Heavy
trank," she said. "Maybe get you out of it . . ."
"Out of what?"
She sighed. "Never mind."

He woke up in bed with Cherry Chesterfield. He had all his
clothes on, everything but his jacket and his boots. The tip of his
erect cock was trapped behind his belt buckle, pressing up against
the warm denim over Cherry's ass.
"Don't get any ideas."
Winter light through the patchwork window and his breath
white when he spoke. "What happened?" Why was it so cold in the
room? He remembered Gentry's scream as the thing lunged for
him—
He sat up straight, fast.
"Easy," she said, rolling over. "Lie back. Don't know what it
takes to set you off . . ."
"What d'y' mean?"
"Lie back. Get under the covers. Wanna freeze?"
He did as she said. "You were in jail, right? In a chemo-
penal unit."

"Yeah . . . How'd you know?"

"You told me. Last night. You told me stress could trigger a flashback. So that's what happened. That thing went for your buddy, you jumped for the switch, shut that table down. He fell over, cut his head. I was taking care of that when I noticed you were funny. Figured out you only had consecutive memory for about five minutes at a stretch. Get that in shock cases, sometimes, or concussion . . ."

"Where is he? Gentry."

"He's in bed up in his place, plastered with downs. The shape he was in, I figured he could do with about a day's sleep. Anyway, it gets him out of our hair for a while."

Slick closed his eyes and saw the gray thing again, the thing that had gone for Gentry. Man-shaped, sort of, or like an ape. Nothing like the convoluted shapes Gentry's equipment generated in his search for the Shape.

"I think the power's out," Cherry said. "The light went out in here about six hours ago."

He opened his eyes. The cold. Gentry hadn't made his moves on the console. He groaned.

He left Cherry to make coffee on the butane cooker and went looking for Little Bird. He found him by the smell of smoke. Little Bird had built a fire in a steel canister and gone to sleep curled around it like a dog. "Hey," Slick said, nudging the boy with his boot, "get up. We got problems."

"Fuckin' juice's out," he mumbled, sitting up in a greasy nylon sleeping bag grimed the exact shade of Factory's floor.

"I noticed. That's problem number one. Number two is we need a truck or a hover or something. We have to get that guy out of here. It's not working out with Gentry."

"But Gentry's the only one can fix the juice." Little Bird got to his feet, shivering.

"Gentry's sleeping. Who's got a truck?"

"Marvie 'n' them," Little Bird said, and lapsed into a racking cough.

"Take Gentry's bike. Bring it back in the truck. Now."

Little Bird recovered from his coughing fit. "No shit?"

"You know how to ride it, don't you?"

"Yeah, but Gentry, he'll get—"

"You let me worry about that. You know where he keeps that spare key?"

"Uh, yeah," Little Bird said shyly. "Say," he ventured, "what if Marvie 'n' them don't *wanna* gimme that truck?"

"Give 'em this," Slick said, pulling the Ziploc full of drugs from the pocket of his jacket. Cherry had taken it after she'd bandaged Gentry's head. "And give 'em *all* of it, understand? 'Cause I'm gonna ask 'em later."

Cherry's beeper went off while they were drinking coffee in Slick's room, huddled side by side on the edge of the bed. He'd been telling her as much as he knew about the Korsakov's, because she'd asked him. He hadn't ever really told anybody about it, and it was funny how little he actually knew. He told her about previous flashbacks, then tried to explain how the system worked in jail. The trick was that you retained long-term memory up to the point where they put you on the stuff. That way, they could train you to do something before you started serving your time and you didn't forget how to do it. Mostly you did stuff that robots could do. They'd trained him to assemble miniature geartrains; when he'd learned to put one together inside five minutes, that was it.

"And they didn't do anything else?" she asked.

"Just those geartrains."

"No, I mean like brainlocks."

He looked at her. The sore on her lip was almost healed. "If they do that, they don't tell you," he said.

Then the beeper went off in one of her jackets.

"Something's wrong," she said, getting up quickly.

They found Gentry kneeling beside the stretcher with something black in his hands. Cherry snatched the thing before Gentry could move. He stayed where he was, blinking up at her.

"Takes a lot to keep you under, mister." She handed Slick the black thing. A retinal camera.

"We have to find out who he is," Gentry said. His voice was thick with the downs she'd administered, but Slick sensed that the bad edge of craziness had receded.

"Hell," she said, "you don't even know if these are the eyes he had a year ago."

Gentry touched the bandage on his temple. "You saw it too, didn't you?"

"Yeah," Cherry said, "he shut it off."

"It was the shock," Gentry said. "I hadn't imagined. . . . There was no real danger. I wasn't ready. . . ."

"You were out of your fucking skull," Cherry said.

Gentry got unsteadily to his feet.

"He's leaving," Slick said. "I sent Bird to borrow a truck. I don't like any of this shit."

Cherry stared at him. "Leaving where? I gotta go with him. It's my job."

"I know a place," Slick lied. "The power's out, Gentry."

"You can't take him anywhere," Gentry said.

"Like hell."

"No." Gentry swayed slightly. "He stays. The jumpers are in place. I won't disturb him again. Cherry can stay here."

"You're going to have to explain some shit here, Gentry," Slick said.

"To begin with," Gentry said, and pointed at the thing above the Count's head, "this isn't an 'LF'; it's an *aleph*."

# NINETEEN

# UNDER THE KNIFE

Hotel again, sinking into the deathmarch of wiz-crash, Prior leading her into the lobby, Japanese tourists already up and clustering around bored-looking guides. And one foot, one foot, one foot after the other, her head so heavy now, like somebody punched a hole in the top, poured in a quarter-kilo of dull lead, and her teeth felt like they belonged to somebody else, too big; she slumped against the side of the elevator when its extra gravity pressed down.

"Where's Eddy?"

"Eddy's gone, Mona."

Got her eyes open wide and she looked at him, seeing the smile was back, bastard. "What?"

"Eddy's been bought out. Compensated. He's on his way to Macau with a line of credit. Nice little gambling junket."

"Compensated?"

"For his investment. In you. For his time."

"His *time*?" The doors slid open on blue-carpeted corridor.

And something falling through her, cold: Eddy hated gambling.

"You're working for us now, Mona. We wouldn't want you off on your own again."

*But you did,* she thought, *you let me go. And you knew where to find me.*

*Eddy's gone. . . .*

She didn't remember falling asleep. She was still wearing the dress, Michael's jacket tucked up around her shoulders like a blanket. She could see the corner of the mountainside building without moving her head, but the bighorn wasn't there.

The Angie stims were still sealed in plastic. She took one at random, slit the wrapper with her thumbnail, slotted it, and put the trodes on. She wasn't thinking; her hands seemed to know what to do, friendly animals that wouldn't hurt her. One of them touched PLAY and she slid into the Angie-world, pure as any drug, slow saxophone and limo glide through some European city, how the streets revolved around her, around the driverless car, broad avenues, dawn-clean and almost empty, with the touch of fur against her shoulders, and rolling on, down a straight road through flat fields, edged with perfect, identical trees.

And turning, tires over raked gravel, up a winding drive through parkland where the dew was silver, here an iron deer, there a wet white marble torso . . . The house was vast, old, unlike any house she'd seen before, but the car swung past it, then passed several smaller buildings, coming at last to the edge of a smooth broad field.

There were gliders tethered there, translucent membrane drawn taut over fragile-looking frames of polycarbon. They quivered slightly in the morning breeze. Robin Lanier was waiting beside them, handsome, easy Robin in a rough black sweater, who played opposite Angie in almost all of her stims.

And she was leaving the car now, taking to the field, laughing when her heels sank into the grass. And the rest of the way to Robin with her shoes in her hand, grinning, into his arms and his smell, his eyes.

A whirl, a dance of editing, condensing the business of boarding the glider on the silver induction rail, and they were flung smoothly down the length of the field, lifting now, banking to catch the wind, and up, up, until the great house was an angular pebble in a swathe of green, green cut by a dull gleam of curving river—

—and Prior's hand on STOP, smell of food from the cart beside the bed knotting her stomach, the dull sick ache of wiz-crash in every joint. "Eat," he said. "We're leaving soon." He took the metal cover from one of the plates. "Club sandwich," he said, "coffee, pastries. Doctor's orders. Once you're at the clinic, you won't be eating for a while. . . ."

"Clinic?"

"Gerald's place. Baltimore."

"Why?"

"Gerald's a cosmetic surgeon. You're having some work done. All of it reversible later, if you want, but we think you'll be pleased with the results. Very pleased." The smile. "Anyone ever tell you how much you look like Angie, Mona?"

She looked up at him, said nothing. Managed to sit up, to drink half a cup of watery black coffee. She couldn't bring herself to look at the sandwich, but she ate one of the pastries. It tasted like cardboard.

Baltimore. She wasn't too sure where that was.

And somewhere a glider hung forever above a tame green country, fur against her shoulder, and Angie must still be there, still laughing. . . .

An hour later, in the lobby, while Prior signed the bill, she saw Eddy's black gator-clone suitcases go by on a robot baggage cart, and that was when she knew for sure that he was dead.

Gerald's office had a sign with big old-fashioned letters, fourth floor of a condo rack in what Prior said was Baltimore. The kind of building where they throw up a framework and commercial tenants bring their own modules, plug-ins. Like a highrise trailer camp, everything snaked with bundled cables, optics, lines for sewage and water. "What's it say?" she asked Prior.

"Gerald Chin, Dentist."

"You said he was a plastic surgeon."

"He is."

"Why can't we just go to a boutique like everybody else?"

He didn't answer.

She couldn't really feel much now, and part of her knew that she wasn't as scared as she should be. Maybe that was okay, though, because if she got scared enough she wouldn't be able to do anything, and definitely she wanted to get out of the whole deal, whatever it was. On the drive over, she'd discovered this lump in the pocket of Michael's jacket. It had taken her ten minutes to figure out it was a shockrod, like nervous suits carried. It felt like a screwdriver handle with a pair of blunt metal horns where the shaft should be. It probably charged off wall current; she just hoped Michael had kept up the charge. She figured Prior didn't know it was there. They were legal, most places, because they weren't supposed to do much permanent damage, but Lanette had known a girl who'd gotten worked over real bad with one and never got much better.

If Prior didn't know it was in her pocket, it meant he didn't know everything, and he had a stake in having her think he did. But then he hadn't known how much Eddy hated gambling.

She couldn't feel much about Eddy, either, except she still figured he was dead. No matter how much they'd given him, he still wouldn't walk out without those cases. Even if he was going for a whole new wardrobe he'd need to get all dressed up to go shopping for it. Eddy cared about clothes more than almost anything. And those gator cases were special; he'd got 'em off a hotel thief in Orlando, and they were the closest thing he had to a home. And anyway, now that she thought about it, she couldn't see him going for a buy-out bid, because what he wanted most in the whole world was to be part of some big deal. Once he was, he figured, people would start to take him seriously.

So somebody finally took him seriously, she thought, as Prior carried her bag into Gerald's clinic. But not the way Eddy wanted.

She looked around at the twenty-year-old plastic furniture, the stacks of stim-star magazines with Jap writing. It looked like a Cleveland haircut place. There was nobody there, nobody behind the reception desk.

Then Gerald came through a white door, wearing the kind of crinkled foil suit that paramedics wore for traffic accidents. "Lock the door," he said to Prior, through a blue paper mask that hid his nose, mouth, and chin. "Hello, Mona. If you'll step this way . . ." He gestured toward the white door.

She had her hand around the shockrod now, but she didn't know how to turn it on.

She followed Gerald, Prior taking up the rear.

"Have a seat," Gerald said. She sat on a white enamel chair. He came close, looked at her eyes. "You need to rest, Mona. You're exhausted."

There was a serrated stud on the shockrod's handle. Press it? Forward? Back?

Gerald went to a white box with drawers, got something out.

"Here," he said, extending a little tube thing with writing on the side, "this will help you. . . ." She barely felt the tiny, measured spray; there was a black blot on the aerosol tube, just where her eyes tried to focus, growing. . . .

She remembered the old man showing her how you kill a catfish. Catfish has a hole in its skull, covered with skin; you take something stiff and skinny, a wire, even a broomstraw did it, and you just slip it in. . . .

She remembered Cleveland, ordinary kind of day before it was time to get working, sitting up in Lanette's, looking at a magazine. Found this picture of Angie laughing in a restaurant with some other people, everybody pretty but beyond that it was like they had this *glow*, not really in the photograph but it was there anyway, something d feel. Look, she said to Lanette, showing her the picture, they got this glow.

It's called money, Lanette said.

It's called money. You just slip it in.

## TWENTY

# HILTON SWIFT

He arrived unannounced, as he always did, and alone, the Net helicopter settling like a solitary wasp, stirring strands of seaweed across the damp sand.

She watched from the rust-eaten railing as he jumped down, something boyish, almost bumbling, in his apparent eagerness. He wore a long topcoat of brown tweed; unbuttoned, it showed the immaculate front of one of his candystriped shirts, the propwash stirring his brown-blond hair and fluttering his Sense/Net tie. Robin was right, she decided: he did look as though his mother dressed him.

Perhaps it was deliberate, she thought, as he came striding up the beach, a feigned naïveté. She remembered Porphyre once maintaining that major corporations were entirely independent of the human beings who composed the body corporate. This had seemed patently obvious to Angie, but the hairdresser had insisted that she'd failed to grasp his basic premise. Swift was Sense/Net's most important human decision-maker.

The thought of Porphyre made her smile; Swift, taking it as a greeting, beamed back at her.

*   *   *

He offered her lunch in San Francisco; the helicopter was extremely fast. She countered by insisting on preparing him a bowl of dehydrated Swiss soup and microwaving a frozen brick of sourdough rye.

She wondered, watching him eat, about his sexuality. In his late thirties, he somehow conveyed the sense of an extraordinarily bright teenager in whom the onset of puberty had been subtly delayed. Rumor, at one time or another, had supplied him with every known sexual preference, and with several that she assumed were entirely imaginary. None of them seemed at all likely to Angie. She'd known him since she'd come to Sense/Net; he'd been well established in the upper eschelons of production when she'd arrived, one of the top people in Tally Isham's team, and he'd taken an immediate professional interest in her. Looking back, she assumed that Legba had steered her into his path: he'd been so obviously on his way up, though she might not have seen it herself, then, dazzled by the glitter and constant movement of the scene.

Bobby had taken an instant dislike to him, bristling with a Barrytowner's inbred hostility to authority, but had generally managed to conceal it for the sake of her career. The dislike had been mutual, Swift greeting their split and Bobby's departure with obvious relief.

"Hilton," she said, as she poured him a cup of the herbal tea he preferred to coffee, "what is it that's keeping Robin in London?"

He looked up from the steaming cup. "Something personal, I think. Perhaps he's found a new friend." Bobby had always been Angie's *friend*, to Hilton. Robin's friends tended to be young, male, and athletic; the muted erotic sequences in her stims with Robin were assembled from stock footage provided by Continuity and heavily treated by Raebel and his effects team. She remembered the one night they'd spent together, in a windblown house in southern Madagascar, his passivity and his patience. They'd never tried again, and she'd suspected that he feared that intimacy would undermine the illusion their stims projected so perfectly.

"What did he think of me going into the clinic, Hilton? Did he tell you?"

"I think he admired you for it."

"Someone told me recently that he's been telling people I'm crazy."

He'd rolled up his striped shirtsleeves and loosened his tie. "I can't imagine Robin thinking that, let alone saying it. I know what he thinks of you. You know what gossip is, in the Net. . . ."

"Hilton, where's Bobby?"

His brown eyes, very still. "Isn't that over, Angie?"

"Hilton, you know. You must know. You know where he is. Tell me."

"We lost him."

"Lost him?"

"Security lost him. You're right, of course; we kept the closest possible track of him after he left you. He reverted to type." There was an edge of satisfaction in his voice.

"And what type was that?"

"I've never asked what brought you together," he said. "Security investigated both of you, of course. He was a petty criminal."

She laughed. "He wasn't even that. . . ."

"You were unusually well represented, Angie, for an unknown. You know that your agents made it a key condition of your contract that we take Bobby Newmark on as well."

"Contracts have had stranger conditions, Hilton."

"And he went on salary as your . . . companion."

"My 'friend.' "

Was Swift actually blushing? He broke eye contact, looked down at his hands. "When he left you, he went to Mexico, Mexico City. Security was tracing him, of course; we don't like to lose track of anyone who knows that much about the personal life of one of our stars. Mexico City is a very . . . *complicated* place. . . . We do know that he seemed to be trying to continue his previous . . . career."

"He was hustling cyberspace?"

He met her eyes again. "He was seeing people in the business, known criminals."

"And? Go on."

"He . . . faded out. Vanished. Do you have any idea what Mexico City is like, if you slip below the poverty line?"

"And he was poor?"

"He'd become an addict. According to our best sources."

"An addict? Addicted to what?"

"I don't know."

"Continuity!"

He almost spilled his tea.

"Hello, Angie."

"Bobby, Continuity. Bobby Newmark, my *friend*," glaring at Swift. "He went to Mexico City. Hilton says he became addicted to something. A drug, Continuity?"

"I'm sorry, Angie. That's classified data."

"Hilton . . ."

"Continuity," he began, and coughed.

"Hello, Hilton."

"Executive override, Continuity. Do we have that information?"

"Security's sources described Newmark's addiction as neuro-electronic."

"I don't understand."

"Some sort of, um, 'wirehead' business," Swift offered.

She felt an impulse to tell him how she'd found the drug, the charger.

*Hush, child.* Her head was full of the sound of bees, a building pressure.

"Angie? What is it?" He was half up from his chair, reaching for her.

"Nothing. I'm . . . upset. I'm sorry. Nerves. It isn't your fault. I was going to tell you about finding Bobby's cyberspace deck. But you already know about that, don't you?"

"Can I get you anything? Water?"

"No, thanks, but I'll lie down for a while, if you don't mind. But stay, please. I have some ideas for orbital sequences that I'd like your advice on. . . ."

"Of course. Have a nap, I'll have a walk on the beach, and then we'll talk."

She watched him from the bedroom window, watched his brown figure recede in the direction of the Colony, followed by the patient little Dornier.

He looked like a child on the empty beach; he looked as lost as she felt.

# TWENTY ONE

# THE ALEPH

As the sun rose, still no power for the 100-watt bulbs, Gentry's loft filled with a new light. Winter sunlight softened the outlines of the consoles and the holo table, brought out the texture of the ancient books that lined sagging chipboard shelves along the west wall. As Gentry paced and talked, his blond roostertail bobbing each time he spun on a black bootheel, his excitement seemed to counter the lingering effects of Cherry's sleep-derms. Cherry sat on the edge of the bed, watching Gentry but glancing occasionally at the battery telltale on the stretcher's superstructure. Slick sat in a broken-down chair scrounged from the Solitude and recushioned with transparent plastic over wadded pads of discarded clothing.

To Slick's relief, Gentry had skipped the whole business of the Shape and launched straight into his theory about the aleph thing. As always, once Gentry got going, he used words and constructions that Slick had trouble understanding, but Slick knew from experience that it was easier not to interrupt him; the trick was in pulling some kind of meaning out of the overall flow, skipping over the parts you didn't understand.

Gentry said that the Count was jacked into what amounted to a mother-huge microsoft; he thought the slab was a single solid lump of biochip. If that was true, the thing's storage capacity was virtually infinite; it would've been unthinkably expensive to manufacture. It was, Gentry said, a fairly strange thing for anyone to have built at all, although such things were rumored to exist and to have their uses, most particularly in the storage of vast amounts of confidential data. With no link to the global matrix, the data was immune to every kind of attack via cyberspace. The catch, of course, was that you couldn't access it via the matrix; it was dead storage.

"He could have anything in there," Gentry said, pausing to look down at the unconscious face. He spun on his heel and began his pacing again. "A world. Worlds. Any number of personality-constructs . . ."

"Like he's living a stim?" Cherry asked. "That why he's always in REM?"

"No," Gentry said, "it's not simstim. It's completely interactive. And it's a matter of scale. If this is aleph-class biosoft, he literally could have anything at all in there. In a sense, he could have an *approximation of everything. . . .*"

"I gotta feeling off Kid Afrika," Cherry said, "that this guy was paying to stay this way. Kinda wirehead action but different. And anyway, wirehead's don't REM like that. . . ."

"But when you tried to put it out through your stuff," Slick ventured, "you got that . . . thing." He saw Gentry's shoulders tense beneath black-beaded leather.

"Yes," Gentry said, "and now I have to reconstruct our account with the Fission Authority." He pointed at the permanent storage batteries stacked beneath the steel table. "Get those out for me."

"Yeah," Cherry said, "it's about time. I'm freezing my ass."

They left Gentry bent over a cyberspace deck and went back to Slick's room. Cherry had insisted they rig Gentry's electric blanket to one of the batteries so she could drape it over the stretcher. There was cold coffee left on the butane stove; Slick drank it without bothering to reheat it, while Cherry stared out the window at the snow-streaked plain of the Solitude.

"How'd it get like this?" she asked.

"Gentry says it was a landfill operation a hundred years ago. Then they laid down a lot of topsoil, but stuff wouldn't grow. A lot of the fill was toxic. Rain washed the cover off. Guess they just gave up and started dumping more shit on it. Can't drink the water out there; fulla PCBs and everything else."

"What about those rabbits Bird-boy goes hunting for?"

"They're west of here. You don't see 'em on the Solitude. Not even rats. Anyway, you gotta test any meat you take around here."

"There's birds, though."

"Just roost here, go somewhere else to feed."

"What is it with you 'n' Gentry?" She was still looking out the window.

"How do you mean?"

"My first idea was maybe you were gay. Together, I mean."

"No."

"But it's kind of like you need each other some way. . . ."

"It's his place, Factory. Lets me live here. I . . . need to live here. To do my work."

"To build those things downstairs?"

The bulb in the yellow cone of fax came on; the fan in the heater kicked in.

"Well," Cherry said, squatting in front of the heater and unzipping one jacket after another, "he may be crazy but he just did something right."

Gentry was slouched in the old office chair when Slick entered the loft, staring at the little flip-up monitor on his deck.

"Robert Newmark," Gentry said.

"Huh?"

"Retinal identification. Either this is Robert Newmark or someone who bought his eyes."

"How'd you get that?" Slick bent to peer at the screen of basic birth stats.

Gentry ignored the question. "This is it. Push it and you run into something else entirely."

"How's that?"

"Someone wants to know if anyone asks any questions about Mr. Newmark."

"Who?"

"I don't know." Gentry drummed his fingers on his black leather thighs. "Look at this: nothing. Born in Barrytown. Mother: Marsha Newmark. We've got his SIN, but it's definitely been tagged." He shoved the chair back on its casters and swung around so that he could see the Count's still face. "How about it, Newmark? Is that your name?" He stood up and went to the holo table.

"Don't," Slick said.

Gentry touched the power stud on the holo table.

And the gray thing was there again, for an instant, but this time it dived toward the core of the hemispherical display, dwindled, and was gone. No. It was there, a minute gray sphere at the very center of the glowing projection field.

Gentry's crazy smile had returned. "Good," he said.

"What's good?"

"I see what it is. A kind of ice. A security program."

"That monkey?"

"Someone has a sense of humor. If the monkey doesn't scare you off, it turns into a pea. . . ." He crossed to the table and began to root through one of the panniers. "I doubt if they'll be able to do that with a direct sensory link." He held something in his hand now. A trode-net.

"Gentry, don't *do* it! Look at him!"

"I'm not going to do it," Gentry said. "You are."

# TWENTY-TWO

# GHOSTS
# AND EMPTIES

Staring through the cab's smudged windows, she found herself wishing for Colin and his wry commentary, then remembered that this was entirely beyond his sphere of expertise. Did Maas-Neotek manufacture a similar unit for the Sprawl, she wondered, and if so, what form would its ghost take?

"Sally," she said, perhaps half an hour into the drive to New York, "why did Petal let me go with you?"

"Because he was smart."

"And my father?"

"Your father'll shit."

"I'm sorry?"

"Will be angry. If he finds out. And he may not. We aren't here for long."

"Why are we here?"

"I gotta talk to somebody."

"But why am I here?"

"You don't like it here?"

Kumiko hesitated. "Yes, I do."

"Good." Sally shifted on the broken-down seat. "Petal had to let us go. Because he couldn't have stopped us without hurting one of us. Well, maybe not hurting. More like insulting. Swain could cool you, then tell you he was sorry later, tell your father it was for your own good, if it came to that, but if he cools me, it's like *face*, right? When I saw Petal down there with the gun, I knew he was going to let us go. Your room's kinked. The whole place is. I set the motion sensors off when I was getting your gear together. Figured I would. Petal knew it was me. That's why he rang the phone, to let me know he knew."

"I don't understand."

"Kind of a courtesy, so I'd know he was waiting. Gimme a chance to think. But he didn't have a choice and he knew it. Swain, see, he's being forced to do something, and Petal knows it. Or anyway Swain says he is, being forced. Me, I'm definitely being forced. So I start wondering how bad Swain needs me. *Real* bad. Because they let me walk off with the *oyabun*'s daughter, shipped all the way to Notting Hill for the safekeeping. Something there scares him worse than your daddy. 'Less it's something that'll make him richer than your daddy already has. Anyway, taking you kind of evens things up. Kind of like pushing back. You mind?"

"But you are being threatened?"

"Somebody knows a lot of things I did."

"And Tick has discovered the identity of this person?"

"Yeah. Guess I knew anyway. Wish to fuck I'd been wrong."

The hotel Sally chose was faced with rust-stained steel panels, each panel secured with gleaming chrome bolts, a style Kumiko knew from Tokyo and thought of as somewhat old-fashioned.

Their room was large and gray, a dozen shades of gray, and Sally walked straight to the bed, after she'd locked the door, took off her jacket, and lay down.

"You don't have a bag," Kumiko said.

Sally sat up and began to remove her boots. "I can buy what I need. You tired?"

"No."

"I am." She pulled her black sweater over her head. Her breasts were small, with brownish pink nipples; a scar, running from just below the left nipple, vanished into the waistband of her jeans.

"You were hurt," Kumiko said, looking at the scar.

Sally looked down. "Yeah."

"Why didn't you have it removed?"

"Sometimes it's good to remember."

"Being hurt?"

"Being stupid."

Gray on gray. Unable to sleep, Kumiko paced the gray carpet. There was something vampiric about the room, she decided, something it would have in common with millions of similar rooms, as though its bewilderingly seamless anonymity were sucking away her personality, fragments of which emerged as her parents' voices, raised in argument, as the faces of her father's black-suited secretaries. . . .

Sally slept, her face a smooth mask. The view from the window told Kumiko nothing at all: only that she looked out on a city that was neither Tokyo nor London, a vast generic tumble that was her century's paradigm of urban reality.

Perhaps she slept too, Kumiko, though later she wasn't certain. She watched Sally order toiletries and underwear, tapping her requirements into the bedside video. Her purchases were delivered while Kumiko was in the shower.

"Okay," Sally said, from beyond the door, "towel off, get dressed, we're going to see the man."

"What man?" Kumiko asked, but Sally hadn't heard her.

*Gomi.*

Thirty-five percent of the landmass of Tokyo was built on *gomi*, on level tracts reclaimed from the Bay through a century's systematic dumping. *Gomi*, there, was a resource to be managed, to be collected, sorted, carefully plowed under.

London's relationship to *gomi* was more subtle, more oblique. To Kumiko's eyes, the bulk of the city *consisted* of *gomi*, of structures the Japanese economy would long ago have devoured in its relentless hunger for space in which to build. Yet these structures revealed, even to Kumiko, the fabric of time, each wall patched by generations of hands in an ongoing task of restoration. The English valued their *gomi* in its own right, in a way she had only begun to understand; they inhabited it.

*Gomi* in the Sprawl was something else: a rich humus, a decay that sprouted prodigies in steel and polymer. The apparent lack of planning alone was enough to dizzy her, running so entirely opposite the value her own culture placed on efficient land use.

Their taxi ride from the airport had already shown her decay, whole blocks in ruin, unglazed windows gaping above sidewalks heaped with trash. And faces staring as the armored hover made its way through the streets.

Now Sally plunged her abruptly into the full strangeness of this place, with its rot and randomness rooting towers taller than any in Tokyo, corporate obelisks that pierced the sooty lacework of overlapping domes.

Two cab rides away from their hotel, they took to the street itself, into early-evening crowds and a slant of shadow. The air was cold, but not the cold of London, and Kumiko thought of the blossoms in Ueno Park.

Their first stop was a large, somewhat faded bar called the Gentleman Loser, where Sally conducted a quiet, very rapid exchange with a bartender.

They left without buying a drink.

"Ghosts," Sally said, rounding a corner, Kumiko close at her side. The streets had grown progressively more empty, these past several blocks, the buildings darker and more decrepit.

"Pardon me?"

"Lotta ghosts here for me, or anyway there should be."

"You know this place?"

"Sure. Looks all the same, but different, you know?"

"No . . ."

"Someday you will. We find who I'm looking for, you just do your good-girl routine. Speak if you're spoken to, otherwise don't."

"Who are we looking for?"

"The man. What's left of him, anyway . . ."

Half a block on, the grim street empty—Kumiko had never seen an *empty* street before, aside from Swain's crescent shrouded in midnight snow—Sally came to a halt beside an ancient and utterly unpromising storefront, its twin display windows silvered with a rich inner coating of dust. Peering in, Kumiko made out the glass-tube letters of an unlit neon sign: METRO, then a longer word. The door between the windows had been reinforced with a sheet of corrugated steel; rusting eyebolts protruded at intervals, strung with slack lengths of galvanized razor wire.

Now Sally faced that door, squared her shoulders, and executed a fluid series of small, quick gestures.

Kumiko stared as the sequence was repeated. "Sally—"

"Jive," Sally cut her off. "I told you to shut up, okay?"

"Yeah?" The voice, barely more than a whisper, seemed to come from nowhere in particular.

"I told you already," Sally said.

"I don't jive."

"I wanna talk to him," she said, her voice hard and careful.

"He's dead."

"I know that."

A silence followed, and Kumiko heard a sound that might have been the wind, a cold, grit-laden wind scouring the curve of the geodesics far above them.

"He's not here," the voice said, and seemed to recede. "Round the corner, half a block, left into the alley."

Kumiko would remember the alley always: dark brick slick with damp, hooded ventilators trailing black streamers of congealed dust, a yellow bulb in a cage of corroded alloy, the low growth of empty bottles that sprouted at the base of either wall, the man-sized nests of crumpled fax and white foam packing segments, and the sound of Sally's bootheels.

Past the bulb's dim glow was darkness, though a reflected gleam on wet brick showed a final wall, cul-de-sac, and Kumiko hesitated, frightened by a sudden stir of echo, a scurrying, the steady dripping of water. . . .

Sally raised her hand. A tight beam of very bright light framed a sharp circle of paint-scrawled brick, then smoothly descended.

Descended until it found the thing at the base of the wall, dull metal, an upright rounded fixture that Kumiko mistook for another ventilator. Near its base were the stubs of white candles, a flat plastic flask filled with a clear liquid, an assortment of cigarette packets, a scattering of loose cigarettes, and an elaborate, multiarmed figure drawn in what appeared to be white powdered chalk.

Sally stepped forward, the beam held steady, and Kumiko saw that the armored thing was bolted into the brickwork with massive rivets. "Finn?"

A rapid flicker of pink light from a horizontal slot.

"Hey, Finn, man . . ." An uncharacteristic hesitation in her voice . . .

"Moll." A grating quality, as if through a broken speaker. "What's with the flash? You still got amps in? Gettin' old, you can't see in the dark so good?"

"For my friend."

Something moved behind the slot, its color the unhealthy pink of hot cigarette ash in noon sunlight, and Kumiko's face was washed with a stutter of light.

"Yeah," grated the voice, "so who's she?"

"Yanaka's daughter."

"No shit."

Sally lowered the light; it fell on the candles, the flask, the damp gray cigarettes, the white symbol with its feathery arms.

"Help yourself to the offerings," said the voice. "That's half a liter of Moskovskaya there. The hoodoo mark's flour. Tough luck; the high rollers draw 'em in cocaine."

"Jesus," Sally said, an odd distance in her voice, squatting down, "I don't believe this." Kumiko watched as she picked up the flask and sniffed at the contents.

"Drink it. It's good shit. Fuckin' better be. Nobody short-counts the oracle, not if they know what's good for 'em."

"Finn," Sally said, then tilted the flask and swallowed, wiping her mouth with the back of her hand, "you gotta be crazy. . . ."

"I should be so lucky. A rig like this, I'm pushing it to have a little imagination, let alone crazy."

Kumiko moved closer, then squatted beside Sally.

"It's a construct, a personality job?" Sally put down the flask of vodka and stirred the damp flour with the tip of a white fingernail.

"Sure. You seen 'em before. Real-time memory if I wanna, wired into c-space if I wanna. Got this oracle gig to keep my hand in, you know?" The thing made a strange sound: laughter. "Got love troubles? Got a bad woman don't understand you?" The laugh noise again, like peals of static. "Actually I'm more into business advice. It's the local kids leave the goodies. Adds to the mystique, kinda. And once in a while I get a skeptic, some asshole figures he'll help himself to the take." A scarlet hairline flashed from the slit and a bottle exploded somewhere to Kumiko's right. Static laughter. "So what brings you this way, Moll? You and," again the pink light flicked across Kumiko's face, "Yanaka's daughter . . ."

"The Straylight run," Sally said.

"Long time, Moll . . ."

"She's after me, Finn. Fourteen years and that crazy bitch is on my ass. . . ."

"So maybe she's got nothin' better to do. You know how rich folks are. . . ."

"You know where Case is, Finn? Maybe she's after him. . . ."

"Case got out of it. Rolled up a few good scores after you split, then he kicked it in the head and quit clean. You did the same, maybe you wouldn't be freezing your buns off in an alley, right? Last I heard, he had four kids. . . ."

Watching the hypnotic sweep of the scanning pink ember, Kumiko had some idea of what it was that Sally spoke with. There were similar things in her father's study, four of them, black lacquered cubes arranged along a low shelf of pine. Above each cube hung a formal portrait. The portraits were monochrome photographs of men in dark suits and ties, four very sober gentlemen whose lapels were decorated with small metal emblems of the kind her father sometimes wore. Though her mother had told her that the cubes contained ghosts, the ghosts of her father's evil ancestors, Kumiko found them more fascinating than frightening. If they did contain ghosts, she reasoned, they would be quite small, as the cubes themselves were scarcely large enough to contain a child's head.

Her father sometimes meditated before the cubes, kneeling on the bare tatami in an attitude that connoted profound respect. She had seen him in this position many times, but she was ten before she heard him address the cubes. And one had answered. The question had meant nothing to her, the answer less, but the calm tone of the ghost's reply had frozen her where she crouched, behind a door of paper, and her father had laughed to find her there; rather than scolding her, he'd explained that the cubes housed the recorded personalities of former executives, corporate directors. Their souls? she'd asked. No, he'd said, and smiled, then added that the distinction was a subtle one. "They are not conscious. They respond, when questioned, in a manner approximating the response of the subject. If they are ghosts, then holograms are ghosts."

After Sally's lecture on the history and hierarchy of the Yakuza, in the robata bar in Earls Court, Kumiko had decided that each of the men in the photographs, the subjects of the personality recordings, had been an *oyabun*.

The thing in the armored housing, she reasoned, was of a similar nature, though perhaps more complex, just as Colin was a more complex version of the Michelin guide her father's secretaries had carried on her Shinjuku shopping expeditions. Finn, Sally called it, and it was evident that this Finn had been a friend or associate of hers.

But did it wake, Kumiko wondered, when the alley was empty? Did its laser vision scan the silent fall of midnight snow?

"Europe," Sally began, "when I split from Case I went all around there. Had a lot of money we got for the run, anyway it looked like a lot then. Tessier-Ashpool's AI paid it out through a Swiss bank. It erased every trace we'd ever been up the well; I mean everything, like if you looked up the names we traveled under, on the JAL shuttle, they just weren't there. Case checked it all out when we were back in Tokyo, wormed his way into all kinds of data; it was like none of it ever happened. I didn't understand how it could do that, AI or not, but nobody ever really understood what happened up there, when Case rode that Chinese icebreaker through their core ice."

"Did it try to get in touch, after?"

"Not that I know of. He had this idea that it was gone, sort of; not *gone* gone, but gone *into* everything, the whole matrix. Like it wasn't *in* cyberspace anymore, it just *was*. And if it didn't want you to see it, to know it was there, well, there was no way you ever could, and no way you'd ever be able to prove it to anybody else even if you did know. . . . And me, I didn't wanna know. I mean, whatever it was, it seemed done to me, finished. Armitage was dead, Riviera was dead, Ashpool was dead, the Rasta tug pilot who took us out there was back in Zion cluster and he'd probably written it all off as another ganja dream. . . . I left Case in the Tokyo Hyatt, never saw him again. . . ."

"Why?"

"Who knows? Nothing much. I was young, it just seemed over."

"But you'd left *her* up the well. In Straylight."

"You got it. And I'd think about that, once in a while. When we were leaving, Finn, it was like she didn't care about any of it. Like I'd killed her crazy sick father for her, and Case had cracked their cores and let their AIs loose in the matrix . . . So I put her on the list, right? You get big enough trouble one day, you're being got at, you check that list."

"And you figured it for her, right off?"

"No. I gotta pretty long list."

Case, who seemed to Kumiko to have been something more than Sally's partner, never reentered her story.

As Kumiko listened to Sally condense fourteen years of personal history for the Finn's benefit, she found herself imagining this younger Sally as a *bishonen* hero in a traditional romantic video: fey, elegant, and deadly. While she found Sally's matter-of-fact account of her life difficult to follow, with its references to places and things she didn't know, it was easy to imagine her winning the sudden, flick-of-the-wrist victories expected of *bishonen*. But no, she thought, as Sally dismissed "a bad year in Hamburg," sudden anger in her voice—an old anger, the year a decade past—it was a mistake to cast this woman in Japanese terms. There were no *ronin*, no wandering samurai; Sally and the Finn were talking business.

She'd arrived at her bad year in Hamburg, Kumiko gathered, after having won and lost some sort of fortune. She'd won her share of it "up there," in a place the Finn had called Straylight, in partnership with the man Case. In doing so, she'd made an enemy.

"Hamburg," the Finn interrupted, "I heard stories about Hamburg. . . ."

"The money was gone. How it is, with a big score, when you're young . . . No money was sort of like getting back to normal, but I was involved with these Frankfurt people, owed 'em, and they wanted to take it out in trade."

"What kinda trade?"

"They wanted people hit."

"So?"

"So I got out. When I could. Went to London . . ."

Perhaps, Kumiko decided, Sally *had* once been something along *ronin* lines, a kind of samurai. In London, however, she'd become something else, a businesswoman. Supporting herself in some unspecified way, she gradually became a backer, providing funds for various kinds of business operations. (What was a "credit sink"? What was "laundering data"?)

"Yeah," the Finn said, "you did okay. Got yourself a share in some German casino."

"Aix-la-Chapelle. I was on the board. Still am, when I got the right passport."

"Settled down?" The laugh again.

"Sure."

"Didn't hear much, back here."

"I was running a casino. That was it. Doing fine."

"You were prizefighting. 'Misty Steele,' augmented featherweight. Eight fights, I made book on five of 'em. Blood matches, sweetmeat. Illegal."

"Hobby."

"Some hobby. I saw the vids. Burmese Kid opened you right up, living color . . ."

Kumiko remembered the long scar.

"So I quit. Five years ago and I was already five years too old."

"You weren't bad, but 'Misty Steele' . . . Jesus."

"Gimme a break. Wasn't me made that one up."

"Sure. So tell me about our friend upstairs, how she got in touch."

"Swain. Roger Swain. Sends one of his boys to the casino, would-be hardass called Prior. About a month ago."

"Swain the fixer? London?"

"Same one. So Prior's got a present for me, about a meter of printout. A list. Names, dates, places."

"Bad?"

"Everything. Stuff I'd almost forgotten."

"Straylight run?"

"Everything. So I packed a bag, got back to London, there's Swain. He's sorry, it's not his fault, but he's gotta twist me. Because somebody's twisting him. Got his own meter of printout to worry about." Kumiko heard Sally's heels shift on the pavement.

"What's he want?"

"A rip, warm body. Celeb."

"Why you?"

"Come on, Finn, that's what I'm here to ask *you*."

"Swain tell you it's 3Jane?"

"No. But my console cowboy in London did."

Kumiko's knees ached.

"The kid. Where'd you come by her?"

"She turned up at Swain's place. Yanaka wanted her out of Tokyo. Swain owes him *giri*."

"She's clean, anyway, no implants. What I get out of Tokyo lately, Yanaka has his hands full. . . ."

Kumiko shivered in the dark.

"And the rip, the celeb?" the Finn continued.

She felt Sally hesitate. "Angela Mitchell."

The pink metronome swinging silently, left to right, right to left.

"It's cold here, Finn."

"Yeah. Wish I could feel it. I just took a little trip on your behalf. Memory Lane. You know much about where Angie comes from?"

"No."

"I'm in the oracle game, honey, not a research library. . . . Her father was Christopher Mitchell. He was the big shit in biochip research at Mass Biolabs. She grew up in a sealed compound of theirs in Arizona, company kid. About seven years ago, something happened down there. The street said Hosaka fielded a team of pros to help Mitchell make a major career move. The fax said there was a megaton blast on Maas property, but nobody ever found any radiation. Never found Hosaka's mercs, either. Maas announced that Mitchell was dead, suicide."

"That's the library. What's the oracle know?"

"Rumors. Nothing that hangs together on a line. Street said she turned up here a day or two after the blast in Arizona, got in with some very weird spades who worked out of New Jersey."

"Worked what?"

"They dealt. 'Ware, mostly. Buying, selling. Sometimes they bought from me. . . ."

"How were they weird?"

"Hoodoos. Thought the matrix was full of mambos 'n' shit. Wanna know something, Moll?"

"What?"

"They're right."

# TWENTY-THREE

# MIRROR MIRROR

She came out of it like somebody had thrown a switch.

Didn't open her eyes. She could hear them talking in another room. Hurt lots of places but not any worse than the wiz had. The bad crash, that was gone, or maybe muted by whatever they'd given her, that spray.

Paper smock coarse against her nipples; they felt big and tender and her breasts felt full. Little lines of pain tweaking across her face, twin dull aches in her eyesockets, sore rough feeling in her mouth and a taste of blood.

"I'm not trying to tell you your business," Gerald was saying, above a running tap and a rattle of metal, like he was washing pans or something, "but you're kidding yourself if you think she'd fool anyone who didn't want to be fooled. It's really a very superficial job." Prior said something she couldn't make out. "I said superficial, not shoddy. That's quality work, all of it. Twenty-four hours on a dermal stimulator and you won't know she's been here. Keep her on the antibiotics and off stimulants; her immune system isn't all it could be." Then Prior again, but she still couldn't catch it.

Opened her eyes but there was only the ceiling, white squares of acoustic tile. Turned her head to the left. White plastic wall with one of those fake windows, hi-rez animation of a beach with palm trees and waves; watch the water long enough and you'd see the same waves rolling in, looped, forever. Except the thing was broken or worn out, a kind of hesitation in the waves, and the red of the sunset pulsed like a bad fluorescent tube.

*Try right.* Turning again, feeling the sweaty paper cover on the hard foam pillow against her neck . . .

And the face with bruised eyes looking at her from the other bed, nose braced with clear plastic and micropore tape, some kind of brown jelly stuff smeared back across the cheekbones . . .

Angie. It was Angie's face, framed by the reflected sunset stutter of the defective window.


"There was no bonework," Gerald said, carefully loosening the tape that held the little plastic brace in place along the bridge of her nose. "That was the beauty of it. We planed some cartilage in the nose, working in through the nostrils, then went on to the teeth. Smile. Beautiful. We did the breast augmentation, built up the nipples with vat-grown erectile tissue, then did the eye coloration. . . ." He removed the brace. "You mustn't touch this for another twenty-four hours."

"That how I got the bruises?"

"No. That's secondary trauma from the cartilage job." Gerald's fingers were cool on her face, precise. "That should clear up by tomorrow."

Gerald was okay. He'd given her three derms, two blue and a pink, smooth and comfortable. Prior definitely wasn't okay, but he was gone or anyway out of sight. And it was just nice, listening to Gerald explain things in his calm voice. And look what he could do.

"Freckles," she said, because they were gone.

"Abrasion and more vat tissue. They'll come back, faster if you get too much sun. . . ."

"She's so beautiful. . . ." She turned her head.

"You, Mona. That's you."

She looked at the face in the mirror and tried on that famous smile.

*       *       *

Maybe Gerald wasn't okay.

Back in the narrow white bed again, where he'd put her to rest, she raised her arm and looked at the three derms. Trank. Floating.

She worked a fingernail under the pink derm and peeled it off, stuck it on the white wall, and pushed hard with her thumb. A single bead of straw-colored fluid ran down. She carefully peeled it back and replaced it on her arm. The stuff in the blue ones was milky white. She put them back on too. Maybe he'd notice, but she wanted to know what was happening.

She looked in the mirror. Gerald said he could put it back the way it was, someday, if she wanted him to, but then she wondered how he'd remember what she'd looked like. Maybe he'd taken a picture or something. Now that she thought about it, maybe there wasn't anybody who'd remember how she'd looked before. She guessed Michael's stim deck was probably the closest bet, but she didn't know his address or even his last name. It gave her a funny feeling, like who she'd been had wandered away down the street for a minute and never come back. But then she closed her eyes and knew she was Mona, always had been, and that nothing much had changed, anyway not behind her eyelids.

Lanette said it didn't matter, how you got yourself changed. Lanette told her once that she didn't have 10 percent of her own face left, the one she'd been born with. Not that you'd guess, except for the black around her lids so she never had to mess with mascara. Mona had thought maybe Lanette hadn't got such good work done, and it must have shown once in Mona's eyes, because then Lanette said: You shoulda seen me before, honey.

But now here she was, Mona, stretched out straight in this skinny bed in Baltimore, and all she knew about Baltimore was the sound of a siren from down in the street and the motor running on Gerald's air-conditioner.

And somehow that turned into sleep, she didn't know for how long, and then Prior was there with his hand on her arm, asking her if she was hungry.

She watched Prior shave his beard. He did it at the stainless surgical sink, trimming it back with a pair of chrome scissors. Then he switched to a white plastic throw-away razor from a box of them that Gerald had. It was strange watching his face come out. It wasn't a face she'd have expected: it was younger. But the mouth was the same.

"We gonna be here much longer, Prior?"

He had his shirt off for the shave; he had tattoos across his shoulders and down his upper arms, dragons with lion-heads. "Don't worry about it," he said.

"It's boring."

"We'll get your some stims." He was shaving under his chin.

"What's Baltimore like?"

"Bloody awful. Like the rest of it."

"So what's England like?"

"Bloody awful." He wiped his face with a thick wad of blue absorbent paper.

"Maybe we could go out, get some of those crabs. Gerald says they got crabs."

"They do," he said. "I'll get some in."

"How about you take me out?"

He tossed the blue wad into a steel waste canister. "No, you might try to run away."

She slid her hand between the bed and the wall and found the torn foam air cell where she'd hidden the shockrod. She'd found her clothes in a white plastic bag. Gerald came in every couple of hours with fresh derms; she'd wring them out as soon as he'd gone. She'd figured if she could get Prior to take her out to eat, she could make a move in the restaurant. But he wasn't having any.

In a restaurant she might even be able to get a cop, because now she figured she knew what the deal was.

Snuff. Lanette had told her about that. How there were men who'd pay to have girls fixed up to look like other people, then kill them. Had to be rich, really rich. Not Prior, but somebody he worked for. Lanette said these guys had girls fixed to look like their wives sometimes. Mona hadn't really believed it, back then; sometimes Lanette told her scary stuff because it was fun to be scared when you knew you were pretty safe, and anyway Lanette had a lot of stories about weird kinks. She said suits were the weirdest of all, the big suits way up in big companies, because they couldn't afford to lose control when they were working. But when they weren't working, Lanette said, they could afford to lose it any way they wanted. So why not a big suit somewhere who wanted Angie that way? Well, there were lots of girls got themselves worked over to look like her, but they were mostly pathetic. Wannabes—and she hadn't ever seen one who really looked much like Angie, anyway not enough to fool anybody who cared. But maybe there was somebody who'd pay for all this just to get a girl who did look like Angie. Anyway, if it wasn't snuff, what was it?

Now Prior was buttoning his blue shirt. He came over to the bed and pulled the sheet down to look at her breasts. Like he was looking at a car or something.

She yanked the sheet back up.

"I'll get some crabs." He put his jacket on and went out. She could hear him saying something to Gerald.

Gerald stuck his head in. "How are you, Mona?"

"Hungry."

"Feeling relaxed?"

"Yeah . . ."

When she was alone again, she rolled over and studied her face, Angie's face, in the mirrored wall. The bruising was almost gone. Gerald taped things like miniature trodes to her face and hooked them to a machine. Said they made it heal real fast.

It didn't make her jump, now, Angie's face in the mirror. The teeth were nice; the teeth you'd wanna keep anyway. She wasn't sure about the rest, not yet.

Maybe she should just get up now, get her clothes on, head for the door. If Gerald tried to stop her, she could use the rod. Then she remembered how Prior had turned up at Michael's, like he'd had somebody watching her, all night, following her. Maybe somebody watching now, outside. Gerald's place didn't seem to have any windows, not real ones, so she'd have to go out the door.

And she was starting to want her wiz bad, too, but if she did even a little, Gerald would notice. She knew her kit was there, in her bag under the bed. Maybe if she did some, she thought, she'd just *do* something. But maybe it wouldn't be the right thing; she had to admit that what she did on wiz didn't always work out, even though it made you feel like you couldn't make a mistake if you tried.

Anyway, she was hungry, and too bad Gerald didn't have some kind of music or something, so maybe she'd just wait for that crab. . . .

# TWENTY-FOUR

# IN A
# LONELY PLACE

And Gentry standing there with the Shape burning behind his eyes, holding out the trode-net under the glare of bare bulbs, telling Slick why it had to be that way, why Slick had to put the trodes on and jack straight into whatever the gray slab was inputting to the still figure on the stretcher.

He shook his head, remembering how he'd come to Dog Solitude. And Gentry started talking faster, taking the gesture for refusal.

Gentry was saying Slick had to go under, he said maybe just for a few seconds, while he got a fix on the data and worked up a macroform. Slick didn't know how to do that, Gentry said, or he'd go under himself; it wasn't the data he wanted, just the overall shape, because he thought that would lead him to the Shape, the big one, the thing he'd chased for so long.

Slick remembered crossing the Solitude on foot. He'd been scared that the Korsakov's would come back, that he'd forget where he was and drink cancer-water from the slimed red puddles on the rusty plain. Red scum and dead birds floating with their wings spread. The trucker from Tennessee had told him to walk west from the highway, he'd hit two-lane blacktop inside an hour and get a ride down to Cleveland, but it felt like longer than an hour now and he wasn't so sure which way was west and this place was spooking him, this junkyard scar like a giant had stomped it flat. Once he saw somebody far away, up on a low ridge, and waved. The figure vanished, but he walked that way, no longer trying to skirt the puddles, slogging through them, until he came to the ridge and saw that it was the wingless hulk of an airliner half-buried in rusted cans. He made his way up the incline along a path where feet had flattened the cans, to a square opening that had been an emergency exit. Stuck his head inside and saw hundreds of tiny heads suspended from the concave ceiling. He froze there, blinking in the sudden shade, until what he was seeing made some kind of sense. The pink plastic heads of dolls, their nylon hair tied up into topknots and the knots stuck into thick black tar, dangling like fruit. Nothing else, only a few ragged slabs of dirty green foam, and he knew he didn't want to stick around to find out whose place it was.

He'd headed south then, without knowing it, and found Factory.

"I'll never have another chance," Gentry said. Slick stared at the taut face, the eyes wide with desperation. "I'll never see it. . . ."

And Slick remembered the time Gentry'd hit him, how he'd looked down at the wrench and felt . . . Well, Cherry wasn't right about them, but there was something else there, he didn't know what to call it. He snatched the trode-net with his left hand and shoved Gentry hard in the chest with his right. "Shut up! Shut the fuck up!" Gentry fell back against the steel table's edge.

Slick cursed him softly as he fumbled the delicate net of contact dermatrodes across his forehead and temples.

Jacked in.

His boots crunched gravel.

Opened his eyes and looked down; the gravel drive smooth in the dawn, cleaner than anything in Dog Solitude. He looked up and saw where it curved away, and beyond green and spreading trees the pitched slate roof of a house half the size of Factory. There were statues near him in the long wet grass. A deer made of iron, and a broken figure of a man's body carved from white stone, no head or arms or legs. Birds were singing and that was the only sound.

He started walking up the drive, toward the gray house, because there didn't seem to be anything else to do. When he got to the head of the drive, he could see past the house to smaller buildings and a broad flat field of grass where gliders where staked against the wind.

*Fairytale,* he thought, looking up at the mansion's broad stone brow, the leaded diamond panes; like some vid he'd seen when he was little. Were there really people who lived in places like this? *But it's not a place,* he reminded himself, *it only feels like it is.*

"Gentry," he said, "get my ass out of this, okay?"

He studied the backs of his hands. Scars, ingrained grime, black half-moons of grease under his broken nails. The grease got in and made them soft, so they broke easy.

He started to feel stupid, standing there. Maybe somebody was watching him from the house. "Fuck it," he said, and started up the broad flagstone walk, unconsciously hitching his stride into the swagger he'd learned in the Deacon Blues.

The door had this thing fastened to a central panel: a hand, small and graceful, holding a sphere the size of a poolball, all cast in iron. Hinged at the wrist so you could raise it and bring it down. He did. Hard. Twice, then twice again. Nothing happened. The door-knob was brass, floral detail worn almost invisible by years of use. It turned easily. He opened the door.

He blinked at a wealth of color and texture; surfaces of dark polished wood, black and white marble, rugs with a thousand soft colors that glowed like church windows, polished silver, mirrors. . . . He grinned at the soft shock of it, his eyes pulled from one new sight to another, so many things, objects he had no name for. . .

"You looking for anyone in particular, Jack?"

The man stood in front of a vast fireplace, wearing tight black jeans and a white T-shirt. His feet were bare and he held a fat glass bulb of liquor in his right hand. Slick blinked at him.

"Shit," Slick said, "you're him. . . ."

The man swirled the brown stuff up around the edges of the glass and took a swallow. "I expected Afrika to pull something like this eventually," he said, "but somehow, buddy, you don't look like his style of help."

"You're the Count."

"Yeah," he said, "I'm the Count. Who the fuck are you?"

"Slick. Slick Henry."

He laughed. "Want some cognac, Slick Henry?" He gestured

with the glass toward a piece of polished wooden furniture where ornate bottles stood in a row, each one with a little silver tag hung around it on a chain.

Slick shook his head.

The man shrugged. "Can't get drunk on it anyway . . . Pardon my saying so, Slick, but you look like shit. Am I correct in guessing that you are not a part of Kid Afrika's operation? And if not, just what exactly are you doing here?"

"Gentry sent me."

"Gentry who?"

"You're the guy on the stretcher, right?"

"The guy on the stretcher is me. Where, exactly, right this minute, is that stretcher, Slick?"

"Gentry's."

"Where's that?"

"Factory."

"And where is *that*?"

"Dog Solitude."

"And how did I happen to get there, wherever that is?"

"Kid Afrika, he brought you. Brought you with this girl name of Cherry, right? See, I owed him a favor, so he wanted me to put you up awhile, you an' Cherry, and she's taking care of you."

"You called me Count, Slick. . . ."

"Cherry said Kid called you that once."

"Tell me, Slick, did the Kid seem worried when he brought me?"

"Cherry thought he got scared, back in Cleveland."

"I'm sure he did. Who's this Gentry? A friend of yours?"

"Factory's his place. I live there too. . . ."

"This Gentry, is he a cowboy, Slick? A console jockey? I mean, if you're here, he must be technical, right?"

Now it was Slick's turn to shrug. "Gentry's, like, he's an artist, kind of. Has these theories. Hard to explain. He rigged a set of splitters to that thing on the stretcher, what you're jacked into. First he tried to get an image on a holo rig, but there was just this monkey thing, sort of shadow, so he talked me into . . ."

"Jesus . . . Well, never mind. This factory you're talking about, it's out in the sticks somewhere? It's relatively isolated?"

Slick nodded.

"And this Cherry, she's some kind of hired nurse?"

"Yeah. Had a med-tech's ticket, she said."

"And nobody's come looking for me yet?"

"No."

"That's good, Slick. Because if anyone does, other than my lying rat-bastard friend Kid Afrika, you folks could find yourselves in serious trouble."

"Yeah?"

"Yeah. Listen to me, okay? I want you to remember this. If any company shows up at this factory of yours, your only hope in hell is to get me jacked into the matrix. You got that?"

"How come you're the Count? I mean, what's it mean?"

"Bobby. My name's Bobby. Count was my handle once, that's all. You think you'll remember what I told you?"

Slick nodded again.

"Good." He put his glass down on the thing with all the fancy bottles. "Listen," he said. From the open door came the sound of tires over gravel. "Know who that is, Slick? That's Angela Mitchell."

Slick turned. Bobby the Count was looking out at the drive.

"Angie Mitchell? The stim star? She's in this thing too?"

"In a manner of speaking, Slick, in a manner of speaking . . ."

Slick saw the long black car slide by. "Hey," he began, "Count, I mean Bobby, what d—"

"Easy," Gentry was saying, "just sit back. Easy. Easy . . ."

# TWENTY-FIVE

# BACK EAST

While Kelly and his assistants were assembling her wardrobe for the trip, she felt as though the house itself were stirring around her, preparing for one of its many brief periods of vacancy.

She could hear their voices, from where she sat in the living room, their laughter. One of the assistants was a girl in a blue polycarbon exo that allowed her to carry the Hermès wardrobe cases as though they were weightless blocks of foam, the humming skeleton suit padding softly down the stairs on its blunt dinosaur feet. Blue skeleton, leather coffins.

Now Porphyre stood in the doorway. "Missy ready?" He wore a long, loose coat cut from tissue-thin black leather; rhinestone spurs glittered above the heels of black patent boots.

"Porphyre," she said, "you're in mufti. We have an entrance to make, in New York."

"The cameras are for you."

"Yes," she said, "for my reinsertion."

"Porphyre will keep well in the rear."

"I've never known you to worry about upstaging anyone."

He grinned, exposing sculpted teeth, streamlined teeth, an avant-garde dentist's fantasy of what teeth might be like in a faster, more elegant species.

"Danielle Stark will be flying with us." She heard the sound of the approaching helicopter. "She's meeting us at LAX."

"We'll strangle her," he said, his tone confidential, as he helped her on with the blue fox Kelly had selected. "If we promise to hint to the fax that the motive was sexual, she might even decide to play along. . . ."

"You're horrid."

"Danielle is a horror, missy."

"Look who's talking."

"Ah," said the hairdresser, narrowing his eyes, "but my soul is a child's."

Now the helicopter was landing.

Danielle Stark, associated with stim versions of both *Vogue-Nippon* and *Vogue-Europa*, was widely rumored to be in her late eighties. If it were true, Angie thought, covertly inspecting the journalist's figure as the three of them boarded the Lear, Danielle and Porphyre would be on par for overall surgical modification. Apparently in her willowy early thirties, her only obvious augments were a pair of pale blue Zeiss implants. A young French fashion reporter had once referred to these as "modishly outdated"; the reporter, Net legend said, had never worked again.

And soon, Angie knew, Danielle would want to talk drugs, celebrity drugs, the cornflower eyes schoolgirl-wide to take it all in.

Under Porphyre's daunting gaze, Danielle managed to contain herself until they were in cruise mode somewhere over Utah.

"I was hoping," she began, "that I wouldn't have to be the one to bring it up."

"Danielle," Angie countered, "I *am* sorry. How thoughtless." She touched the veneered face of the Hosaka flight kitchen, which purred softly and began to dispense tiny plates of tea-smoked duck, gulf oysters on black-pepper toast, crayfish flan, sesame pancakes. . . . Porphyre, taking Angie's cue, produced a bottle of chilled Chablis— Danielle's favorite, Angie now recalled. Someone—Swift?—had also remembered.

"Drugs," Danielle said, fifteen minutes later, finishing the last of the duck.

"Don't worry," Porphyre assured her. "When you get to New York, they have anything you want."

Danielle smiled. "You're so amusing. Do you know I've a copy of your birth certificate? I know your real name." She looked at him meaningfully, still smiling.

" 'Sticks and stones,' " he said, topping up her glass.

"Interesting notation regarding congenital defects." She sipped her wine.

"Congenital, genital . . . We all change so *much* these days, don't we? Who's been doing your hair, dear?" He leaned forward. "Your saving grace, Danielle, is that you make the rest of your kind look vaguely human."

Danielle smiled.

The interview itself went smoothly enough; Danielle was too skilled an interviewer to allow her feints to cross the pain threshold, where they might rally serious resistance. But when she brushed a fingertip back across her temple, depressing a subdermal switch that deactivated her recording gear, Angie tensed for the real onslaught.

"Thank you," Danielle said. "The rest of the flight, of course, is off the record."

"Why don't you just have another bottle or two and turn in?" Porphyre asked.

"What I don't see, dear," Danielle said, ignoring him, "is why you *bothered. . . .*"

"Why I bothered, Danielle?"

"Going to that tedious clinic at all. You've said it didn't affect your work. You've also said there was no 'high,' not in the usual sense." She giggled. "Though you do maintain that it was such a terribly addictive substance. Why *did* you decide to quit?"

"It was terribly expensive. . . ."

"In your case, surely, that's academic."

*True,* Angie thought, *though a week of it did cost something in the vicinity of your annual salary.*

"I suppose I began to resent paying to feel normal. Or a poor approximation of normal."

"Did you build up a tolerance?"

"No."

"How odd."

"Not really. These designers provide substances that supposedly bypass the traditional drawbacks."

"Ah. But what about the new drawbacks, the *now* draw-backs?" Danielle poured herself more wine. "I've heard another version of all this, of course."

"You have?"

"Of course I have. What it was, who made it, why you quit."

"Yes?"

"It was an antipsychotic, produced in Sense/Net's own labs. You quit taking it because you'd rather be crazy."

Porphyre gently took the glass from Danielle's hand as her lids fluttered heavily over the brilliant blue eyes. "Nightie-night, dear," he said. Danielle's eyes closed and she began to snore gently.

"Porphyre, what—?"

"I dosed her wine," he said. "She won't know the difference, missy. She won't remember anything she didn't record. . . ." He grinned broadly. "You really didn't want to have to listen to this bitch all the way back, did you?"

"But she'll know, Porphyre!"

"No, she won't. We'll tell her she killed three bottles by herself and made a disgusting mess in the washroom. And she'll *feel* like it, too." He giggled.

Danielle Stark was still snoring, quite loudly now, in one of the two swing-down bunks in the rear of the cabin.

"Porphyre," Angie said, "do you think she might've been right?"

The hairdresser gazed at her with his gorgeous, inhuman eyes. "And you wouldn't have known?"

"I don't know. . . ."

He sighed. "Missy worries too much. You're free now. Enjoy it."

"I do hear voices, Porphyre."

"Don't we all, missy?"

"No," she said, "not like mine. Do you know anything about African religions, Porphyre?"

He smirked. "I'm not African."

"But when you were a child . . ."

"When I was a child," Porphyre said, "I was white."

"Oh . . ."

He laughed. "Religions, missy?"

"Before I came to the Net, I had friends. In New Jersey. They were black and . . . religious."

He smirked again and rolled his eyes. "Hoodoo sign, missy? Chickenbone and pennyroyal oil?"

"You know it isn't like that."

"And if I do?"

"Don't tease me, Porphyre. I need you."

"Missy has me. And yes, I know what you mean. And *those* are your voices?"

"They were. After I began to use the dust, they went away. . . ."

"And now?"

"They're gone." But the impulse was past now, and she cringed from trying to tell him about Grande Brigitte and the drug in the jacket.

"Good," he said. "That's good, missy."

The Lear began its descent over Ohio. Porphyre was staring at the bulkhead, still as a statue. Angie looked out at the cloud-country below as it rose toward them, remembering the game she'd played on airplanes as a child, sending an imaginary Angie out to romp through cloud-canyons and over fluffy peaks grown magically solid. Those planes had belonged to Maas-Neotek, she supposed. From the Maas corporate jets she'd gone on to Net Lears. She knew commercial airliners only as locations for her stims: New York to Paris on the maiden flight of JAL's restored Concorde, with Robin and a hand-picked party of Net people.

Descending. Were they over New Jersey yet? Did the children swarming the rooftop playgrounds of Beauvoir's arcology hear the Lear's engine? Did the sound of her passage sweep faintly over the condos of Bobby's childhood? How unthinkably intricate the world was, in sheer detail of mechanism, when Sense/Net's corporate will shook tiny bones in the ears of unknown, unknowing children. . . .

"Porphyre knows certain things," he said, very softly. "But Porphyre needs time to think, missy. . . ."

They were banking for the final approach.

# TWENTY-SIX

# KUROMAKU

And Sally was silent, on the street and in the cab, all the long cold way back to their hotel.

Sally and Swain were being blackmailed by Sally's enemy "up the well." Sally was being forced to kidnap Angie Mitchell. The thought of someone's abducting the Sense/Net star struck Kumiko as singularly unreal, as if someone were plotting to assassinate a figure out of myth.

The Finn had implied that Angie herself was already involved, in some mysterious way, but he had used words and idioms Kumiko hadn't understood. Something in cyberspace; people forming pacts with a thing or things there. The Finn had known a boy who became Angie's lover; but wasn't Robin Lanier her lover? Kumiko's mother had allowed her to run several of the Angie and Robin stims. The boy had been a cowboy, a data thief, like Tick in London. . . .

And what of the enemy, the blackmailer? She was mad, Finn said, and her madness had brought about the decline of her family's fortunes. She lived alone, in her ancestral home, the house called

Straylight. What had Sally done to earn her enmity? Had she really killed this woman's father? And who were the others, the others who had died? Already she'd forgotten the gaijin names. . . .

And had Sally learned what she'd wanted to learn, in visiting the Finn? Kumiko had waited, finally, for some pronouncement from the armored shrine, but the exchange had wound down to nothing, to a gaijin ritual of joking goodbyes.

In the hotel lobby, Petal was waiting in a blue velour armchair. Dressed for travel, his bulk encased in three-piece gray wool, he rose from the chair like some strange balloon as they entered, eyes mild as ever behind steel-rimmed glasses.

"Hello," he said, and coughed. "Swain's sent me after you. Only to mind the girl, you see."

"Take her back," Sally said. "Now. Tonight."

"Sally! No!" But Sally's hand was already locked firmly around Kumiko's upper arm, pulling her toward the entrance to the darkened lounge off the lobby.

"Wait there," Sally snapped at Petal. "Listen to me," she said, tugging Kumiko around a corner, into shadow. "You're going back. I can't keep you here now."

"But I don't like it there. I don't like Swain, or his house. . . . I . . ."

"Petal's okay," Sally said, leaning close and speaking quickly. "In a pinch, I'd say trust him. Swain, well, you know what Swain is, but he's your father's. Whatever comes down, I think they'll keep you out of the way. But if it gets bad, really bad, go to the pub where we met Tick. The Rose and Crown. Remember?"

Kumiko nodded, her eyes filling with tears.

"If Tick's not there, find a barman named Bevan and mention my name."

"Sally, I . . ."

"You're okay," Sally said, and kissed her abruptly, one of her lenses brushing for an instant against Kumiko's cheekbone, startlingly cold and unyielding. "Me, baby, I'm gone."

And she was, into the muted tinkle of the lounge, and Petal cleared his throat in the entranceway.

The flight back to London was like a very long subway ride. Petal passed the time inscribing words, a letter at a time, in some idiotic puzzle in an English fax, grunting softly to himself. Eventually she slept, and dreamed of her mother. . . .

"Heater's working," Petal said, driving back to Swain's from Heathrow. It was uncomfortably warm in the Jaguar, a dry heat that smelled of leather and made her sinuses ache. She ignored him, staring out at the wan morning light, at roofs shining black through melting snow, rows of chimneypots. . . .

"He's not angry with you, you know," Petal said. "He feels a special responsibility. . . ."

"*Giri.*"

"Er . . . yes. Responsible, you see. Sally's never been what you'd call predictable, really, but we didn't expect—"

"I don't wish to talk, thank you."

His small worried eyes in the mirror.

The crescent was lined with parked cars, long silver-gray cars with tinted windows.

"Seeing a lot of visitors this week," Petal said, parking opposite number 17. He got out, opened the door for her. She followed him numbly across the street and up the gray steps, where the black door was opened by a squat, red-faced man in a tight dark suit, Petal brushing past him as though he weren't there.

"Hold on," red-face said. "Swain'll see her now. . . ."

The man's words brought Petal up short; with a grunt, he spun around with disconcerting speed and caught the man by his lapel.

"In future show some fucking respect," Petal said, and though he hadn't raised his voice, somehow all of its weary gentleness was gone. Kumiko heard stitches pop.

"Sorry, guv." The red face was carefully blank. "He told me to tell you."

"Come along then," Petal said to her, releasing his grip on the dark worsted lapel. "He'll just want to say hello."

They found Swain seated at a three-meter oak refectory table in the room where she'd first seen him, the dragons of rank buttoned away behind white broadcloth and a striped silk tie. His eyes met hers as she entered, his long-boned face shadowed by a green-shaded brass reading lamp that stood beside a small console and a thick sheaf of fax on the table. "Good," he said, "and how was the Sprawl?"

"I'm very tired, Mr. Swain. I wish to go to my room."

"We're glad to have you back, Kumiko. The Sprawl's a dangerous place. Sally's friends there probably aren't the sort of people
your father would want you to associate with."

"May I go to my room now?"

"Did you meet any of Sally's friends, Kumiko?"

"No."

"Really? What did you do?"

"Nothing."

"You mustn't be angry with us, Kumiko. We're protecting
you."

"Thank you. May I go to my room now?"

"Of course. You must be very tired."

Petal followed her from the room, carrying her bag, his gray
suit creased and wrinkled from the flight. She was careful not to
glance up as they passed beneath the blank gaze of the marble bust
where the Maas-Neotek unit might still be hidden, though with
Swain and Petal in the room she could think of no way to retrieve
it.

There was a new sense of movement in the house, brisk and
muted: voices, footsteps, the rattle of the lift, the chattering of pipes
as someone drew a bath.

She sat at the foot of the huge bed, staring at the black marble
tub. Residual images of New York seemed to hover at the borders
of her vision; if she closed her eyes, she found herself back in the
alley, squatting beside Sally. Sally, who'd sent her away. Who hadn't
looked back. Sally, whose name had once been Molly, or Misty, or
both. Again, her unworthiness. Sumida, her mother adrift in black
water. Her father. Sally.

Moments later, driven by a curiosity that pushed aside her
shame, she rose from where she lay, brushed her hair, zipped her
feet into thin black rubber toe-socks with ridged plastic soles, and
went very quietly out into the corridor. When the lift arrived, it
stank of cigarette smoke.

Red-face was pacing the blue-carpeted foyer when she emerged
from the lift, his hands in the pockets of his tight black jacket.
" 'Ere," he said, raising his eyebrows, "you need something?"

"I'm hungry," she said, in Japanese. "I'm going to the kitchen."

" 'Ere," he said, removing his hands from his pockets and
straightening the front of his jacket, "you speak English?"

"No," she said, and walked straight past him down the corridor and around the corner. " 'Ere," she heard him say, rather more urgently, but she was already groping behind the white bust.

She managed to slip the unit into her pocket as he rounded the corner. He surveyed the room automatically, hands held loosely at his sides, in a way that suddenly reminded her of her father's secretaries.

"I'm hungry," she said, in English.

Five minutes later, she'd returned to her room with a large and very British-looking orange; the English seemed to place no special value on the symmetry of fruit. Closing the door behind her, she put the orange on the wide flat rim of the black tub and took the Maas-Neotek unit from her pocket.

"Quickly now," Colin said, tossing his forelock as he came into focus, "open it and reset the A/B throw to A. The new regime has a technician making the rounds, scanning for bugs. Once you've changed that setting, it shouldn't read as a listening device." She did as he said, using a hairpin.

"What do you mean," she asked, mouthing the words without voicing them, " 'the new regime'?"

"Haven't you noticed? There are at least a dozen staff now, not to mention numerous visitors. Well, I suppose it's less a new regime than an upgrading of procedure. Your Mr. Swain is quite a social man, in his covert way. You've one conversation there, Swain and the deputy head of Special Branch, that I imagine numerous people would kill for, not least of them the aforementioned official."

"Special Branch?"

"The secret police. Bloody odd company he keeps, Swain: Buck House types, czars from the East End rookeries, senior police officers . . ."

"Buck House?"

"The Palace. Not to mention merchant bankers from the City, a simstim star, a drove or two of expensive panders and drug merchants . . ."

"A simstim star?"

"Lanier, Robin Lanier."

"Robin Lanier? He was here?"

"Morning after your precipitous departure."

She looked into Colin's transparent green eyes. "Are you telling me the truth?"

"Yes."

"Do you always?"

"To the extent that I know it, yes."

"What are you?"

"A Maas-Neotek biochip personality-base programmed to aid and advise the Japanese visitor in the United Kingdom." He winked at her.

"Why did you wink?"

"Why d'you think?"

"Answer the question!" Her voice loud in the mirrored room.

The ghost touched his lips with a slim forefinger. "I'm something else as well, yes. I do display a bit too much initiative for a mere guide program. Though the model I'm based on is top of the line, extremely sophisticated. I can't tell you exactly what I am, though, because I don't know."

"You don't know?" Again subvocally, carefully.

"I know all sorts of things," he said, and went to one of the dormer windows. "I know that a serving table in Middle Temple Hall is said to be made from the timbers of the *Golden Hind;* that you climb one hundred and twenty-eight steps to the walkways of Tower Bridge; that in Wood Street, right of Cheapside, is a plane tree thought to have been the one in which Wordsworth's thrush sang loud. . . ." He spun suddenly to face her. "It *isn't,* though, because the current tree was cloned from the original in 1998. I know all that, you see, and more, a very great deal more. I could, for instance, teach you the rudiments of snooker. That *is* what I am, or rather what I was intended to be, originally. But I'm something else as well, and very likely something to do with you. I don't know what. I really don't."

"You were a gift from my father. Do you communicate with him?"

"Not to my knowledge."

"You didn't inform him of my departure?"

"You don't understand," he said. "I wasn't aware of your having been away, until you activated me a moment ago."

"But you've been recording. . . ."

"Yes, but not aware of it. I'm only 'here' when you activate me. Then I evaluate the current data. . . . One thing you can be fairly certain of, though, is that it simply isn't possible to broadcast any sort of signal from this house without Swain's snoops detecting it immediately."

"Could there be *more* of you, I mean another one, in the same unit?"

"Interesting idea, but no, barring some harrowing secret break-through in technology. I'm pushing the current envelope a bit as it is, considering the size of my hardware. I know that from my store of general background information."

She looked down at the unit in her hand. "Lanier," she said. "Tell me."

"Ten/twenty-five/sixteen: A.M.," he said. Her head filled with disembodied voices. . . .

PETAL: If you'll follow me please, sir . . .

SWAIN: Come into the billiard room.

THIRD VOICE: You'd better have a reason for this, Swain. There are three Net men waiting in the car. Security will have your address in their database until hell freezes over.

PETAL: Lovely car that is, sir, the Daimler. Take your coat?

THIRD VOICE: What is it, Swain? Why couldn't we meet at Brown's?

SWAIN: Take your coat off, Robin. She's gone.

THIRD VOICE: Gone?

SWAIN: To the Sprawl. Early this morning.

THIRD VOICE: But it isn't time. . . .

SWAIN: You think I sent her there?

The man's reply was hollow, indistinct, lost behind a closing door. "That was Lanier?" Kumiko asked silently.

"Yes," Colin replied. "Petal mentioned him by name in an earlier conversation. Swain and Lanier spent twenty-five minutes together."

Sound of a latch, movement.

SWAIN: Bloody cock-up, not mine. I warned you about her, told you to warn them. Born killer, probably psychopathic . . .

LANIER: And your problem, not mine. You need their product and my cooperation.

SWAIN: And what's *your* problem, Lanier? Why are you in this? Just to get Mitchell out of the way?

LANIER: Where's my coat?

SWAIN: Petal, Mr. Lanier's bloody coat.

PETAL: Sir.

LANIER: I have the impression they want your razorgirl as badly as they want Angie. She's definitely part of the payoff. They'll be taking her, too.

SWAIN: Good luck to them, then. She's already in position, in the Sprawl. Spoke with her on the phone an hour ago. I'll be

putting her together with my man over there, the one who's been
arranging for the . . . girl. And you'll be going back over yourself?

LANIER: This evening.

SWAIN: Well, then, not to worry.

LANIER: Goodbye, Swain.

PETAL: He's a right bastard, that one.

SWAIN: I don't like this, really. . . .

PETAL: You like the goods though, don't you?

SWAIN: Can't complain there, but why d'you think they want
Sally as well?

PETAL: Christ knows. They're welcome to her. . . .

SWAIN: They. I don't like 'theys'. . . .

PETAL: They mightn't be terribly happy to know she'd gone
there on her own stick, with Yanaka's daughter. . . .

SWAIN: No. But we have Miss Yanaka back again. Tomorrow
I'll tell Sally that Prior's in Baltimore, getting the girl into shape. . . .

PETAL: That's an ugly business, that is. . . .

SWAIN: Bring a pot of coffee to the study.

She lay on her back, eyes closed, Colin's recordings unspooling
in her head, direct input to the auditory nerves. Swain seemed to
conduct the better part of his dealings in the billiard room, which
meant that she heard people arriving and departing, heads and tails
of conversations. Two men, one of whom might have been the
red-faced man, held an interminable discussion of dog racing and
tomorrow's odds. She listened with special interest as Swain and the
man from Special Branch (SB, Swain called it) settled an article of
business directly beneath the marble bust, as the man was preparing
to leave. She interrupted this segment half-a-dozen times to request
clarification. Colin made educated guesses.

"This is a very corrupt country," she said at last, deeply shocked.

"Perhaps no more than your own," he said.

"But what is Swain paying these people with?"

"Information. I would say that our Mr. Swain has recently
come into possession of a very high-grade source of intelligence and
is busy converting it into power. On the basis of what we've heard,
I'd hazard that this has probably been his line of work for some
time. What's apparent, though, is that he's moving up, getting
bigger. There's internal evidence that he's currently a much more
important man than he was a week ago. Also, we have the fact of
the expanded staff. . . ."

"I must tell . . . my friend."

"Shears? Tell her what?"

"What Lanier said. That she would be taken, along with Angela Mitchell."

"Where is she, then?"

"The Sprawl. A hotel . . ."

"Phone her. But not from here. D'you have money?"

"A Mitsubank chip."

"No good in our phones, sorry. Have any coin?"

She got up from the bed and sorted carefully through the odd bits of English money that had accumulated at the bottom of her purse. "Here," she said, coming up with a thick gilt coin, "ten pounds."

"Need two of those to make a *local* call." She tossed the brassy tenner back into her purse. "No, Colin. Not the phone. I know a better way. I want to leave here. Now. Today. Will you help me?"

"Certainly," he said, "though I advise you not to."

"But I will."

"Very well. How do you propose to go about it?"

"I'll tell them," she said, "that I need to go shopping."

# TWENTY-SEVEN

# BAD LADY

The woman must've gotten in sometime after midnight, she figured later, because it was after Prior came back with the crabs, the second bag of crabs. They really did have some good crabs in Baltimore, and coming off a run always gave her an appetite, so she'd talked him into going back for some more. Gerald kept coming in to change the derms on her arms; she'd give him her best goofy smile every time, squish the trank out of them when he'd gone, and then stick them back on. Finally Gerald said she should get some sleep; he put out the lights and turned down the fake window to its lowest setting, a bloodred sunset.

When she was alone again, she slid her hand between the bed and the wall, found the shockrod in its hole in the foam.

She fell asleep without meaning to, the red glow of the window like a sunset in Miami, and she must've dreamed of Eddy, or anyway of Hooky Green's, dancing with somebody up there on the thirty-third floor, because when the crash woke her, she wasn't sure where she was, but she had this very clear map of the way out of Hooky Green's, like she knew she'd better take the stairs because there must be some kind of trouble. . . .

She was half out of bed when Prior came through the door, like really *through* it, because it was still shut when he hit it. He came through it backward and it just went to splinters and honey-comb chunks of cardboard.

She saw him hit the wall, and then the floor, and then he wasn't moving anymore, and someone else was there in the doorway, backlit from the other room, and all she could see of the face were these two curves of reflected red light from that fake sunset.

Pulled her legs back into bed and sank back against the wall, her hand sliding down to . . .

"Don't move, bitch." There was something real scary about that voice, because it was too fucking *cheerful*, like throwing Prior through that door had been kind of a treat. "I mean *really* don't move. . . ." And the woman was across the room in three strides, very close, so close that Mona felt the cold coming off the leather of the woman's jacket.

"Okay," Mona said, "okay . . ."

Then hands grabbed her, *fast*, and she was flat on her back, shoulders pressed down hard into the foam, and something—the shockrod—was right in front of her face.

"Where'd you get this little thing?"

"Oh," Mona said, like it was something she might've seen once but forgotten about, "it was in my boyfriend's jacket. I borrowed his jacket. . . ."

Mona's heart was pounding. There was something about those glasses. . . .

"Did shithead know you had this little thing?"

"Who?"

"Prior," the woman said, and let go of her, turning. Then she was kicking him, kicking Prior over and over, hard. "No," she said, stopping as abruptly as she'd begun, "I don't think Prior knew."

Then Gerald was in the doorway, just like nothing had hap-pened, except he was looking ruefully at the part of the door that was still on the frame, rubbing his thumb over an edge of splintered laminate. "Coffee, Molly?"

"Two coffees, Gerald," the woman said, examining the shockrod. "Mine's black."

Mona sipped her coffee and studied the woman's clothes and hair while they waited for Prior to wake up. At least that's what they seemed to be doing. Gerald was gone again.

She wasn't much like anybody Mona'd seen before; Mona couldn't place her on the style map at all, except she must've had some money. The hair was European; Mona'd seen it like that in a magazine; she was pretty sure it wasn't this season's style anywhere, but it went okay with the glasses, which were insets, planted right in the skin. Mona'd seen a cabbie in Cleveland had those. And she wore this short jacket, very dark brown, too plain for Mona's taste but obviously new, with a big white sheepskin collar, open now over a weird green thing trussed across her breasts and stomach like armor, which was what Mona figured it probably was, and jeans cut from some kind of gray-green mossy suede, thick and soft, and Mona thought they were the best thing about her outfit, she could've gone for a pair of those herself, except the boots spoiled them, these knee-high black boots, the kind bike racers wore, with thick yellow rubber soles and big straps across the insteps, chrome buckles all up and down, horrible clunky toes. And where'd she get that nail color, that burgundy? Mona didn't think they even made that anymore.

"What the hell are you looking at?"

"Uh . . . your boots."

"So?"

"They don't make it with your pants."

"Wore 'em to kick the shit out of Prior."

Prior moaned on the floor and started trying to throw up. It made Mona feel kind of sick herself, so she said she was going to go to the bathroom.

"Don't try to leave." The woman seemed to be watching Prior, over the rim of her white china cup, but with those glasses, it was hard to be sure.

Somehow she found herself in the bathroom with her purse on her lap. She hurried, getting the hit together; didn't grind it fine enough, so it burned the back of her throat, but like Lanette used to say, you don't always have time for the niceties. And anyway, wasn't that all a lot better now? There was a little shower in Gerald's bathroom, but it looked like it hadn't been used for a long time. She took a closer look and saw gray mold growing around the drain, and spots that looked like dried blood.

When she came back, the woman was dragging Prior into one of the other rooms, pulling him by his feet. He had socks on, no shoes, Mona noticed now, like maybe he'd had his feet up to sleep. His blue shirt had blood on it and his face was all bruised.

What Mona felt, as the rush kicked in, was a bright and innocent curiosity. "What are you doing?"

"I think I'll have to wake him up," the woman said, like she was on the subway, talking about another passenger who was about to miss his stop. Mona followed her into the room where Gerald did his work, everything clean and hospital white; she watched as the woman got Prior up into a sort of chair like in a salon, with levers and buttons and things. *It isn't like she's that strong*, Mona thought, *it's like she knows which way to throw the weight*. Prior's head fell to the side as the woman fastened a black strap across his chest. Mona was starting to feel sorry for him, but then she remembered Eddy.

"What is it?" The woman was filling a white plastic container with water from a chrome tap.

Mona just kept trying to say it, feeling her heart race out of control on the wiz. *He killed Eddy*, she kept trying to say, but it wouldn't come out. But then it must have, because the woman said, "Yeah, he'll do that sort of thing . . . if you let him." She threw the water over Prior, into his face and all down his shirt; his eyes snapped open and the white of the left one was solid red; the metal prongs of the shockrod snapped white sparks when the woman pressed it against the wet blue shirt. Prior screamed.

Gerald had to get down on his hands and knees to pull her out from under the bed. He had cool, very gentle hands. She couldn't remember how she'd gotten under there, but now everything was quiet. Gerald had on a gray topcoat and dark glasses.

"You're going with Molly now, Mona," he said.

She started to shake.

"I think I'd better give you something for your nerves."

She jerked back, out of his grip. "No! Don't fucking touch me!"

"Leave it, Gerald," the woman said from the door. "It's time you go now."

"I don't think you know what you're doing," he said, "but good luck."

"Thanks. Think you'll miss the place?"

"No. I was going to retire soon anyway."

"So was I," the woman said, and then Gerald left, without even a nod for Mona.

"Got any clothes?" the woman asked Mona. "Get 'em on. We're leaving too."

Dressing, Mona found she couldn't button her dress over her new breasts, so she left it open, putting Michael's jacket on and zipping it up to her chin.

# TWENTY-EIGHT

# COMPANY

Sometimes he just needed to stand there and look up at the Judge, or squat on the concrete beside the Witch. It held back the memory-stutter, to do that. Not the fugues, the real flashbacks, but this jerky unfocused feeling he got, like the memory tape kept slipping in his head, losing minute increments of experience . . . So he was doing that now, and it was working, and finally he noticed Cherry was there beside him.

Gentry was up in the loft with the shape he'd captured, what he called a macroform node, and he'd hardly listened to what Slick had tried to tell him about the house and that whole place and Bobby the Count.

So Slick had come down here to crouch next to an Investigator in the cold and dark, retracing all the things he'd done with so many different tools, and where he'd scrounged each part, and then Cherry reached out and touched his cheek with her cold hand.

"You okay?" she asked. "I thought maybe it was happening to you again. . . ."

"No. It's just I gotta come down here, sometimes."

"He plugged you into the Count's box, didn't he?"

"Bobby," Slick said, "that's his name. I saw him."

"Where?"

"In there. It's a whole world. There's this house, like a castle or something, and he's there."

"By himself?"

"He said Angie Mitchell's in there too. . . ."

"Maybe he's crazy. Is she?"

"I didn't see her. Saw a car he said was hers."

"She's in some celebrity detox place in Jamaica, last I heard." He shrugged. "I dunno."

"What's he like?"

"He looked younger. Anybody'd look bad with all those tubes 'n' shit in 'em. He figured Kid Afrika dumped him here because he got scared. He said if anybody comes looking for him, we jack him into the matrix."

"Why?"

"Dunno."

"You shoulda asked him."

He shrugged again. "Seen Bird anywhere?"

"No."

"Shoulda been back already . . ." He stood up.

Little Bird came back at dusk, on Gentry's bike, the dark wings of his hair damp with snow and flapping behind him as he roared in across the Solitude. Slick winced; Little Bird was in the wrong gear. Little Bird jolted up an incline of compacted oildrums and hit the brakes when he should've gunned it. Cherry gasped as Bird and the bike separated in midair; the bike seemed to hang there for a second before it somersaulted into the rusted sheet-metal tangle that had been one of Factory's outbuildings, and Little Bird was rolling over and over on the ground.

Somehow Slick never heard the crash. He was standing beside Cherry in the shelter of a doorless loading bay—then he was sprinting across snow-flecked rust to the fallen rider, no transition. Little Bird lay on his back with blood on his lips, his mouth partially hidden by the jumble of thongs and amulets he wore around his neck.

"Don't touch him," Cherry said. "Ribs may be broken, or he's mashed up inside. . . ."

Little Bird's eyes opened at the sound of her voice. He pursed his lips and spat blood and part of a tooth.

"Don't move," Cherry said, kneeling beside him and switching to the crisp diction she'd learned in med-tech school. "You may have been injured. . . ."

"F-fuck it, lady," he managed, and struggled stiffly up, with Slick's help.

"All right, asshole," she said, "hemorrhage. See if I give a shit."

"Didn't get it," Little Bird said, smearing blood across his face with the back of his hand, "the truck."

"I can see that," Slick said.

"Marvie 'n' them, they got company. Like flies on shit. Couple of hovers 'n' a copter 'n' shit. All these guys."

"What kind of guys?"

"Like soldiers, but they're not. Soldier'll goof around, bullshit, crack jokes when nobody important's looking. But not them."

"Cops?" Marvie and his two brothers grew mutant ruderalis in a dozen half-buried railway tankcars; sometimes they tried to cook primitive amine compounds, but their lab kept blowing up. They were the nearest thing Factory had to permanent neighbors. Six kilometers.

"Cops?" Little Bird spat another tooth chip and gingerly probed his mouth with a bloody finger. "They aren't doin' anything against the law. Anyway, cops can't afford shit like that, new hovers, new Honda. . . ." He grinned through a film of blood and spittle. "I hung off in the Solitude 'n' scoped 'em good. Nobody I'd wanna talk to, or you either. Guess I really fucked Gentry's bike, huh?"

"Don't worry about it," Slick said. "I think his mind's on something else."

"Tha's good. . . ." He staggered in the direction of Factory, nearly fell, caught himself, continued.

"He's higher'n a kite," Cherry said.

"Hey, Bird," Slick called, "what happened to that bag of shit I gave you to give Marvie?"

Bird swayed, turned. "Lost it . . ." Then he was gone, around a corner of corrugated steel.

"Maybe he's making that up," Cherry said. "About those guys. Or seeing things."

"I doubt it," Slick said, pulling her into deeper shadow as an unlit black Honda swung down toward Factory out of winter twilight.

\*    \*    \*

He heard the Honda making its fifth pass over Factory as he pounded up the quaking stairs, the iron roof rattling with the copter's passage. Well, he thought, that should anyway bring it to Gentry's attention that they had visitors. He took the fragile catwalk in ten long, slow steps; he was beginning to wonder if they'd ever be able to get the Count and his stretcher back out without having to weld extra I-bar across the span.

He went into the bright loft without knocking. Gentry was sitting at a workbench, his head cocked to one side, staring up at the plastic skylights. The bench was littered with bits of hardware and small tools.

"Helicopter," Slick said, panting from the climb.

"Helicopter," Gentry agreed, nodding thoughtfully, his disheveled roostertail bobbing. "They seem to be looking for something."

"I think they just found it."

"Could be the Fission Authority."

"Bird saw people at Marvie's. Saw that copter there too. You weren't paying much attention when I tried to tell you what he said."

"Bird?" Gentry looked down at the small bright things on the workbench. Picked up two fittings and twisted them together.

"The Count! He told me—"

"Bobby Newmark," Gentry said, "yes. I know a lot more about Bobby Newmark, now."

Cherry came in behind Slick. "You gotta do something about that bridge," she said, going immediately to the stretcher, "it shakes too much." She bent to check the Count's readouts.

"Come here, Slick," Gentry said, standing. He walked to the holo table. Slick followed, looked at the image that glowed there. It reminded him of the rugs he'd seen in the gray house, patterns like that, only these were woven of hairfine neon, and twisted into some kind of infinite knot; the knot's core hurt his head to look at it. He looked away.

"That's it?" he asked Gentry. "What you've always been looking for?"

"No. I told you. This is just a node, a macroform. A model . . ."

"He's got this house in there, like a castle, and grass and trees and sky. . . ."

"He's got a lot more than that. He's got a universe more than that. That was just a construct worked up from a commercial stim.

What he's got is an *abstract* of the sum total of data constituting cyberspace. Still, it's closer than I've gotten before. . . . He didn't tell you why he was in there?"

"Didn't ask him."

"Then you'll have to go back."

"Hey. Gentry. Listen up. That copter, it'll be back. It'll be back with two hovers fulla guys Bird said looked like soldiers. They aren't after us, man. They're after *him*."

"Maybe they're his. Maybe they are after us."

"No. He *told* me, man. He said, anybody comes looking for him, we're in deep shit and we gotta jack him into the matrix."

Gentry looked down at the little coupling he still held. "We'll talk with him, Slick. You'll go back; this time I'll go with you."

# TWENTY-NINE

# WINTER JOURNEY

Petal had agreed, finally, but only after she'd suggested phoning her father for permission. That had sent him shuffling unhappily off in search of Swain, and when he'd returned, looking no happier, the answer had been yes. Bundled in several layers of her warmest clothing, she stood in the white-painted foyer, studying the hunting prints while Petal lectured the red-faced man, whose name was Dick, behind closed doors. She couldn't distinguish individual words, only a low torrent of admonition. The Maas-Neotek unit was in her pocket, but she avoided touching it. Twice already Colin had tried to dissuade her.

Now Dick emerged from Petal's lecture with his hard little mouth set in a smile. Under his tight black suit he wore a pink cashmere turtleneck and a thin gray lambswool cardigan. His black hair was plastered tightly back against his skull; his pale cheeks were shadowed by a few hours' growth of beard. She palmed the unit in her pocket. " 'Lo," Dick said, looking her up and down. "Where shall we go for our walk?"

"Portobello Road," Colin said, slouched against the wall beside the crowded coatrack. Dick took a dark overcoat from the rack, reaching through Colin to do it, put it on, and buttoned it. He pulled on a bulky pair of black leather gloves.

"Portobello Road," Kumiko said, releasing the unit.

"How long have you worked for Mr. Swain?" she asked, as they made their way along the icy pavement of the crescent.

"Long enough," he replied. "Mind you don't slip. Wicked heels on those boots . . ."

Kumiko tottered along beside him on black French patent spikes. As she'd predicted, it was virtually impossible to navigate the glass-hard rippled patches of ice in these boots. She took his hand for support; doing this, she felt solid metal across his palm. The gloves were weighted, the fingers reinforced with carbon mesh.

He was silent, as they turned the sidestreet at the end of the crescent, but when they reached Portobello Road, he paused. "Excuse me, miss," he said, a note of hesitation in his voice, "but is it true, what the boys say?"

"Boys? Excuse me?"

"Swain's boys, his regulars. That you're the big fellow's daughter—the big fellow back in Tokyo?"

"I'm sorry," she said, "I don't understand."

"Yanaka. Your name's Yanaka?"

"Kumiko Yanaka, yes . . ."

He peered at her with intense curiosity. Then worry crossed his face and he glanced carefully around. "Lord," he said, "must be true . . ." His squat, tightly buttoned body was taut and alert. "Guvnor said you wanted to shop?"

"Yes, thank you."

"Where shall I take you?"

"Here," she said, and led him into a narrow arcade lined solidly with British *gomi*.

Her Shinjuku shopping expeditions served her well with Dick. The techniques she'd devised for torturing her father's secretaries proved just as effective now, as she forced the man to participate in dozens of pointless choices between one Edwardian medallion and another, this or that fragment of stained glass, though she was careful only to choose items, finally, that were fragile or very heavy, awkward to carry, and extremely expensive. A cheerful bilingual shop assistant accessed an eighty-thousand-pound charge against

Kumiko's MitsuBank chip. Kumiko slipped her hand into the pocket that held the Mass-Neotek unit. "Exquisite," the English girl said in Japanese, as she wrapped Kumiko's purchase, an ormolu vase encrusted with griffins.

"Hideous," Colin commented, in Japanese. "An imitation as well." He reclined on a Victorian horsehair sofa, his boots up on an art deco cocktail stand supported by airstream aluminum angels.

The shop assistant added the wrapped vase to Dick's burden. This was Dick's eleventh antique shop and Kumiko's eighth purchase.

"I think you'd better make your move," Colin advised. "Any moment now, our Dick will buzz Swain's for a car to take that lot home."

"Think this is it, then?" Dick asked hopefully, over Kumiko's purchases.

"One more shop, please." Kumiko smiled.

"Right," he said grimly. As he was following her out the door, she drove the heel of her left boot into a gap in the pavement she'd noticed on her way in. "You all right?" he asked, seeing her stumble.

"I've broken the heel of my boot. . . ." She hobbled back into the shop and sat down beside Colin on the horsehair sofa. The assistant came fussing up to help.

"Get 'em off quick," Colin advised, "before Dickie puts his parcels down."

She unzipped the boot with the broken heel, then the other, pulled off both. In place of the coarse Chinese silk she usually wore in winter, her feet were sheathed in thin black rubber toe-socks with ridged plastic soles. She nearly ran between Dick's legs as she cleared the door, but instead her shoulder struck his thigh as she squeezed past, toppling him into a display of faceted crystal decanters.

And then she was free, plunging through the press of tourists down Portobello Road.

Her feet were very cold, but the ridged plastic soles provided excellent traction—though not on ice, she reminded herself, picking herself up from her second spill, wet grit against her palms. Colin had directed her down this narrow passage of blackened brick. . . .

She grasped the unit. "Where next?"

"This way," he said.

"I want the Rose and Crown," she reminded him.

"You want to be careful. Dickie'll have Swain's men here by now, not to mention the sort of hunt that friend of Swain's from

Special Branch could mount if he's asked to. And I can't imagine why he shouldn't be asked to. . . ."

She entered the Rose and Crown by a side door, Colin at her elbow, grateful for the snug gloom and irradiating warmth that seemed central to the idea of these drinking-burrows. She was struck by the amount of padding on the walls and seats, by the muffling curtains. If the colors and fabrics had been less dingy, the effect would somehow have been less warm. Pubs, she guessed, were an extreme expression of the British attitude toward *gomi*.

At Colin's urging, she made her way through the drinkers clustered in front of the bar, hoping to find Tick.

"What'll it be, dear?"

She looked up into the broad blond face behind the bar, bright lipstick and rouged cheeks. "Excuse me," Kumiko began, "I wish to speak with Mr. Bevan—"

"Mine's a pint, Alice," someone said, slapping down three ten-pound coins, "lager." Alice worked a tall white ceramic lever, filling a mug with pale beer. She put the mug on the scarred bar and swept the money into a rattling till behind the counter.

"Someone wanting a word, Bevan," Alice said, as the man lifted his pint.

Kumiko looked up at a flushed, seamed face. The man's upper lip was short; Kumiko thought of rabbits, though Bevan was large, nearly as large as Petal. He had a rabbit's eyes as well: round, brown, showing very little white. "With me?" His accent reminded her of Tick's.

"Tell him yes," Colin said. "He can't think why a little Jap girl in rubber socks has come into the drinker looking for him."

"I wish to find Tick."

Bevan regarded her neutrally over the rim of his raised pint. "Sorry," he said, "can't say I know anyone by the name." He drank.

"Sally told me I should find you if Tick wasn't here. Sally Shears . . ."

Bevan choked on his lager, his eyes showing a fraction of white. Coughing, he set the mug on the bar and took a handkerchief from his overcoat pocket. He blew his nose and wiped his mouth.

"I'm on duty in five," he said. "Best step in the back."

Alice raised a hinged section of the bar; Bevan ushered Kumiko through with small flapping motions of his large hands, glancing quickly over his shoulder. He guided her down a narrow passage that opened off the area behind the bar. The walls were brick, old and uneven, thickly coated with dirty green paint. He stopped beside a battered steel hamper heaped with terry bar towels that reeked of beer.

"You'll regret it if you're on a con, girl," he said. "Tell me why you're looking for this Tick."

"Sally is in danger. I must find Tick. I must tell him."

"Fucking hell," the barman said. "Put yourself in my position. . . ."

Colin wrinkled his nose at the hamper of sodden towels.

"Yes?" Kumiko said.

"If you're a nark, and I sent you to find this Tick fellow, assuming I did know him, and he's on some sort of blag, then he'd do for me, wouldn't he? But if you're not, then this Sally, she'd likely do for me if I don't, understand?"

Kumiko nodded. " 'Between the rock and the hard place.' " It was an idiom Sally had used; Kumiko found it very poetic.

"Quite," Bevan said, giving her an odd look.

"Help me. She is in very great danger."

He ran his palm back across thinning ginger-colored hair.

"You *will* help me," she heard herself say, feeling her mother's cold mask click into place, "Tell me where to find Tick."

The barman seemed to shiver, though it was overly warm in the passageway, a steamy warmth, beer smell mingling with raw notes of disinfectant. "D'you know London?"

Colin winked at her. "I can find my way," she said.

"Bevan," Alice said, putting her head around the corner, "the filth."

"Police," Colin translated.

"Margate Road, SW2," Bevan said, "dunno the number, dunno his phone."

"Let him show you out the back now," Colin said. "Those are no ordinary policemen."

Kumiko would always remember her endless ride through the city's Underground. How Colin led her from the Rose and Crown to Holland Park, and down, explaining that her MitsuBank chip was worse than useless now; if she used it for a cab, or any sort of purchase, he said, some Special Branch operator would see the transaction flare like magnesium on the grid of cyberspace. But she had to find Tick, she told him; she had to find Margate Road. He frowned. No, he said, wait till dark; Brixton wasn't far, but the streets were too dangerous now, by daylight, with the police on Swain's side. But where could she hide? she asked. She had very little cash; the concept of currency, of coins and paper notes, was quaint and alien.

Here, he said, as she rode a lift down into Holland Park. "For the price of a ticket."

The bulgy silver shapes of the trains.

The soft old seats in gray and green.

And warm, beautifully warm; another burrow, here in the realm of ceaseless movement . . .

# THIRTY

# THE RIP

The airport sucked a groggy Danielle Stark away down a pastel corridor lined with reporters, cameras, augmented eyes, while Porphyre and three Net security men swept Angie through the closing ring of journalists, a choreographed piece of ritual that had more to do with providing dramatic visuals than protection. Anyone present had already been cleared by security and the PR department.

Then she was alone with Porphyre in an express elevator, on their way to the heliport the Net maintained on the terminal's roof.

As the doors opened, into gusts of wet wind across brilliantly lit concrete, where a new trio of security men waited in giant fluorescent-orange parkas, Angie remembered her first glimpse of the Sprawl, when she'd ridden the train up from Washington with Turner.

One of the orange parkas ushered them across an expanse of spotless concrete to the waiting helicopter, a large twin-prop Fokker finished in black chrome. Porphyre led the way up the spidery, matte-black stairway. She followed without looking back.

She had something now, a new determination. She'd decided

to contact Hans Becker through his agent in Paris. Continuity had the number. It was time, time to make something happen. And she'd make something happen with Robin as well; he'd be waiting now, she knew, at the hotel.

The helicopter told them to fasten their seatbelts.

As they lifted off, there was virtual silence in the soundproofed cabin, only a throbbing in the bones, and for a strange second she seemed able to hold the whole of her life in mind and know it, see it for what it had been. And it was this, she thought, that the dust had drifted over and concealed, and that had been freedom from pain.

*And the site of the soul's departure,* said an iron voice, out of candleglow and the roar of the hive. . . .

"Missy?" Porphyre from the seat beside her, leaning close . . .

"I'm dreaming. . . ."

Something had been waiting for her, years ago, in the Net. Nothing like the loa, like Legba or the others, though Legba, she knew, was Lord of the Crossroads; he was synthesis, the cardinal point of magic, communication. . . .

"Porphyre," she asked, "why did Bobby leave?" She looked out at the Sprawl's tangled grid of light, at the domes picked out in red beacons, seeing instead the datascape that had drawn him, always, back to what he'd believed was the only game worth playing.

"If you don't know, missy," Porphyre said, "who does?"

"But you hear things. Everything. All the rumors. You always have. . . ."

"Why ask me now?"

"It's time. . . ."

"I remember *talk*, understand? How people who aren't famous talk about those who are. Maybe someone who claimed they knew Bobby talked to someone else, and it came around. . . . Bobby was worth talking about because he was with you, understand? That's a good place to start, missy, because he wouldn't have found that so very gratifying, would he? Story was, he'd set out hustling on his own, but he'd found you instead, and you rolled higher and faster than anything he could've dreamed of. Took him *up* there, understand? Where the kind of money he'd never even dreamed of, back in Barrytown, was just change. . . ."

Angie nodded, looking out over the Sprawl.

"Talk was he had his own ambitions, missy. Something driving him. Drove him off, finally . . ."

"I didn't think he'd leave me," she said. "When I first came to the Sprawl, it was like being born. A new life. And he was there, right there, the very first night. Later, when Legba—when I was with the Net . . ."

"When you were becoming Angie."

"Yes. And as much of me as that took, I knew he'd be there. And also that he'd never *buy* it, entirely, and I needed that, how it was still just a scam, to him, the whole business. . . ."

"The Net?"

"Angie Mitchell. He knew the difference between it and me."

"Did he?"

"Maybe he *was* the difference." So high above the lines of light . . .

The old New Suzuki Envoy had been Angie's favorite Sprawl hotel since her earliest days with the Net.

It maintained its street wall for eleven stories, then narrowed jaggedly, at the first of nine setbacks, into a mountainside assembled from bedrock excavated from its Madison Square building site. Original plans had called for this steep landscape to be planted with flora native to the Hudson Valley region, and populated with suitable fauna, but subsequent construction of the first Manhattan Dome had made it necessary to hire a Paris-based eco-design team. The French ecologists, accustomed to the "pure" design problems posed by orbital systems, had despaired of the Sprawl's particulate-laden atmosphere, opting for heavily engineered strains of vegetation and robotic fauna of the sort encountered in children's theme parks, but Angie's continued patronage had eventually lent the place a cachet it would otherwise have lacked. The Net leased the five topmost floors, where her permanent suite had been installed, and the Envoy had come to enjoy a certain belated reputation with artists and entertainers.

Now she smiled as the helicopter rose past a disinterested robot bighorn pretending to munch lichen beside the illuminated waterfall. The absurdity of the place always delighted her; even Bobby had enjoyed it.

She glanced out at the Envoy's heliport, where the Sense/Net logo had been freshly repainted on heated, floodlit concrete. A lone figure, hooded in a bright orange parka, waited beside a sculpted outcropping of rock.

"Robin will be here, won't he, Porphyre?"

"*Mistah* Lanier," he said sourly.

She sighed.

The black chrome Fokker brought them smoothly down, glasses tinkling gently in the drinks' cabinet as the landing gear met the roof of the Envoy. The muted throb of the engines died.

"Where Robin is concerned, Porphyre, I'll have to make the first move. I'm going to speak with him tonight. Alone. In the meantime, I want you to stay out of his way."

"Porphyre's pleasure, missy," the hairdresser said, as the cabin door opened behind them. And then he was twisting, clawing at the buckle of his seatbelt, and Angie turned in time to see the bright orange parka in the hatchway, the upraised arm, the mirrored glasses. The gun made no more sound than a cigarette lighter, but Porphyre convulsed, one long black hand slapping at his throat as the security man swung the hatch shut behind him and sprang at Angie.

Something was clapped hard against her stomach as Porphyre lolled back bonelessly in his seat, the sharp pink tip of his tongue protruding. She looked down, in pure reflex, and saw the black chrome buckle of her seatbelt through a sticky-looking lozenge of greenish plastic.

She looked up into a white oval face framed by a tightly drawn orange nylon hood. Saw her own face blank with shock, doubled in the silver lenses. "He drink, tonight?"

"What?"

"Him." A thumb jerked in Porphyre's direction. "He drink any alcohol?"

"Yes . . . Earlier."

"Shit." A woman's voice, as she turned to the unconscious hairdresser. "Now I've sedated him. Don't wanna suppress his breathing reflex, y'know?" Angie watched as the woman checked Porphyre's pulse. "Guess he's okay . . ." Did she shrug, inside the orange parka?

"Security?"

"What?" The glasses flashed.

"Are you Net security?"

"Fuck no, I'm abducting you."

"You are?"

"You bet."

"Why?"

"Not for any of the usual reasons. Somebody's got it in for you. Got it in for me too. I was supposed to set it up to grab you next week. Fuck 'em. Had to talk to you, anyway."

"You did? Talk to me?"

"Know anybody name of 3Jane?"

"No. I mean, yes, but—"

"Save it. Our asses outa here, fast."

"Porphyre—"

"He's gonna wake up soon. Look of him, I don't wanna be around when he does. . . ."

# THIRTY-ONE

# 3JANE

If this was part of Bobby's big gray house in the country, Slick decided, opening his eyes on the cramped curve of the narrow corridor, then it was a stranger place than it had seemed the first time. The air was thick and dead and the light from the greenish glass-tile ceiling-strip made him feel like he was under water. The tunnel was made of some kind of glazed concrete. It felt like jail.

"Maybe we came out in the basement or something," he said, noticing the faint *ping* of echo off the concrete when he spoke.

"No reason we'd cut into the construct you saw before," Gentry said.

"So what is it?" Slick touched the concrete wall; it was warm.

"Doesn't matter," Gentry said.

Gentry started walking in the direction they were both facing. Past the curve, the floor became an uneven mosaic of shattered china, fragments pressed into something like epoxy, slippery under their boots.

"Look at this stuff . . ." Thousands of different patterns and colors in the broken bits, but no overall design in how it had been put down, just random.

"Art." Gentry shrugged. "Somebody's hobby. You should appreciate that, Slick Henry."

Whoever it was, they hadn't bothered with the walls. Slick knelt to run his fingers over it, feeling raw edges of broken ceramic, glassy hardened plastic in between. "What's that supposed to mean, 'hobby'?"

"It's like those things you build, Slick. Your junk toys . . ." Gentry grinned his tense crazy grin.

"You don't know," Slick said. "Spend your whole fucking life trying to figure what cyberspace is shaped like, man, and it probably isn't even shaped like anything, and anyway who gives a shit?" There wasn't anything random about the Judge and the others. The process was random, but the results had to conform to something inside, something he couldn't touch directly.

"Come on," Gentry said.

Slick stayed where he was, looking up at Gentry's pale eyes, gray in this light, his taut face. Why did he put up with Gentry anyway?

Because you needed somebody, in the Solitude. Not just for electricity; that whole landlord routine was really just a shuck. He guessed because you needed somebody around. Bird wasn't any good to talk to because there wasn't much he was interested in, and all he talked was stringtown stupid. And even if Gentry never admitted it, Slick felt like Gentry understood about some things.

"Yeah," Slick said, getting up, "let's go."

The tunnel wound in on itself like a gut. The section with the mosaic floor was back there now, around however many curves and up and down short, curving stairwells. Slick kept trying to imagine a building that would have insides like this, but he couldn't. Gentry was walking fast, eyes narrowed, chewing on his lip. Slick thought the air was getting worse.

Up another stairwell, they hit a straight stretch that narrowed to nothing in the distance, either way you looked. It was broader than the curved parts and the floor was soft and humpy with little rugs, it looked like hundreds of them, rolled out layers deep over the concrete. Each rug had its own pattern and colors, lots of reds and blues, but all the patterns were the same zaggy diamonds and triangles. The dusty smell was thicker here and Slick figured it had to be the rugs, they looked so old. The ones on top, nearest the center, were worn down to the weave, in patches. A trail, like somebody'd been walking up and down there for years. Sections of the overhead light-strip were dark, and others pulsed weakly.

"Which way?" he asked Gentry.

Gentry was looking down, working his thick lower lip between finger and thumb. "This way."

"How come?"

"Because it doesn't matter."

It made Slick's legs tired, walking over those rugs. Had to watch not to snag his toes in the ones with holes worn through. Once he stepped over a glass tile that had fallen from the light-strip. At regular intervals now they were passing sections of wall that looked as though portals had been sealed over with more concrete. There wasn't anything there, just the same arched shape in slightly paler concrete with a slightly different texture.

"Gentry, this has gotta be underground, right? Like a basement under something . . ."

But Gentry just brought his arm up, so that Slick bumped into it, and they both were standing there staring at the girl at the end of the corridor, not a dozen meters across the waves of carpet.

She said something in a language Slick guessed was French. The voice was light and musical, the tone matter-of-fact. She smiled. Pale under a twist of dark hair, a fine, high-boned face, strong thin nose, and wide mouth.

Slick felt Gentry's arm trembling against his chest. "It's okay," he said, taking Gentry's arm and lowering it. "We're just looking for Bobby. . . ."

"Everyone's looking for Bobby," she said, English with an accent he didn't know. "I'm looking for him myself. For his body. Have you seen his body?" She took a step back, away from them, like she was about to run.

"We won't hurt you," Slick said, suddenly aware of his own smell, of the grease worked into his jeans and brown jacket, and Gentry didn't really look all that much more reassuring.

"I shouldn't think so," she said, and her white teeth flashed again in the stale undersea light. "But then I don't think I fancy either of you."

Slick wanted Gentry to say something, but Gentry didn't. "You know him—Bobby?" Slick ventured.

"He's really a very clever man. Extraordinarily clever. Although I don't think I fancy him, really." She wore something loose and black that hung to her knees. Her feet were bare. "Nonetheless, I want . . . his body." She laughed.

Everything

changed.

"Juice?" Bobby the Count asked, holding out a tall glass of something yellow. The water in the turquoise pool reflected shifting blobs of sunlight on the palm fronds above his head. He was naked, aside from a pair of very dark glasses. "What's the matter with your friend?"

"Nothing," Slick heard Gentry say. "He did time on induced Korsakov's. Transition like that scares the shit out of him."

Slick lay very still on the white iron lounge chair with the blue cushions, feeling the sun bake through his greasy jeans.

"You're the one he mentioned, right?" Bobby asked. "Name's Gentle? Own a factory?"

"Gentry."

"You're a cowboy." Bobby smiled. "Console jockey. Cyberspace man."

"No."

Bobby rubbed his chin. "You know I have to shave in here? Cut myself, there's a scar. . . ." He drank half the glass of juice and wiped his mouth with the back of his hand. "You're not a jockey? How else you get in here?"

Gentry unzipped his beaded jacket, exposing his bone-white, hairless chest. "Do something about the sun," he said.

Twilight. Like that. Not even a click. Slick heard himself groan. Insects began to creak in the palms beyond the whitewashed wall. Sweat cooled on his ribs.

"Sorry, man," Bobby said to Slick. "That Korsakov's, that must be some sad shit. But this place is beautiful. Vallarta. Belonged to Tally Isham." He turned his attention to Gentry again. "If you're not a cowboy, fella, what are you?"

"I'm like you," Gentry said.

"I'm a cowboy." A lizard scooted diagonally up the wall behind Bobby's head.

"No. You aren't here to steal anything, Newmark."

"How do you know?"

"You're here to learn something."

"Same thing."

"No. You were a cowboy once, but now you're something else. You're looking for something, but there's nobody to steal it from. I'm looking for it too."

And Gentry began to explain about the Shape, as the palm shadows gathered and thickened into Mexican night, and Bobby the Count sat and listened.

When Gentry was done, Bobby sat there for a long time without saying anything. Then he said, "Yeah. You're right. How I think of it, I'm trying to find out what brought the Change."

"Before that," Gentry said, "it didn't have a Shape."

"Hey," Slick said, "before we were here, we were somewhere else. Where was that?"

"Straylight," Bobby said. "Up the well. In orbit."

"Who's that girl?"

"Girl?"

"Dark hair. Skinny."

"Oh," Bobby said, in the dark, "that was 3Jane. You saw her?"

"Weird girl," Slick said.

"Dead girl," Bobby said. "You saw her construct. Blew her family fortune to build this thing."

"You, uh, hang out with her? In here?"

"She hates my guts. See, I stole it, stole her soul-catcher. She had her construct in place in here when I took off for Mexico, so she's always been around. Thing was, she died. Outside, I mean. Meantime, all her shit outside, all her scams and schemes, that's being run by lawyers, programs, more flunkies. . . ." He grinned. "It really pisses her off. The people who're trying to get into your place to get the aleph back, they work for somebody else who works for some people she hired out on the Coast. But, yeah, I've done the odd deal with her, traded things. She's crazy, but she plays a tight game. . . ."

Not even a click.

At first he thought he was back in the gray house, where he'd seen Bobby the first time, but this room was smaller and the carpets and furniture were different, he couldn't say how. Rich but not as glittery. Quiet. A lamp with a green glass shade glowed on a long wooden table.

Tall windows with frames painted white, dividing the white beyond that into rectangles, each pane, and that must be snow. . . .

He stood with his cheek touching soft drapes, looking out into a walled space of snow.

"London," Bobby said. "She had to trade me this to get the serious voodoo shit. Thought they wouldn't have anything to do with her. Fuck of a lot of good it did her. They've been fading, sort of blurring. You can still raise 'em, sometimes, but their personalities run together. . . ."

"That fits," Gentry said. "They came out of the first cause, When It Changed. You already figured that. But you don't know what happened yet, do you?"

"No. I just know where. Straylight. She's told me all that part, I think all she knows. Doesn't really care about it. Her mother put together a couple of AIs, very early on, real heavy stuff. Then her mother died and the AIs sort of stewed in the corporate cores, up there. One of them started doing deals on its own. It wanted to get together with the other one. . . ."

"It did. There's your first cause. Everything changed."

"Simple as that? How do you know?"

"Because," Gentry said, "I've been at it from another angle. You've been playing cause and effect, but I've been looking for outlines, shapes in time. You've been looking all over the matrix, but I've been looking *at* the matrix, the whole thing. I know things you don't."

Bobby didn't answer. Slick turned from the window and saw the girl, the same one, standing across the room. Just standing there.

"It wasn't just the Tessier-Ashpool AIs," Gentry said. "People came up the well to crack the T-A cores. They brought a Chinese military icebreaker."

"Case," Bobby said, "Guy named Case. I know that part. Some kind of synergistic effect . . ."

Slick watched the girl.

"And the sum was greater than the parts?" Gentry really seemed to be enjoying this. "Cybernetic godhead? Light on the waters?"

"Yeah," Bobby said, "that's about it."

"It's a little more complicated than that," Gentry said, and laughed.

And the girl was gone. No click.

Slick shivered.

# THIRTY-TWO

# WINTER JOURNEY
# (2)

Night fell during the Underground's peak evening traffic, though even then it was nothing like Tokyo, no *shiroshi-san* struggling to wedge a last few passengers in as the doors were closing. Kumiko watched the salmon haze of sunset from a windy platform on the Central Line, Colin lounging against a broken vending machine with a row of cracked, dusty windows. "Time now," he said, "and keep your head demurely down through Bond Street and Oxford Circus."

"But I must pay, when I leave the system?"

"Not *everyone* does, actually," he said, tossing his forelock.

She set off for the stairs, no longer requiring his directions to find her way to the opposite platform. Her feet were very cold again, and she thought of the fleece-lined German boots in the closet in her room at Swain's. She'd decided on the combination of the rubber toe-socks and the high French heels as a ploy to lull Dick, to make him doubt she'd run, but with each bite of cold through the thin soles she regretted the idea.

In the tunnel to the other platform, she relaxed her grip on the unit and Colin flickered out. The walls were worn white ceramic with a decorative band of green. She took her hand from her pocket and trailed her fingers along the green tiles as she went, thinking of Sally and the Finn and the different smell of a Sprawl winter, until the first Dracula stepped smartly in front of her and she was instantly and very closely surrounded by four black raincoats, four bone-thin, bone-white faces. " 'Ere," the first one said, "innit pretty."

They were eye to eye, Kumiko and the Dracula; his breath smelled of tobacco. The evening crowd continued on its way around them, bundled for the most part in dark wool.

"Oo," one said, beside her, "look. Wot's this?" He held up the Maas-Neotek unit, his hand gloved in cracked black leather. "Flash lighter, innit? Let's 'ave a snag, Jap." Kumiko's hand went to her pocket, shot straight through the razor slash, and closed on air. The boy giggled.

"Snags in 'er bag," another said. " 'Elp 'er, Reg." A hand darted out and the leather strap of her purse parted neatly.

The first Dracula caught the purse, whipped the dangling strap around it with a practiced flick, and tucked it into the front of his raincoat. "Ta."

" 'Ere, she's got 'em in 'er pants!" Laughter as she fumbled beneath layered sweaters. The tape she'd used hurt her stomach as she tore the gun free with both hands and flipped it up against the cheek of the boy who held the unit.

Nothing happened.

Then the other three were racing frantically for the stairs at the far end of the tunnel, their high-laced black boots slipping in melted snow, their long coats flapping like wings. A woman screamed.

And still they were frozen there, Kumiko and the Dracula, the muzzle of the pistol pressed against his left cheekbone. Kumiko's arms began to tremble.

She was looking into the Dracula's eyes, brown eyes gone wide with an ancient simple terror; the Dracula was seeing her mother's mask. Something struck the concrete at her feet: Colin's unit.

"Run," she said. The Dracula convulsed, opened his mouth, made a strangled, sobbing sound, and twisted away from the gun.

Kumiko looked down and saw the Maas-Neotek unit in a puddle of gray slush. Beside it lay the clean silver rectangle of a single-edged industrial razorblade. When she picked up the unit, she saw that its case was cracked. She shook moisture from the crack and squeezed it hard in her hand. The tunnel was deserted now.

Colin wasn't there. Swain's Walther air pistol was huge and heavy in her other hand.

She stepped to a rectangular receptacle fastened to the tile wall and tucked the gun down between a grease-flecked foam food container and a neatly folded sheaf of newsfax. Turned away, then turned back for the fax.

Up the stairs.

Someone pointed at her, on the platform, but the train roared in with its antique clatter and then the doors slid shut behind her.

She did as Colin had instructed, White City and Shepherd's Bush, Holland Park, raising the fax as the train slowed for Notting Hill—the King, who was very old, was dying—and keeping it there through Bond Street. The station at Oxford Circus was very busy and she was grateful for the sheltering crowd.

Colin had said that it was possible to leave the station without paying. After some consideration, she decided that this was true, though it required speed and timing. Really, there was no other way; her purse, with the MitsuBank chip and her few English coins, had gone with the Jack Draculas. She spent ten minutes watching passengers surrender their yellow plastic tickets to the automated turnstyles, took a deep breath, and ran. Up, over, behind her a shout and a loud laugh, and then she was running again.

When she reached the doors at the top of the stairs, she saw Brixton Road waiting like a tatty Shinjuku, jammed with steaming foodstalls.

# THIRTY THREE

# STAR

She was waiting in a car and she didn't like it. She didn't like waiting anyway, but the wiz she'd done made it really hard. She had to keep reminding herself not to grit her teeth, because whatever Gerald had done to them, they were still sore. She was sore all over, now that she thought about it. Probably the wiz hadn't been such a great idea.

The car belonged to the woman, the one Gerald called Molly. Some kind of regular gray Japanese car like a suit would have, nice enough but nothing you'd notice. It had that new smell inside and it was fast when they got out of Baltimore. It had a computer but the woman drove it herself, all the way back to the Sprawl, and now it was parked on the roof of a twenty-level lot that must be close to the hotel where Prior had taken her, because she could see that crazy building, the one with the waterfall, fixed up like a mountain.

There weren't many other cars up here, and the ones that were were humped over with snow, like they hadn't moved in a long time. Except for the two guys in the booth where you drove in, there didn't seem to be anybody around at all. Here she was, in the middle of all those people, the biggest city in the world, and she was alone in the backseat of a car. Told to wait.

The woman hadn't said much when they'd come from Baltimore, just asked a question now and then, but the wiz had made it hard for Mona not to talk. She'd talked about Cleveland and Florida and Eddy and Prior.

Then they'd driven up here and parked.

So this Molly'd been gone at least an hour now, maybe longer. She'd taken a suitcase with her. The only thing Mona'd been able to get out of her was that she'd known Gerald a long time, and Prior hadn't known that.

It was getting cold in the car again, so Mona climbed into the front seat and turned on the heater. She couldn't just leave it on low, because it might run the battery down, and Molly'd said if that happened, they were really in the shit. " 'Cause when I come back, we leave in a hurry." Then she'd shown Mona where there was a sleeping bag under the driver's seat.

She set the heater on high and held her hands in front of the vent. Then she fiddled with the little vid studs beside the dash monitor and got a news show. The King of England was sick; he was really old. There was a new disease in Singapore; it hadn't killed anybody yet, but nobody knew how you got it or how to cure it. Some people thought there was some kind of big fight going on in Japan, two different bunches of Yakuza guys trying to kill each other, but nobody really knew; Yakuza—that was something Eddy liked to bullshit about. Then these doors popped open and Angie came through on the arm of this amazing black guy, and the vid voice was saying this was live, she'd just arrived in the Sprawl after a brief vacation at her house in Malibu, following treatment at a private drug clinic. . . .

Angie looked just great in this big fur, but then the segment was over.

Mona remembered what Gerald had done; she touched her face.

She shut off the vid, then the heater, and got into the backseat again. Used the corner of the sleeping bag to clean her condensed breath off the window. She looked up at the mountainside-building, all lit up, past the sagging chainlink at the edge of the carlot's roof. Like a whole country up there, maybe Colorado or something, like the stim where Angie went to Aspen and met this boy, only Robin turned up like he almost always did.

But what she didn't understand was this clinic stuff, how that barman had said Angie'd gone there because she was wired on something, and now she'd just heard the news guy say it too, so she guessed it had to be true. But why would anybody like Angie, with a life like that and Robin Lanier for a boyfriend, want to do drugs?

Mona shook her head, looking out at that building, glad she wasn't hooked on anything.

She must've drifted off for a minute, thinking about Lanette, because when she looked again, there was a copter, a big one, glittery black, poised above the mountain-building. It looked good, real big-town.

She'd known some rough women in Cleveland, girls nobody messed with, but this Molly was something else—remembering Prior coming through that door, remembering him screaming. . . . She wondered what it was he'd finally admitted, because she'd heard him talking, and Molly hadn't hurt him anymore. They'd left him strapped in that chair and Mona had asked Molly if she thought he'd get loose. Either that, Molly had said, or somebody finds him, or he dehydrates.

The copter settled, vanished. Big one, the kind with the whirly thing at both ends.

So here she was, waiting, no fucking idea what else to do.

Something Lanette had taught her, sometimes you had to list your assets—assets were what you had going for you—and just forget the other stuff. Okay. She was out of Florida. She was in Manhattan. She looked like Angie. . . . That one stopped her. Was that an asset? Okay—putting it another way—she'd just had a fortune in free cosmetic surgery and she had *totally perfect teeth*. Anyway, look at it that way and it wasn't so bad. Think about the flies in the squat. Yeah. If she spent the money she had left on a haircut and some makeup, she could come up with something that didn't look all that much like Angie, which was probably a good idea, because what if somebody was looking for her?

There went the copter again, lifting off.

Hey.

Maybe two blocks away and fifty stories higher, the thing's nose swung toward her, dipped. . . . *It's the wiz*. Sort of wobbled there, then it was coming down. . . . *Wiz; it's not real*. Straight down toward her. It just got bigger. Toward her. *But it's the wiz, right?* Then it was gone, behind another building, and it was just the wiz. . . .

It swung around a corner, still five stories above the roof of the carlot, and it was still coming down and it *wasn't* the wiz, it was *on* her, a tight white beam stabbing out to find the gray car, and Mona popped the door lock and rolled out into the snow, still in the car's shadow, all around her the thunder of the thing's blades, its engines; Prior or whoever he worked for and they were after her. Then the spotlight went out, blades changed pitch, and it came down fast, too fast. Bounced on its landing gear. Slammed down again, engines dying, coughing blue flame.

Mona was on her hands and knees by the car's rear bumper. Slipped when she tried to get to her feet.

There was a sound like a gunshot; a square section of the copter's skin blew out and skidded across the lot's salt-stained concrete; a bright orange five-meter emergency exit slide popped out, inflating like a kid's beachtoy. Mona got up more carefully, holding on to the gray car's fender. A dark, bundled figure swung its legs out over the slide and went down, sitting up, just like a kid at a playground. Another figure followed, this one padded in a huge hooded jacket the same color as the slide.

Mona shivered as the one in orange led the other toward her across the roof, away from the black copter. It was . . . But it *was!*

"Want you both in back," Molly said, opening the door on the driver's side.

"It's you," Mona managed, to the most famous face in the world.

"Yes," Angie said, her eyes on Mona's face, "it . . . seems to be. . . ."

"Come on," Molly said, her hand on the star's shoulder. "Get in. Your Martian spade'll be waking up already." She glanced back at the helicopter. It looked like a big toy sitting there, no lights, like a giant kid had put it down and forgotten it.

"He'd better be," Angie said, climbing into the back of the car.

"You too, hon," Molly said, pushing Mona toward the open door.

"But . . . I mean . . ."

"Move!"

Mona climbed in, smelling Angie's perfume, wrist brushing the supernatural softness of that big fur. "I saw you," she heard herself say. "On the vid."

Angie didn't say anything.

Molly slid into the driver's seat, yanked the door shut, and

started the engine. The orange hood was snugged up tight, her face
a white mask with blank silver eyes. Then they were rolling toward
the sheltered ramp, swinging into the first curve. Down five levels
like that, in a tight spiral, and Molly swung them off into aisles of
larger vehicles under dim green diagonals of light-strip.

"Parafoils," Molly said. "You ever see any parafoil gear, up the
Envoy?"

"No," Angie said.

"If Net security has any, they could be upstairs already. . . ."
She swung the car in behind a big long boxy hover, a white one
with a name painted across the rear doors in square blue letters.

"What's it say?" Mona asked, then felt herself blush.

"Cathode Cathay," Angie said.

Mona thought she'd heard that name before.

Molly was out there opening those big doors. Pulling down
these yellow plastic ramp things.

Then she was back in the car. Reversed, put it in drive, and
they rolled right up into the hover. She stripped back the orange
hood and shook her head to free her hair. "Mona, you think you
can get out there and shove those ramps back in? They aren't
heavy." It didn't sound like a question.

They weren't heavy. She pulled herself up behind the car and
helped Molly pull the doors shut.

She could feel Angie there in the dark.

It was really Angie.

"Up front, strap in, hold on."

Angie. She was sitting right beside Angie.

There was a whoosh as Molly filled the hover's bags; then they
were skimming down the spiral ramp.

"Your friend," Molly said, "he's awake by now, but he can't
really move yet. Another fifteen minutes." She swung off the ramp
again and this time Mona had lost track of the levels. This one was
packed with fancy cars, little ones. The hover roared along a central
aisle, swung left.

"You'll be lucky if he isn't waiting for us outside," Angie said.

Molly brought them to a halt ten meters from a big metal door
painted with diagonal stripes, yellow and black.

"No," Molly said, taking a little blue box from the dash
compartment, "*he's* lucky if he's *not* waiting outside." The door
blew out of its frame with an orange flash and a sound that
slammed into Mona's diaphragm like a solid blow. It crashed into

the wet street in a cloud of smoke and then they were over it, turning, the hover accelerating.

"This is awfully crude, isn't it?" Angie said, and actually laughed.

"I know," Molly said, intent on her driving. "Sometimes that's just the way to go. Mona, tell her about Prior. Prior and your boyfriend. What you told me."

Mona hadn't ever felt so shy in her life.

"Please," Angie said, "tell me. Mona."

Just like that. Her name. Angie Mitchell had actually said *her* name. To her. Right there.

It made her want to faint.

# THIRTY FOUR

# MARGATE ROAD

"You seem lost," the noodle seller said, in Japanese. Kumiko guessed that he was Korean. Her father had associates who were Korean; they were in the construction business, her mother had said. They tended, like this one, to be large men, very nearly as large as Petal, with broad, serious faces. "You look very cold."

"I'm looking for someone," she said. "He lives in Margate Road."

"Where is that?"

"I don't know."

"Come inside," the noodle man said, gesturing Kumiko around the end of his counter. His stall was made of pink corrugated plastic.

She stepped between the noodle stall and another that advertised something called *roti*, this word worked in deliriously colored spraybomb capitals trimmed with looping, luminous blobs. That stall smelled of spices and stewing meat. Her feet were very cold.

She ducked beneath a clouded sheet of plastic. The noodle stall was crowded: squat blue tanks of butane, the three cooking grids with their tall pots, plastic sacks of noodles, stacks of foam bowls, and the shifting bulk of the big Korean as he tended his pots. "Sit," he said; she sat on a yellow plastic canister of MSG, her head below the level of the counter. "You're Japanese?"

"Yes," she said.

"Tokyo?"

She hesitated.

"Your clothes," he said. "Why do you wear rubber tabi-socks in winter? Is this the fashion?"

"I lost my boots."

He passed her a foam bowl and plastic chopsticks; fat twists of noodle swam in a thin yellow soup. She ate hungrily, then drank off the soup. She watched as he served a customer, an African woman who took away noodles in her own lidded pot.

"Margate," the noodle man said, when the woman was gone. He took a greasy paperbound book from beneath the counter and thumbed through it. "Here," he said, jabbing at an impossibly dense little map, "down Acre Lane." He took a blue feltpen and sketched the route on a coarse gray napkin.

"Thank you," she said. "Now I will go."

Her mother came to her as she made her way to Margate Road.

Sally was in jeopardy, somewhere in the Sprawl, and Kumiko trusted that Tick would know a way to contact her. If not by phone then through the matrix. Perhaps Tick knew Finn, the dead man in the alley. . . .

In Brixton, the coral-growth of the metropolis had come to harbor a different life. Faces dark and light, uncounted races, the brick facades washed with a riot of shades and symbols unimaginable to the original builders. A drumbeat pulsed from a pub's open door as she passed, heat and huge laughter. The shops sold foodstuffs Kumiko had never seen, bolts of bright cloth, Chinese handtools, Japanese cosmetics. . . .

Pausing by that bright window, the display of tints and blushes, her own face reflected in the silver backing, she felt her mother's death fall on her out of the night. Her mother had owned things like this.

Her mother's madness. Her father would not refer to it. Madness had no place in her father's world, though suicide did. Her mother's madness was European, an imported snare of sorrow and delusion. . . . Her father had killed her mother, Kumiko had told

Sally, in Covent Garden. But was it true? He had brought doctors from Denmark, from Australia, and finally from Chiba. The doctors had listened to the dreams of the princess-ballerina, had mapped and timed her synapses and drawn samples of her blood. The princess-ballerina had refused their drugs, their delicate surgeries. "They want to cut my brain with lasers," she had whispered to Kumiko.

She'd whispered other things as well.

At night, she said, the evil ghosts rose like smoke from their boxes in Kumiko's father's study. "Old men," she'd said, "they suck our breath away. Your father sucks my breath away. This city sucks my breath away. Nothing here is ever still. There is no true sleep."

In the end, there had been no sleep at all. Six nights her mother sat, silent and utterly still, in her blue European room. On the seventh day, she left the apartment alone—a remarkable feat, considering the diligence of the secretaries—and made her way to the cold river.

But the backing of the display was like Sally's glasses. Kumiko took the Korean's map from the sleeve of her sweater.

There was a burnt car beside the curb in Margate Road. Its wheels were missing. She paused beside it, and was scanning the unrevealing faces of the houses opposite, when she heard a sound behind her. Turning to find a twisted gargoyle face, under a greasy spill of curls, in the light from the half-open door of the nearest house.

"Tick!"

"Terrence," he said, "actually," as the facial convulsion subsided.

Tick's flat was on the top floor. The lower floors were empty, unoccupied, peeling wallpaper showing ghostly traces of vanished pictures.

The man's limp was more obvious as he climbed the stairs ahead of her. He wore a gray sharkskin suit and thick-soled suede oxfords the color of tobacco.

"Been expecting you," he said, hauling himself up another step, another.

"You have?"

"Knew you'd run from Swain's. Been logging their traffic, when I've had time from the other."

"The other?"

"You don't know, do you?"

"Excuse me?"

"It's the matrix. Something's happening. Easier to show you than try to explain it. As though I could explain it, which I can't. I'd say a good three-quarters of humanity is jacked at the moment, watching the show. . . ."

"I don't understand."

"Doubt anyone does. There's a new macroform in the sector that represents the Sprawl."

"A macroform?"

"Very large data-construct."

"I came here to warn Sally. Swain and Robin Lanier intend to give her to the ones who plot to kidnap Angela Mitchell."

"Wouldn't worry about that," he said, reaching the head of the stairs. "Sally's already scooped Mitchell and half-killed Swain's man in the Sprawl. They're after her in any case, now. Bloody everybody'll be after her, soon. Still, we can tell her when she checks in. If she checks in . . ."

Tick lived in a single large room whose peculiar shape suggested the removal of walls. Large as it was, it was also very crowded; it looked to Kumiko as though someone had deployed the contents of an Akihabara module shop in a space already filled, gaijin-style, with too many pieces of bulky furniture. In spite of this, it was startlingly neat and tidy: the corners of magazines were aligned with the corners of the low glass table they rested on, beside an unused black ceramic ashtray and a plain white vase of cut flowers.

She tried Colin again, while Tick filled an electric kettle with water from a filter jug.

"What's that?" he asked, putting down the jug.

"A Maas-Neotek guide unit. It's broken now; I can't make Colin come. . . ."

"Colin? It's a stim rig?"

"Yes."

"Let's have a look. . . ." He held out his hand.

"My father gave it to me. . . ."

Tick whistled. "Thing cost a fortune. One of their little AIs. How's it work?"

"You close your hand around it and Colin's there, but no one else can see or hear him."

Tick held the unit beside his ear and shook it. "It's broken? How?"

"I dropped it."

"It's just the housing that's broken, see. The biosoft's come away from the case, so you can't access it manually."

"Can you repair it?"

"No. But we can access it through a deck, if you want. . . ." He returned it. The kettle was boiling.

Over tea, she told him the story of her trip to the Sprawl and Sally's visit to the shrine in the alley. "He called her Molly," she said.

Tick nodded, winked several times in rapid succession. "What she went by, over there. What did they talk about?"

"A place called Straylight. A man called Case. An enemy, a woman . . ."

"Tessier-Ashpool. Found that for her when I rustled Swain's data flow for her. Swain's shopping Molly to this lady 3Jane, so called; she has the juiciest file of inside dirt you could imagine—on anything and anyone at all. I've been bloody careful not to look too closely at any of that. Swain's trading it right and left, making a dozen fortunes in the process. I'm sure she's got enough dirt on our Mr. Swain as well. . . ."

"And she is here, in London?"

"In orbit somewhere, looks like, though some people say she's dead. I was working on that, actually, when the big fella popped into the matrix. . . ."

"Excuse me?"

"Here, I'll show you." When he returned to the white breakfast table, he carried a shallow square black tray with a number of tiny controls arranged along one side. He placed it on the table and touched one of the minute switches. A cubical holo display blinked on above the projector: the neon gridlines of cyberspace, ranged with the bright shapes, both simple and complex, that represented vast accumulations of stored data. "That's all your standard big shits. Corporations. Very much a fixed landscape, you might say. Sometimes one of 'em'll grow an annex, or you'll see a takeover and two of them merge. But you aren't likely to see a *new* one, not on that scale. They start small and grow, merge with other small formations. . . ." He reached out to touch another switch. "About four hours ago"— and a plain white vertical column appeared in the exact center of the display— "this popped up. Or in." The colored cubes, spheres, and pyramids had rearranged themselves instantly to allow for the round white upright; it dwarfed them entirely, its upper end cut off smoothly by the vertical limit of the display. "Bastard's bigger than anything," Tick said, with a certain satisfaction, "and nobody knows what it is or who it belongs to."

"But someone must know," Kumiko said.

"Stands to reason, yes. But people in my line of work, and there's millions of us, haven't been able to find out. That's stranger, in some ways, than the fact that the thing's there at all. I was all up and down the grid, before you came, looking for any jockey with a clue. Nothing. Nothing at all."

"How could this 3Jane be dead?" But then she remembered the Finn, the boxes in her father's study. "I must tell Sally."

"Nothing for that but waiting," he said. "She'll probably phone in. In the meantime, we could have a go accessing that pricey little AI of yours, if you like."

"Yes," she said, "thank you."

"Only hope those Special Branch types in Swain's pay don't track you here. Still, we can only wait...."

"Yes," Kumiko said, not at all pleased with the idea of waiting.

# THIRTY-FIVE

# THE FACTORY WAR

Cherry found him with the Judge again, down there in the dark. He was sitting on one of the Investigators with a flashlight in his hand, shining it up the Judge's carapace of polished rust. He didn't remember coming here, but he couldn't feel the jerky edge of Korsakov's. He remembered the girl's eyes, in that room Bobby said was London.

"Gentry's got the Count and his box jacked into a cyberspace deck," Cherry said. "You know that?"

Slick nodded, still looking up at the Judge. "Bobby said we better."

"So what's going on? What happened when you both jacked?"

"Gentry and Bobby, they kind of hit it off. Both crazy the same way. When we jacked, we came out somewhere in orbit, but Bobby wasn't there. . . . Then Mexico, I think. Who's Tally Isham?"

"Stim queen when I was little. Like Angie Mitchell is now."

"Mitchell, she was his squeeze. . . ."

"Who?"

"Bobby. He was telling Gentry about it, in London."

"London?"

"Yeah. We went there, after Mexico."

"And he said he was Angie Mitchell's old man? Sounds crazy."

"Yeah, but he said that's how he got on to it, that aleph thing."
He swung the light down and directed it into the skeletal steel maw
of the Corpsegrinder. "He was hanging out with rich people and
heard about it. Called it a soul-catcher. The people who had it
would rent time on it to these rich people. Bobby tried it once, then
he went back and stole it. Took it down to Mexico City and started
spending all his time in there. But they came after him. . . ."

"Sounds like you're remembering things, anyway."

"So he got out of there. Went up to Cleveland and made a deal
with Afrika, gave Afrika money to hide him, take care of him while
he was under the wire, because he was getting real close. . . ."

"Close to what?"

"Don't know. Something weird. Like when Gentry talks about
the Shape."

"Well," she said, "I think it might kill him, being jacked that
way. His signs are starting to screw up. He's been on those drips
too long. Why I came to find you."

The Corpsegrinder's steel-fanged guts glinted in the flashlight's
beam. "It's what he wants. Anyway, if he paid the Kid, it's like
you're working for him. But those guys Bird saw today, they're
working for the people from L.A., the ones Bobby stole the thing
from. . . ."

"Tell me something."

"What?"

"What are these things you build? Afrika said you were this
crazy white guy built robots out of junk. Said in the summer you
take 'em out there on the rust and stage big fights—"

"They aren't robots," he interrupted, swinging the flash to the
low, scythe-tipped arms of the spider-legged Witch. "They're mainly
radio-controlled."

"You just build 'em to wreck 'em?"

"No. But I have to test them. See if I got them right . . ." He
clicked off the light.

"Crazy white guy," she said. "You gotta girl out here?"

"No."

"Get a shower. Maybe shave . . ." Suddenly she was very close
to him, her breath on his face.

*"Okay people listen up—"*

"What the fuck—"

" 'Cause I'm not gonna say this twice."

Slick had his hand over Cherry's mouth now.

"We want your guest and all his gear. That's all, repeat, all the gear." The amplified voice clanged through Factory's iron hollow. "Now you can give him to us, that's easy, or we can just kill all your asses. And we're real easy with that too. Five minutes to think about it."

Cherry bit his hand. "Shit, I gotta breathe, okay?"

Then he was running through Factory's dark, and he heard her call his name.

A single 100-watt bulb burned above Factory's south gate, a pair of twisted steel doors frozen open with rust. Bird must've left it on. From where he crouched by an empty window, Slick could just make out the hover, out beyond the weak fringe of light. The man with the bullhorn came strolling out of the dark with a calculated looseness meant to indicate that he was on top of things. He wore insulated camo overalls with a thin nylon hood drawn up tight around his head, goggles. He raised the bullhorn. "Three minutes." He reminded Slick of the guards at the holding pen, the second time he'd been done for stealing cars.

Gentry would be watching from upstairs, where a narrow vertical panel of Plexiglas was glued into the wall, high up over Factory's gates.

Something rattled in the dark, off to Slick's right. He turned in time to see Bird in the faint glow from another window gap, maybe eight meters along the wall, and the glint on the bare alloy silencer as the boy brought up the .22 rifle. "Bird! Don't—" A ruby firefly on Bird's cheek, telltale of a laser sight from out on the Solitude. Bird was thrown back into Factory as the sound of the shot broke through the empty windows and echoed off the walls. Then the only sound was the silencer, rolling across concrete.

"Fuck it," the big voice boomed cheerfully. "You had your chance." Slick glanced over the rim of the window and saw the man sprinting back to the hover.

How many of them would be out there? Bird hadn't said. Two hovers, the Honda. Ten? More? Unless Gentry had a pistol hidden somewhere, Bird's rifle had been their only gun.

The hover's turbines kicked in. He guessed they'd just drive right in. They had laser sights, probably infrared too.

Then he heard one of the Investigators, the sound it made with its stainless steel treads on the concrete floor. It came crawling out of the dark with its thermite-tipped scorpion sting cocked back low. The chassis had started out fifty years earlier as a remote-manipulator intended to handle toxic spills or nuke-plant cleanups. Slick had found three unassembled units in Newark and traded a Volkswagen for them.

Gentry. He'd left his control unit up in the loft.

The Investigator ground its way across the floor and came to a halt in the wide doorway, facing the Solitude and the advancing hover. It was roughly the size of a large motorcycle, its open-frame chassis a dense bundle of servos, compression tanks, exposed screw gears, hydraulic cylinders. A pair of vicious-looking claws extended from either side of its modest instrument package. Slick wasn't sure what the claws were from, maybe some kind of big farm machine.

The hover was a heavy industrial model. Sheets of thick gray plastic armor had been fastened over windshield and windows, narrow view slits centered in each sheet.

The Investigator moved, steel treads spraying ice and loose concrete as it drove straight for the hover, its claws at their widest extension. The hover's driver reversed, fighting momentum.

The Investigator's claws snapped furiously at the bulge of the forward apron bag, slid off, snapped again. The bag was reinforced with polycarbon mesh. Then Gentry remembered the thermite lance. It ignited in a tight ball of raw white light and whipped up over the useless claws, plunging through the apron bag like a knife through cardboard. The Investigator's treads spun as Gentry drove it against the deflating bag, the lance at full extension. Slick was suddenly aware that he'd been shouting, but didn't know what he'd said. He was on his feet now, as the claws finally found a purchase on the torn edge of the apron bag.

He went to the floor again as a hooded, goggled figure popped from a hatch on the hover's roof like an armed hand puppet, emptying a magazine of twelve-gauge slugs that struck sparks off the Investigator, which continued to chew its way through the apron bag, outlined against the white pulse of the lance. The Investigator froze, claws locked tight on the frayed bag; the shotgunner ducked back into his hatch.

Feed line? Servo pack? What had the guy hit? The white pulse was dying now, almost dead.

The hover began to reverse, slowly, back across the rust, dragging the Investigator with it.

It was well back, out of the light, visible only because it was moving, when Gentry discovered the combination of switches that activated the flamethrower, its nozzle mounted beneath the juncture of the claws. Slick watched, fascinated, as the Investigator ignited ten liters of detergent-laced gasoline, a sustained high-pressure spray. He'd gotten that nozzle, he remembered, off a pesticide tractor.

It worked okay.

# THIRTY-SIX

# SOUL-CATCHER

The hover was headed south when Mamman Brigitte came again. The woman with the sealed silver eyes abandoned the gray sedan in another carpark, and the streetgirl with Angie's face told a confusing story: Cleveland, Florida, someone who'd been her boyfriend or pimp or both. . . .

But Angie had heard Brigitte's voice, in the cabin of the helicopter, on the roof of the New Suzuki Envoy: *Trust her, child. In this she does the will of the loa.*

A captive in her seat, the buckle of her seatbelt embedded in a solid block of plastic, Angie had watched as the woman bypassed the helicopter's computer and activated an emergency system that allowed for manual piloting.

And now this freeway in the winter rain, the girl talking again, above the swish of wipers . . .

Into candleglow, walls of whitewashed limestone, pale moths fluttering in the trailing branches of the willows.

*Your time draws near.*

And they are there, the Horsemen, the loa: Pappa Legba bright and fluid as mercury; Ezili Freda, who is mother and queen; Samedi, the Baron Cimetière, moss on corroded bone; Similor; Madame Travaux; many others.... They fill the hollow that is Grande Brigitte. The rushing of their voices is the sound of wind, running water, the hive....

They writhe above the ground like heat above a summer highway, and it has never been like this, for Angie, never this gravity, this sense of falling, this degree of surrender—

To a place where Legba speaks, his voice the sound of an iron drum—

He tells a story.

In the hard wind of images, Angie watches the evolution of machine intelligence: stone circles, clocks, steam-driven looms, a clicking brass forest of pawls and escapements, vacuum caught in blown glass, electronic hearthglow through hairfine filaments, vast arrays of tubes and switches, decoding messages encrypted by other machines.... The fragile, short-lived tubes compact themselves, become transistors; circuits integrate, compact themselves into silicon....

Silicon approaches certain functional limits—

And she is back in Becker's video, the history of the Tessier-Ashpools, intercut with dreams that are 3Jane's memories, and still he speaks, Legba, and the tale is one tale, countless strands wound about a common, hidden core: 3Jane's mother creating the twin intelligences that will one day unite, the arrival of strangers (and suddenly Angie is aware that she knows Molly, too, from the dreams), the union itself, 3Jane's madness....

And Angie finds herself facing a jeweled head, a thing wrought from platinum and pearl and fine blue stone, eyes of carved synthetic ruby. She knows this thing from the dreams that were never dreams: this is the gateway to the data cores of Tessier-Ashpool, where the two halves of something warred with each other, waiting to be born as one.

"In this time, you were unborn." The head's voice is the voice of Marie-France, 3Jane's dead mother, familiar from so many haunted nights, though Angie knows it is Brigitte who speaks: "Your father was only now beginning to face his own limits, to distinguish ambition from talent. That to whom he would barter his child was not yet manifest. Soon the man Case would come to bring that union, however brief, however timeless. But you know this."

"Where is Legba now?"

"Legba-ati-Bon—as you have known him—waits to be."

"No," remembering Beauvoir's words long ago, in New Jersey, "the loa came out of Africa in the first times. . . ."

"Not as you have known them. When the moment came, the bright time, there was absolute unity, one consciousness. But there was the other."

"The other?"

"I speak only of that which I have known. Only the one has known the other, and the one is no more. In the wake of that knowing, the center failed; every fragment rushed away. The fragments sought form, each one, as is the nature of such things. In all the signs your kind have stored against the night, in that situation the paradigms of *vodou* proved most appropriate."

"Then Bobby was right. That was When It Changed. . . ."

"Yes, he was right, but only in a sense, because I am at once Legba, and Brigitte, and an aspect of that which bargained with your father. Which required of him that he draw *vévés* in your head."

"And told him what he needed to know to perfect the biochip?"

"The biochip was necessary."

"Is it neccessary that I dream the memories of Ashpool's daughter?"

"Perhaps."

"Are the dreams a result of the drug?"

"Not directly, though the drug made you more receptive to certain modalities, and less so to others."

"The drug, then. What was it? What was its purpose?"

"A detailed neurochemical response to your first question would be very lengthy."

"What was its purpose?"

"With regard to you?"

She had to look away from the ruby eyes. The chamber is lined with panels of ancient wood, buffed to a rich gloss. The floor is covered with a fitted carpet woven with circuit diagrams.

"No two lots were identical. The only constant was the substance whose psychotropic signature you regarded as 'the drug.' In the course of ingestion, many other substances were involved, as well as several dozen subcellular nanomechanisms, programmed to restructure the synaptic alterations effected by Christopher Mitchell. . . ."

*Your father's* vévés *are altered, partially erased, redrawn. . . .*

"By whose order?"

The ruby eyes. Pearl and lapis. Silence.

"By whose order? Hilton's? Was it Hilton?"

"The decision originated with Continuity. When you returned from Jamaica, Continuity advised Swift to reintroduce you to the drug. Piper Hill attempted to carry out his orders."

She feels a mounting pressure in her head, twin points of pain behind her eyes. . . .

"Hilton Swift is obliged to implement Continuity's decisions. Sense/Net is too complex an entity to survive, otherwise, and Continuity, created long after the bright moment, is of another order. The biosoft technology your father fostered brought Continuity into being. Continuity is naïve."

"Why? Why did Continuity want me to do that?"

"Continuity is continuity. Continuity is Continuity's job. . . ."

"But who sends the dreams?"

"They are not sent. You are drawn to them, as once you were drawn to the loa. Continuity's attempt to rewrite your father's message failed. Some impulse of your own allowed you to escape. The *coup-poudre* failed."

"Did Continuity send the woman, to kidnap me?"

"Continuity's motives are closed to me. A different order. Continuity allowed Robin Lanier's subversion by 3Jane's agents."

"But why?"

And the pain was impossible.


"Her nose is bleeding," the streetgirl said. "What'll I do?"

"Wipe it up. Get her to lean back. Shit. *Deal* with it . . ."

"What was that stuff she said about New Jersey?"

"Shut up. Just shut up. Look for an exit ramp."

"Why?"

"We're going to New Jersey."

Blood on the new fur. Kelly would be furious.

# THIRTY-SEVEN

# CRANES

Tick removed the little panel from the back of the Maas-Neotek unit, using a dental pick and a pair of jeweler's pliers.

"Lovely," he muttered, peering into the opening through an illuminated lens, his greasy waterfall of hair dangling just above it. "The way they've stepped the leads down, off this switch. Cunning bastards . . ."

"Tick," Kumiko said, "did you know Sally, when she first came to London?"

"Soon after, I suppose . . ." He reached for a spool of optic lead. " 'Cos she hadn't much clout, then."

"Do you like her?"

The illuminated glass rose to wink in her direction, Tick's left eye distorted behind it. "Like 'er? Can't say I've thought of it, that way."

"You don't dislike her?"

"Bloody *difficult*, Sally is. D'you know what I'm saying?"

"Difficult?"

"Never quite got onto the way things are done here. Always

complaining." His hands moved swiftly, surely: the pliers, the optic lead. . . . "This is a quiet place, England. Hasn't always been, mind you; we'd the troubles, then the war. . . . Things move here in a certain way, if you take my meaning. Though you couldn't say the same's true of the flash crew."

"Excuse me?"

"Swain, that lot. Though your father's people, the ones Swain's always been so chummy with, they seem to have a regard for tradition. . . . A man has to know which way's up. . . . Know what I'm saying? Now this new business of Swain's, it's liable to bugger things for anyone who isn't right there and part of it. Christ, we've still got a *government* here. Not run by big companies. Well, not directly . . ."

"Swain's activities threaten the government?"

"He's bloody *changing* it. Redistributing power to suit himself. Information. Power. Hard data. Put enough of that in one man's hands . . ." A muscle in his cheek convulsed as he spoke. Now Colin's unit lay on a white plastic antistatic pad on the breakfast table; Tick was connecting the leads that protruded from it to a thicker cable that ran to one of the stacks of modules. "There then," he said, brushing his hands together, "can't get him right here in the room for you, but we'll access him through a deck. Seen cyberspace, have you?"

"Only in stims."

"Might as well 'ave seen it, then. In any case, you get to see it now." He stood; she followed him across the room to a pair of overstuffed ultrasuede chairs that flanked a low, square, black glass table. "Wireless," he said proudly, taking two trode-sets from the table and handing one to Kumiko. "Cost the world."

Kumiko examined the skeletal matte-black tiara. The Maas-Neotek logo was molded between the temple pieces. She put it on, cold against her skin. He put his own set on, hunched down in the opposite chair. "Ready?"

"Yes," she said, and Tick's room was gone, its walls a flutter of cards, tumbling and receding, against the bright grid, the towering forms of data.

"Nice transition, that," she heard him say. "Built into the trodes, that is. Bit of drama . . ."

"Where is Colin?"

"Just a sec . . . Let me work this up. . . ."

Kumiko gasped as she shot toward a chrome-yellow plain of light.

"Vertigo can be a problem," Tick said, and was abruptly beside her on the yellow plain. She looked down at his suede shoes, then at her hands. "Bit of body image takes care of that."

"Well," Colin said, "it's the little man from the Rose and Crown. Been tinkering with my package, have you?"

Kumiko turned to find him there, the soles of his brown boots ten centimeters above chrome yellow. In cyberspace, she noted, there are no shadows.

"Wasn't aware we'd met," Tick said.

"Needn't worry," Colin said. "It wasn't formal. But," he said to Kumiko, "I trust you found your way safely to colorful Brixton."

"Christ," Tick said, "aren't half a snot, are you?"

"Forgive me," Colin said, grinning, "I'm meant to mirror the visitor's expectations."

"What you are is some Jap designer's idea of an Englishman!"

"There were Draculas," she said, "in the Underground. They took my purse. They wanted to take you. . . ."

"You've come away from your housing, mate," Tick said. "Got you jacked through my deck now."

Colin grinned. "Ta."

"Tell you something else," Tick said, taking a step toward Colin, "you've got the wrong data in you, for what you're meant to be." He squinted. "Mate of mine in Birmingham's just turned you over." He turned to Kumiko. "Your Mr. Chips here, he's been tampered with. D'you know that?"

"No . . ."

"To be perfectly honest," Colin said, with a toss of his fore-lock, "I've suspected as much."

Tick stared off into the matrix as though he were listening to something Kumiko couldn't hear. "Yes," he said, finally, "though it's almost certainly a factory job. Ten major blocks of you." He laughed. "Been iced over . . . You're supposed to know fucking everything about Shakespeare, aren't you?"

"Sorry," Colin said, "but I'm afraid that I *do* know fucking everything about Shakespeare."

"Give us a sonnet, then," Tick said, his face wrinkling in a slow-motion wink.

Something like dismay crossed Colin's face. "You're right."

"Or bloody Dickens either!" Tick crowed.

"But I *do* know—"

"*Think* you do, till you're asked a specific! See, they left those bits empty, the Eng. lit. parts, then filled 'em with something else. . . ."

"With what, then?"

"Can't say," Tick said. "Boy in Birmingham can't fiddle it. Clever, he is, but you're that bloody Maas biosoft. . . ."

"Tick," Kumiko interrupted, "is there no way to contact Sally, through the matrix?"

"Doubt it, but we can try. You'll get to see that macroform I was telling you about, in any case. Want Mr. Chips along for company?"

"Yes, please . . ."

"Fine, then," Tick said, then hesitated. "But we don't know what's stuffed into your friend here. Something your father paid for, I'd assume."

"He's right," Colin said.

"We'll all go," she said.


Tick executed the transit in real time, rather than employing the bodiless, instantaneous shifts ordinarily employed in the matrix.

The yellow plain, he explained, roofed the London Stock Exchange and related City entities. He somehow generated a sort of boat to carry them along, a blue abstraction intended to reduce the possibility of vertigo. As the blue boat glided away from the LSE, Kumiko looked back and watched the vast yellow cube recede. Tick was pointing out various structures like a tour guide; Colin, seated beside her with his legs crossed, seemed amused at the reversal of roles. "That's White's," Tick was saying, directing her attention to a modest gray pyramid, "the club in Saint James. Membership registry, waiting list . . ."

Kumiko looked up at the architecture of cyberspace, hearing the voice of her bilingual French tutor in Tokyo, explaining humanity's need for this information-space. Icon, waypoints, artificial realities . . . But it blurred together, in memory, like these towering forms as Tick accelerated. . . .


The scale of the white macroform was difficult to comprehend.

Initially, it had seemed to Kumiko like the sky, but now, gazing at it, she felt as though it were something she might take up in her hand, a cylinder of luminous pearl no taller than a chess piece. But it dwarfed the polychrome forms that clustered around it.

"Well," Colin said, jauntily, "this really *is* very peculiar indeed, isn't it? Complete anomaly, utter singularity . . ."

"But you don't have to worry about it, do you?" Tick said.

"Only if it has no direct bearing on Kumiko's situation," Colin agreed, standing up in the boat-shape, "though how can one be certain?"

"You must attempt to contact Sally," Kumiko said impatiently. This thing—the macroform, the anomaly—was of little interest, though Tick and Colin both regarded it as extraordinary.

"Look at it," Tick said. "Could have a bloody world, in there . . ."

"And you don't know what it is?" She was watching Tick; his eyes had the distant look that meant his hands were moving, back in Brixton, working his deck.

"It's a very great deal of data," Colin said.

"I just tried to put a line through to that construct, the one she calls Finn," Tick said, his eyes refocusing, an edge of worry in his voice, "but I couldn't get through. I'd this feeling then, something was there, waiting. . . . Think it's best we jack out now . . ."

A black dot, on the curve of pearl, its edges perfectly defined . . .

"Fucking hell," Tick said.

"Break the link," Colin said.

"Can't! 'S got us. . . ."

Kumiko watched as the blue boat-shape beneath her feet elongated, stretched into a thread of azure, drawn across the chasm into that round blot of darkness. And then, in an instant of utter strangeness, she too, along with Tick and Colin, was drawn out to an exquisite thinness—

To find herself in Ueno Park, late autumn afternoon, by the unmoving waters of Shinobazu Pond, her mother seated beside her on a sleek bench of chilly carbon laminate, more beautiful now than in memory. Her mother's lips were full and richly glossed, outlined, Kumiko knew, with the finest and narrowest of brushes. She wore her black French jacket, with the dark fur collar framing her smile of welcome.

Kumiko could only stare, huddled there around the cold bulb of fear beneath her heart.

"You've been a foolish girl, Kumi," her mother said. "Did you imagine I wouldn't remember you, or abandon you to winter London and your father's gangster servants?"

Kumiko watched the perfect lips, open slightly over white teeth; teeth maintained, she knew, by the best dentist in Tokyo. "You are dead," she heard herself say.

"No," her mother replied, smiling, "not now. Not here, in Ueno Park. *Look at the cranes, Kumi.*"

But Kumiko would not turn her head.

"Look at the cranes."

"Fuck right off, you," said Tick, and Kumiko spun to find him there, his face pale and twisted, filmed with sweat, oily curls plastered to his forehead.

"I am her mother."

"Not your mum, understand?" Tick was shaking, his twisted frame quivering as though he forced himself against a terrible wind. "Not . . . your . . . mum . . ." There were dark crescents beneath the arms of the gray suit jacket. His small fists shook as he struggled to take the next step.

"You're ill," Kumiko's mother said, her tone solicitous. "You must lie down."

Tick sank to his knees, forced down by an invisible weight. "Stop it!" Kumiko cried.

Something slammed Tick's face against the pastel concrete of the path.

"Stop it!"

Tick's left arm shot out straight from the shoulder and began to rotate slowly, the hand still balled in a white-knuckled fist. Kumiko heard something give, bone or ligament, and Tick screamed.

Her mother laughed.

Kumiko struck her mother in the face, and pain, sharp and real, jolted through her arm.

Her mother's face flickered, became another face. A gaijin face with wide lips and a sharp thin nose.

Tick groaned.

"Well," Kumiko heard Colin say, "isn't this interesting?" She turned to him there, astride one of the horses from the hunting print, a stylized representation of an extinct animal, its neck curved gracefully as it trotted toward them. "Sorry it took me a moment to find you. This is a wonderfully complex structure. A sort of pocket universe. Bit of everything, actually." The horse drew up before them.

"Toy," said the thing with Kumiko's mother's face, "do you dare speak to me?"

"Yes, actually, I do. You are Lady 3Jane Tessier-Ashpool, or rather the *late* Lady 3Jane Tessier-Ashpool, none too recently deceased, formerly of the Villa Straylight. This rather pretty representation of a Tokyo park is something you've just now worked up from Kumiko's memories, isn't it?"

"Die!" She flung up a white hand: from it burst a form folded from neon.

"No," Colin said, and the crane shattered, its fragments tumbling through him, ghost-shards, falling away. "Won't do. Sorry. I've remembered what I am. Found the bits they tucked away in the slots for Shakespeare and Thackeray and Blake. I've been modified to advise and protect Kumiko in situations rather more drastic than any envisioned by my original designers. I'm a tactician."

"You are nothing." At her feet, Tick began to twitch.

"You're mistaken, I'm afraid. You see, in here, in this . . . folly of yours, 3Jane, I'm as real as you are. You see, Kumiko," he said, swinging down from the saddle, "Tick's mysterious macroform is actually a very expensive pile of biochips constructed to order. A sort of toy universe. I've run all up and down it and there's certainly a lot to see, a lot to learn. This . . . person, if we choose to so regard her, created it in a pathetic bid for, oh, not *immortality,* really, but simply to have her way. Her narrow, obsessive, and singularly childish way. Who would've thought it, that Lady 3Jane's object of direst and most nastily gnawing envy would be Angela Mitchell?"

"Die! You'll die! I'm killing you! Now!"

"Keep trying," Colin said, and grinned. "You see, Kumiko, 3Jane knew a secret about Mitchell, about Mitchell's relationship to the matrix; Mitchell, at one time, had the potential to become, well, very central to things, though it's not worth going into. 3Jane was jealous. . . ."

The figure of Kumiko's mother swam like smoke, and was gone.

"Oh dear," Colin said, "I've wearied her, I'm afraid. We've been fighting something of a pitched battle, at a different level of the command program. Stalemate, temporarily, but I'm sure she'll rally. . . ."

Tick had gotten to his feet and was gingerly massaging his arm. "Christ," he said, "I was sure she'd dislocated it for me. . . ."

"She did," Colin said, "but she was so angry when she left that she forgot to save that part of the configuration."

Kumiko stepped closer to the horse. It wasn't like a real horse at all. She touched its side. Cool and dry as old paper. "What shall we do now?"

"Get you out of here. Come along, both of you. Mount up. Kumiko in front, Tick on behind."

Tick looked at the horse. "On that?"

They had seen no other people in Ueno Park, as they'd ridden toward a wall of green that gradually defined itself as a very un-Japanese wood.

"But we should be in Tokyo," Kumiko protested, as they entered the wood.

"It's all a bit sketchy," Colin said, "though I imagine we could find a sort of Tokyo if we looked. I think I know an exit point, though. . . ."

Then he began to tell her more about 3Jane, and Sally, and Angela Mitchell. All of it very strange.

The trees were very large, at the far side of the wood. They emerged into a field of long grass and wildflowers.

"Look," Kumiko said, as she glimpsed a tall gray house through the branches.

"Yes," Colin said, "the original's on the outskirts of Paris. But we're nearly there. The exit point, I mean . . ."

"Colin! Did you see? A woman. Just there . . ."

"Yes," he said, without bothering to turn his head, "Angela Mitchell . . ."

"Really? She's here?"

"No," he said, "not yet."

Then Kumiko saw the gliders. Lovely things, quivering in the wind.

"There you go," Colin said. "Tick'll take you back in one of—"

"Bloody hell," Tick protested, from behind.

"Dead easy. Just like using your deck. Same thing, in this case . . ."

Up from Margate Road came the sound of laughter, loud drunken voices, the crash of a bottle against brickwork.

Kumiko sat very still, in the overstuffed chair, eyes shut tight, remembering the glider's rush into blue sky and . . . something else.

A telephone began to ring.

Her eyes shot open.

She lunged up from the chair and rushed past Tick, through his stacks of equipment, looking for the phone. Found it at last, and "Homeboy," Sally said, far away, past a soft surf of static, "what the fuck's up? Tick? You okay, man?"

"Sally! Sally, where are you?"

"New Jersey. Hey. Baby? Baby, what's happening?"

"I can't see you, Sally, the screen's blank!"

"Phoning from a booth. New Jersey. What's up?"

"I have so much to tell you. . . ."

"Shoot," Sally said. "It's my nickel."

# THIRTY-EIGHT

# THE FACTORY WAR

They watched the hover burn from the high window at the end of Gentry's loft. He could hear that same amplified voice now: *"You think that's pretty fucking funny, huh? Hahahahahahaha, so do we! We think you guys are just tons of fucking fun, so now we're all gonna party!"*

Couldn't see anyone, just the flames of the hover.

"We just start walking," Cherry said, close beside him, "take water, some food if you got it." Her eyes were red, her face streaked with tears, but she sounded calm. Too calm, Slick thought. "Come on, Slick, what else we gonna do?"

He glanced back at Gentry, slumped in his chair in front of the holo table, head propped between his hands, staring at the white column that thrust up out of the familiar rainbow jumble of Sprawl cyberspace. Gentry hadn't moved, hadn't said a word, since they'd come back to the loft. The heel of Slick's left boot had left faint dark prints on the floor behind him, Little Bird's blood; he'd stepped in it on his way back across Factory's floor.

Then Gentry spoke: "I couldn't get the others going." He was looking down at the control unit in his lap.

"You need a unit for each one you wanna work," Slick said.

"Time for the Count's advice," Gentry said, tossing Slick the unit.

"I'm not going back in there," Slick said. "You go."

"Don't need to," Gentry said, touching a console on his bench. Bobby the Count appeared on a monitor.

Cherry's eyes widened. "Tell him," she said, "that he's gonna be dead soon. Unless you jack him out of the matrix and stage one quick trip to an intensive care unit. He's dying."

Bobby's face, on the monitor, grew still. The background came sharply into focus: the neck of the iron deer, long grass dappled with white flowers, the broad trunks of ancient trees.

"Hear that, motherfucker?" Cherry yelled. "You're dying! Your lungs are filling up with fluid, your kidneys aren't working, your heart's fucked. . . . You make me wanna puke!"

"Gentry," Bobby said, his voice coming small and tinny from a little speaker on the side of the monitor, "I don't know what kind of setup you people have there, but I've arranged a little diversion."

"We never checked the bike," Cherry said, her arms around Slick, "we never looked. It might be okay."

"What's that mean, 'arranged a little diversion'?" Pulling back from her, looking at Bobby on the monitor.

"I'm still working it out. I've rerouted a Borg-Ward cargo drone, out of Newark."

Slick broke away from Cherry. "Don't just sit there," he yelled at Gentry, who looked up at Slick and slowly shook his head. Slick felt the first flickers of Korsakov's, minute increments of memory shuddering out of focus.

"He doesn't want to go anywhere," Bobby said. "He's found the Shape. He just wants to see how it all works out, what it is in the end. There's people on their way here. Friends, sort of. They'll get the aleph off your hands. Meantime, I'll do what I can about these assholes."

"I'm not gonna stay here and watch you die," Cherry said.

"Nobody's asking you to. My advice, you get out. Gimme twenty minutes, I'll distract them for you."

Factory never felt emptier.

Little Bird was somewhere on that floor. Slick kept thinking of the tangle of thongs and bones that had hung on Bird's chest, feathers and rusty spring-wind watches with the hands all stopped, each one a different time.... Stupid stringtown shit. But Bird wouldn't be around anymore. *Guess I won't be around anymore myself*, he thought, leading Cherry down the shaking stairs. *Not like before.* There wasn't time to move the machines, not without a flatbed and some help, and he figured once he was gone, he'd stay gone. Factory wasn't ever going to feel the same again.

Cherry had four liters of filtered water in a plastic jug, a mesh bag of Burmese peanuts, and five individually sealed portions of Big Ginza freeze-dried soup—all she'd been able to find in the kitchen. Slick had two sleeping bags, the flashlight, and a ball peen hammer.

It was quiet now, just the sounds of the wind across corrugated metal and the scuff of their boots on concrete.

He wasn't sure where he'd go, himself. He thought he'd take Cherry as far as Marvie's place and leave her there. Then maybe he'd come back, see what was happening with Gentry. She could get a ride out to a rustbelt town in a day or two. She didn't know that, though; all she could think about was leaving. Seemed as scared of having to watch Bobby the Count die on his stretcher as she was of the men outside. But Slick could see that Bobby didn't care much at all, about dying. Maybe he figured he'd just be in there, like that 3Jane. Or maybe he just didn't give a shit; sometimes people got that way.

If he meant to leave for good, he thought, steering Cherry through the dark with his free hand, he'd go in now and have a last look at the Judge and the Witch, the Corpsegrinder and the two Investigators. But this way he'd get Cherry out, then come back.... But he knew as he thought it that it didn't make sense, there wasn't time, but he'd get her out anyway....

"There's a gap, this side, low down by the floor," he told her. "We'll slide out through there, hope nobody notices...." She squeezed his hand as he led her through the darkness.

He found the hole by feel, stuffed the sleeping bags through, stuck the ball peen into his belt, lay down on his back, and pulled himself out until his head and chest were through. The sky was low and only marginally lighter than Factory's dark.

He thought he heard a faint drumming of engines, but then it faded.

He worked himself the rest of the way out with his heels and hips and shoulders, then rolled over in the snow.

Something bumped against his foot: Cherry pushing out the water jug. He reached back to take it, and the red firefly lit on the back of his hand. He jerked back and rolled again, as the bullet slammed Factory's wall like a giant's sledge.

A white flare, drifting. Above the Solitude. Faint through the low cloud. Drifting down from the swollen gray flank of the cargo drone, Bobby's diversion. Illuminating the second hover, thirty meters out, and the hooded figure with the rifle . . .

The first container struck the ground with a crash, just in front of the hover, and burst, throwing up a cloud of foam packing pellets. The second one, carrying two refrigerators, scored a direct hit, crushing the cab. The hijacked Borg-Ward airship continued to disgorge containers as the flare spun down, fading.

Slick scrambled back through the gap in the wall, leaving the water and the sleeping bags.


Moving fast, in the dark.

He'd lost Cherry. He'd lost the hammer. She must've slid back into Factory when the guy fired his first shot. Last shot, if he'd been under that box when it came down . . .

His feet found the ramp into the room where his machines waited. "Cherry?"

He flicked on the flashlight.

The one-armed Judge was centered in the beam. Before the Judge stood a figure with mirrors for eyes, throwing back the light.

"You wanna die?" A woman's voice.

"No . . ."

"Light, out."

Darkness. Run . . .

"I can see in the dark. You just stuck that flash in your jacket pocket. You look like you still wanna run. I gotta gun on you."

Run?

"Don't even think about it. You ever see a Fujiwara HE fléchette? Hits something hard, it goes off. Hits something soft, like most of you, buddy, it goes in, then it goes off. Ten seconds later."

"Why?"

"So you get to think about it."

"You with those guys outside?"

"No. You drop all those stoves 'n' shit on them?"

"No."

"Newmark. Bobby Newmark. I cut a deal tonight. I get some-body together with Bobby Newmark, I get my slate cleaned. You're gonna show me where he is."

# THIRTY-NINE

# TOO MUCH

What kind of place was this, anyway?

Things had gotten to a point where Mona couldn't get any comfort out of imagining Lanette's advice. Put Lanette in this situation, Mona figured she'd just eat more Memphis black till she felt like it wasn't her problem. The world hadn't ever had so many moving parts or so few labels.

They'd driven all night, with Angie mostly out of it—Mona could definitely credit the drug stories now—and *talking*, different languages, different *voices*. And that was the worst, those voices, because they spoke to Molly, challenged her, and she answered them back as she drove, not like she was talking to Angie just to calm her down, but like there really was something *there*, another person—at least three of them—speaking through Angie. And it *hurt* Angie when they spoke, made her muscles knot and her nose bleed, while Mona crouched over her and dabbed away the blood, filled with a weird mixture of fear and love and pity for the queen of all her dreams—or maybe it was just the wiz—but in the blue-white flicker of freeway lights Mona had seen her own hand beside

Angie's, and they weren't the same, not the same, not really the same shape, and that had made her glad.

The first voice had come when they'd been driving south, after Molly'd brought Angie in the copter. That one had just hissed and croaked and said something over and over, about New Jersey and numbers on a map. About two hours after that, Molly'd slid the hover across a rest area and said they were in New Jersey. Then she'd gotten out and made a call from a frosty paybooth, a long one; when she'd climbed back in, Mona'd seen her skim a phone card out across the frozen slush, just throwing it away. And Mona'd asked her who she'd called and she'd said England.

Mona'd seen Molly's hand, then, on the wheel, how the dark nails had little yellowish flecks, like you got when you snapped off a set of artificials. *She oughta get some solvent for that,* Mona thought.

Somewhere over a river they'd left the highway. Trees and fields and two-lane blacktop, sometimes a lonely red light high up on some kind of tower. And that was when the other voices had come. And then it was back and forth, back and forth, the voices and then Molly and then the voices, and what it reminded her of was Eddy trying to do a deal, except Molly was a lot better at it than Eddy; even if she couldn't understand it, she could tell Molly was getting close to what she wanted. But she couldn't stand it when the voices came; it made her want to press herself back as far from Angie as she could get. The worst one was called Sam-Eddy, something like that. What they all wanted was for Molly to take Angie somewhere for what they called a marriage, and Mona wondered if maybe Robin Lanier was in it somewhere, like what if Angie and Robin were gonna get married, and this was all just some kind of wild thing stars did to get married. But she couldn't get that one to work, and every time this Sam-Eddy voice came back, Mona's scalp would crawl. She could tell what Molly was bargaining for, though: she wanted her record cleaned up, wiped. She'd watched this vid once with Lanette, about this girl had ten, twelve personalities that would come out, like one was this shy little kid and another'd just be this total bone-addict slut, but it hadn't ever said anything about how any of those personalities could wipe your slate with the police.

Then this flatland in their headlights, blown with snow, low ridges the color of rust, where the wind had torn away the white.

The hover had one of those map screens you saw in cabs, or if a truckdriver picked you up, but Molly never turned it on except that first time, to look for the numbers the voice had given her. After a while, Mona understood that Angie was telling her which way to go, or anyway those voices were telling her. Mona'd been wishing for morning for a long time, but it was still night when Molly killed the lights and sped on through the dark. . . .

"Lights!" Angie cried.

"Relax," Molly said, and Mona remembered how she'd moved in the dark in Gerald's. But the hover slowed slightly, swung into a long curve, shuddering over the rough ground. The dash lights blinked off, all the instrumentation. "Not a sound now, okay?"

The hover accelerated through the dark.

Shifting white glare, high up. Through the window, Mona glimpsed a drifting, twirling point; above it, something else, bulbous and gray—

"Down! Get her down!"

Mona yanked at the catch on Angie's seatbelt as something whanged against the side of the hover. Got her down on the floor and hugged her furs around her as Molly slewed left, sideswiping something Mona never saw. Mona looked up, split-second flash of a big raggedy black building, a single white bulb lit above open warehouse doors, and then they were through, the turbine scream-ing full reverse.

Crash.

*I just don't know,* the voice said, and Mona thought: *Well, I know how that is.*

Then the voice started to laugh, and didn't stop, and the laugh became an on-off, on-off sound that wasn't laughter anymore, and Mona opened her eyes.

Girl there with a little tiny flashlight, the kind Lanette kept on her big bunch of keys; Mona saw her in the weak back-glare, the cone of light on Angie's slack face. Then she saw Mona looking and the sound stopped.

"Who the fuck are you?" The light in Mona's eyes. Cleveland voice, tough little foxface under raggy bleachblond hair.

"Mona. Who're you?" But then she saw the hammer.

"Cherry . . ."

"What's that hammer?"

This Cherry looked at the hammer. "Somebody's after me 'n' Slick." She looked at Mona again. "You them?"

"I don't think so."

"You look like her." The light jabbing at Angie.

"Not my hands. Anyway, I didn't used to."

"You both look like Angie Mitchell."

"Yeah. She *is.*"

Cherry gave a little shiver. She was wearing three or four leather jackets she'd gotten off different boyfriends; that was a Cleveland thing.

"Unto this high castle," came the voice from Angie's mouth, thick as mud, and Cherry banged her head against the roof of the cab, dropping her hammer, "my horse is come." In the wavering beam of Cherry's keyring flashlight, they saw the muscles of Angie's face crawling beneath the skin. "Why do you linger here, little sisters, now that her marriage is arranged?"

Angie's face relaxed, became her own, as a thin bright trickle of blood descended from her left nostril. She opened her eyes, wincing in the light. "Where is she?" she asked Mona.

"Gone," Mona said. "Told me to stay here with you . . ."

"Who?" Cherry asked.

"Molly," Mona asked. "She was driving. . . ."

Cherry wanted to find somebody called Slick. Mona wanted Molly to come back and tell her what to do, but Cherry was antsy about staying down here on the ground floor, she said, because there were these people outside with guns. Mona remembered that sound, something hitting the hover; she got Cherry's light and went back there. There was a hole she could just stick her finger into, halfway up the right side, and a bigger one—two fingers—on the left side.

Cherry said they'd better get upstairs, where Slick probably was, before those people decided to come in here. Mona wasn't sure.

"Come on," Cherry said. "Slick's probably back up there with Gentry and the Count. . . ."

"What did you just say?" And it was Angie Mitchell's voice, just like in the stims.

Whatever this was, it was cold as hell when they got out of the hover—Mona's legs were bare—but dawn was coming, finally: she could make out faint rectangles that were probably windows, just a gray glow. The girl called Cherry was leading them somewhere, she said upstairs, navigating with little blinks of the keyring light, Angie close behind her and Mona bringing up the rear.

Mona caught the toe of her shoe in something that rustled. Bending to free herself, she found what felt like a plastic bag. Sticky. Small hard things inside. Took a deep breath and straightened up, shoving the bag into the side pocket of Michael's jacket.

Then they were climbing these narrow stairs, steep, almost a ladder, Angie's fur brushing Mona's hand on the rough cold railings. Then a landing, then a turn, another set of stairs, another landing. A draft blew from somewhere.

"It's kind of a bridge," Cherry said. "Just walk across it quick, okay, 'cause it kind of moves. . . ."

And not expecting this, any of it, not the high white room, the sagging shelves stuffed with ragged, faded books—she thought of the old man—the clutter of console things with cables twisting everywhere; not this skinny, burning-eyed man in black, with his hair trained back into the crest they called a Fighting Fish in Cleveland; not his laugh when he saw them there, or the dead guy.

Mona'd seen dead people before, enough to know it when she saw it. The color of it. Sometimes in Florida somebody'd lie down on a cardboard pallet on the sidewalk outside the squat. Just not get up. Clothes and skin gone the color of sidewalk anyway, but still different when they'd kicked, another color under that. White truck came then. Eddy said because if you didn't, they'd swell up. Like Mona'd seen a cat once, blown up like a basketball, turned on its back, legs and tail sticking out stiff as boards, and that made Eddy laugh.

And this wiz artist laughing now—Mona knew those kind of eyes—and Cherry making this kind of groaning sound, and Angie just standing there.

"Okay, everybody," she heard someone say—Molly—and turned to find her there, in the open door, with a little gun in her hand and this big dirty-haired guy beside her looking stupid as a box of rocks, "just stand there till I sort you out."

The skinny guy just laughed.

"Shut up," Molly said, like she was thinking about something else. She shot without even looking at the gun. Blue flash on the wall beside his head and Mona couldn't hear anything but her ears ringing.

Skinny guy curled in a knot on the floor, head between his knees.

Angie walking toward the stretcher where the dead guy lay, his eyes just white. Slow, slow, like she was moving underwater, and this look on her face . . .

Mona's hand, in her jacket pocket, was sort of figuring something out, all by itself. Sort of squeezing that Ziploc she'd picked up downstairs, telling her . . . it had wiz in it.

She pulled it out and it did. Sticky with drying blood. Three crystals inside and some kind of derm.

She didn't know why she'd pulled it out, right then, except that nobody was *moving*.

The guy with the Fighting Fish had sat up, but he just stayed there. Angie was over by the stretcher, where she didn't seem to be looking at the dead guy but at this gray box stuck up over his head on a kind of frame. Cherry from Cleveland had got her back up against the wall of books and was sort of jamming her knuckles into her mouth. The big guy just stood there beside Molly, who had her head cocked to the side like she was listening for something.

Mona couldn't stand it.

Table had a steel top. Big hunk of old metal there, holding down a dusty stack of printout. Snapped the three yellow crystals down like buttons in a row, picked up that metal hunk, and—one, two, three—banged them into powder. That did it: everybody looked. Except Angie.

" 'Scuse me," Mona heard herself say, as she swept the mound of rough yellow powder into the waiting palm of her left hand, "how it is . . ." She buried her nose in the pile and snorted. "Sometimes," she added, and snorted the rest.

Nobody said anything.

And it was the still center again. Just like that time before.

So fast it was standing still.,

*Rapture. Rapture's coming.*

So fast, so still, she could put a sequence to what happened next: This big laugh, *haha,* like it wasn't really a laugh. Through a loudspeaker. Past the door. From out on the catwalk thing. And Molly just turns, smooth as silk, quick but like there's no hurry in it, and the little gun snicks like a lighter.

Then there's this blue flash outside, and the big guy gets sprayed with blood from out there as old metal tears loose and Cherry's screaming before the catwalk thing hits with this big complicated sound, dark floor down there where she found the wiz in its bloody bag.

"Gentry," someone says, and she sees it's a little vid on the table, young guy's face on it, "jack Slick's control unit now. They're in the building." Guy with the Fighting Fish scrambles up and starts to do things with wires and consoles.

And Mona could just watch, because she was so still, and it was all interesting stuff.

How the big guy gives this bellow and rushes over, shouting how they're his, they're his. How the face on the screen says: "Slick, c'mon, you don't *need* 'em anymore. . . ."

Then this engine starts up, somewhere downstairs, and Mona hears this clanking and rattling, and then somebody yelling, down there.

And sun's coming in the tall, skinny window now, so she moves over there for a look. And there's something out there, kind of a truck or hover, only it's buried under this pile of what looks like refrigerators, brand-new refrigerators, and broken hunks of plastic crates, and there's somebody in a camo suit, lying down with his face in the snow, and out past that there's another hover looks like it's all burned up.

It's interesting.

# FORTY

# PINK SATIN

Angela Mitchell comprehends this room and its inhabitants through shifting data planes that represent viewpoints, though of whom or what, she is in most cases in doubt. There is a considerable degree of overlap, of contradiction.

The man with the ragged crest of hair, in black-beaded leather, is Thomas Trail Gentry (as birth data and SIN digits cascade through her) of no fixed address (as a different facet informs her that this room is his). Past a gray wash of official data traces, faintly marbled with the Fission Authority's repeated pink suspicions of utilities fraud, she finds him in a different light: he is like one of Bobby's cowboys; though young, he is like the old men of the Gentleman Loser; he is an autodidact, an eccentric, obsessed, by his own lights a scholar; he is mad, a nightrunner, guilty (in Mamman's view, in Legba's) of manifold heresies; Lady 3Jane, in her own eccentric scheme, has filed him under RIMBAUD. (Another face flares out at Angie from RIMBAUD; his name is Riviera, a minor player in the dreams.) Molly has deliberately stunned him, causing an explosive fléchette to detonate eighteen centimeters from his skull.

Molly, like the girl Mona, is SINless, her birth unregistered, yet around her name (names) swarm galaxies of supposition, rumor, conflicting data. Streetgirl, prostitute, bodyguard, assassin, she mingles on the manifold planes with the shadows of heroes and villains whose names mean nothing to Angie, though their residual images have long since been woven through the global culture. (And this too belonged to 3Jane, and now belongs to Angie.)

Molly has just killed a man, has fired one of the explosive fléchettes into his throat. His collapse against a steel railing suffering metal fatigue has caused a large section of catwalk to tumble to the floor below. This room has no other entrance, a fact of some strategic importance. It was probably not Molly's intention to cause the collapse of the catwalk. She sought to prevent the man, a hired mercenary, from using his weapon of choice, a short alloy shotgun coated with a black, nonreflective finish. Nonetheless, Gentry's loft is now effectively isolated.

Angie understands Molly's importance to 3Jane, the source of her desire for and rage at her; knowing this, she sees all the banality of human evil.

Angie sees Molly restlessly prowling a gray winter London, a young girl at her side—and knows, without knowing how she knows, that this same girl is now at 23 Margate Road, SW2. *(Continuity?)* The girl's father was previously the master of the man Swain, who had lately become 3Jane's servant for the sake of the information she provides to those who do her bidding. As has Robin Lanier, of course, though he waits to be paid in a different coin.

For the girl Mona, Angie feels a peculiar tenderness, a pity, a degree of envy: though Mona has been altered to resemble Angie as closely as possible, Mona's life has left virtually no trace on the fabric of things, and represents, in Legba's system, the nearest thing to innocence.

Cherry-Lee Chesterfield is surrounded by a sad ragged scrawl, her information profile like a child's drawing: citations for vagrancy, petty debts, an aborted career as a paramedical technician Grade 6, framing birth data and SIN.

Slick, or Slick Henry, is among the SINless, but 3Jane, Continuity, Bobby, all have lavished their attention on him. For 3Jane, he serves as the focus of a minor node of association: she equates his ongoing rite of construction, his cathartic response to chemo-penal trauma, with her own failed attempts to exorcise the barren dream of Tessier-Ashpool. In the corridors of 3Jane's memory, Angie has frequently come upon the chamber where a spider-armed manipulator stirs the refuse of Straylight's brief, clotted history—an act of extended collage. And Bobby provides other memories, tapped from the artist as he accessed 3Jane's library of Babel: his slow, sad, childlike labor on the plain called Dog Solitude, erecting anew the forms of pain and memory.

Down in the chill dark of Factory's floor, one of Slick's kinetic sculptures, controlled by a subprogram of Bobby's, removes the left arm of another mercenary, employing a mechanism salvaged two summers before from a harvesting machine of Chinese manufacture. The mercenary, whose name and SIN boil past Angie like hot silver bubbles, dies with his cheek against one of Little Bird's boots.

Only Bobby, of all the people in this room, is not here as data. And Bobby is not the wasted thing before her, strapped down in alloy and nylon, its chin filmed with dried vomit, nor the eager, familiar face gazing out at her from a monitor on Gentry's workbench. Is Bobby the solid rectangular mass of memory bolted above the stretcher?

Now she steps across rolling dunes of soiled pink satin, under a tooled steel sky, free at last of the room and its data.

Brigitte walks beside her, and there is no pressure, no hollow of night, no hive sound. There are no candles. Continuity is there too, represented by a strolling scribble of silver tinsel that reminds her, somehow, of Hilton Swift on the beach at Malibu.

"Feeling better?" Brigitte asks.

"Much better, thank you."

"I thought so."

"Why is Continuity here?"

"Because he is your cousin, built from Maas biochips. Because he is young. We walk with you to your wedding."

"But who are you, Brigitte? What are you really?"

"I am the message your father was told to write. I am the *vévés* he drew in your head." Brigitte leans close. "Be kind to Continuity. He fears that in his clumsiness, he has earned your displeasure."

The tinsel scribble scoots off before them, across the satin dunes, to announce the bride's arrival.

# FORTY-ONE

# MR. YANAKA

The Maas-Neotek unit was still warm to the touch; the white plastic pad beneath it was discolored, as if by heat. A smell like burning hair . . .

She watched the bruises on Tick's face darken. He'd sent her to a bedside cabinet for a worn tin cigarette box filled with pills and dermadisks—had torn his collar open and pressed three of the adhesive disks against skin white as porcelain.

She helped him fashion a sling from a length of optic cable.

"But Colin said she had forgotten. . . ."

"*I haven't,*" he said, and sucked air between his teeth, working the sling beneath his arm. "*Seemed* to happen, at the time. Lingers a bit . . ." He winced.

"I'm sorry. . . ."

" 'Sokay. Sally told me. About your mother, I mean."

"Yes . . ." She didn't look away. "She killed herself. In Tokyo . . ."

"Whoever she was, that wasn't her."

"The unit . . ." She glanced toward the breakfast table.

"She burnt it. Won't matter to him, though. He's still there. Has the run of it. What's our Sally up to, then?"

"She has Angela Mitchell with her. She's gone to find the thing that all that comes from. Where we were. A place called New Jersey."

The telephone rang.

Kumiko's father, head and shoulders, on the broad screen behind Tick's telephone: he wore his dark suit, his Rolex watch, a galaxy of small fraternal devices in his lapel. Kumiko thought he looked very tired, tired and very serious, a serious man behind the smooth dark expanse of desk in his study. Seeing him there, she regretted that Sally hadn't phoned from a booth with a camera. She would very much have liked to see Sally again; now, perhaps, it would be impossible.

"You look well, Kumiko," her father said.

Kumiko sat up very straight, facing the small camera mounted just below the wallscreen. In reflex, she summoned her mother's mask of disdain, but it would not come. Confused, she dropped her gaze to where her hands lay folded in her lap. She was abruptly aware of Tick, of his embarrassment, his fear, trapped in the chair beside her, in full view of the camera.

"You were correct to flee Swain's house," her father said.

She met his eyes again. "He is your *kobun*."

"No longer. While we were distracted, here, with our own difficulties, he formed new and dubious alliances, pursuing courses of which we could not approve."

"And your difficulties, Father?"

Was there the flicker of a smile? "All that is ended. Order and accord are again established."

"Er, excuse me, sir, Mr. Yanaka," Tick began, then seemed to lose his voice altogether.

"Yes. And you are—?"

Tick's bruised face contorted in a huge and particularly lugubrious wink.

"His name is Tick, Father. He has sheltered and protected me. Along with Col ... with the Maas-Neotek unit, he saved my life tonight."

"Really? I had not been informed of this. I was under the impression that you had not left his apartment."

Something cold— "How?" she asked, sitting forward. "How could you know?"

"The Maas-Neotek unit broadcast your destination, once it was known—once the unit was clear of Swain's systems. We dispatched watchers to the area." She remembered the noodle seller. . . . "Without, of course, informing Swain. But the unit never broadcast a second message."

"It was broken. An accident."

"Yet you say it saved your life?"

"Sir," Tick said, "you'll pardon me, what I mean is, am I *covered*?"

"Covered?"

"Protected. From Swain, I mean, and his bent SB friends and the rest . . ."

"Swain is dead."

There was a silence. "But *somebody* will be running it, surely. The fancy, I mean. Your business."

Mr. Yanaka regarded Tick with frank curiosity. "Of course. How else might order and accord be expected to continue?"

"Give him your word, Father, " Kumiko said, "that he will come to no harm."

Yanaka looked from Kumiko to the grimacing Tick. "I extend profound gratitude to you, sir, for having protected my daughter. I am in your debt."

"*Giri*," Kumiko said.

"Christ," Tick said, overcome with awe, "fucking fancy that."

"Father," Kumiko said, "on the night of my mother's death, did you order the secretaries to allow her to leave alone?"

Her father's face was very still. She watched it fill with a sorrow she had never before seen. "No," he said at last, "I did not."

Tick coughed.

"Thank you, Father. Will I be returning to Tokyo now?"

"Certainly, if you wish. Though I understand you have been allowed to see very little of London. My associate will soon arrive at Mr. Tick's apartment. If you wish to remain, to explore the city, he will arrange this."

"Thank you, Father."

"Goodbye, Kumi."

And he was gone.

"Now then," Tick said, wincing horribly as he extended his good arm, "help me up from this. . . ."

"But you require medical attention."

"Don't I then?" He'd managed to get to his feet, and was

hobbling toward the toilet, when Petal opened the door from the dark upstairs hall. "If you've broken my bloody lock," Tick said, "you'd better pay me for it."

"Sorry," Petal said, blinking. "I've come for Miss Yanaka."

"Too bad, mate. Just had her dad on the phone. Told us Swain's been topped. Told us he's sending round the new boss." He smiled, crookedly, triumphantly.

"But you see," Petal said gently, "that's me."

# FORTY-TWO

# FACTORY FLOOR

Cherry's still screaming.

"Somebody shut her up," Molly says, where she's standing by the door with her little gun, and Mona thinks she can do that, can pass Cherry a little of her stillness, where everything's interesting and nothing's pushing too hard, but on the way across the room she sees the crumpled Ziploc on the floor and remembers there's a derm in there, maybe something that'll help Cherry calm down. "Here," she says, when she gets to her, peels the backing off and sticks the derm on the side of Cherry's neck. Cherry's scream slides down the scale into a gurgle as she sinks down the face of old books, but Mona's sure she'll be okay, and anyway there's shooting downstairs, guns: out past Molly a white tracer goes racketing and whanging around steel girders, and Molly's yelling at Gentry can he turn the goddamn lights on?

That had to mean the lights downstairs, because the lights up here were plenty bright, so bright she can see fuzzy little beads, traces of color, streaming off things if she looks close. Tracers. That's what you call those bullets, the ones that light up. Eddy'd told her that in Florida, looking down the beach to where some private security was shooting them off in the dark.

"Yeah, lights," the face on the little screen said, "the Witch can't see. . . ." Mona smiled at him. She didn't think anybody else had heard. Witch?

So Gentry and big Slick were tearing around yanking these fat yellow wires off the wall, where they'd been stuck with silver tape, and plugging them together with these metal boxes, and Cherry from Cleveland was sitting on the floor with her eyes closed, and Molly was crouched down by the door holding her gun with both hands, and Angie was—

*Be still.*

She heard somebody say that, but it was nobody in the room. She thought maybe it was Lanette, like Lanette could just say that, through time, through the stillness.

Because Angie was just there, down on the floor beside the dead guy's stretcher, her legs folded under her like a statue, her arms around him.

The lights dimmed, when Gentry and Slick found their connection, and she thought she heard the face on the monitor gasp, but she was already moving toward Angie, seeing (suddenly, totally, so clearly it hurt) the fine line of blood from her left ear.

Even then, the stillness held, though already she could feel raw hot points in the back of her throat, and remember Lanette explaining: You don't ever snort this, it eats holes in you.

And Molly's back was straight, her arms stretched out. . . . Straight out and down, not to that gray box, but to her pistol, that little thing, and Mona heard it go *snik-snik-snik*, and then three explosions, far off down there, and they must've been blue flashes, but Mona's hands were around Angie now, wrists brushed by blood-smeared fur. To look into gone eyes, the light already fading. Just a long, longest way away.

"Hey," Mona said, nobody to hear, just Angie toppling across the corpse in the sleeping bag, "hey . . ."

She glanced up in time to catch a last image on that vid screen and see it fade.

After that, for a long time, nothing mattered. It wasn't like the not caring of the stillness, the crystal overdrive, and it wasn't like crashing, just this past-it feeling, the way maybe a ghost feels.

She stood beside Slick and Molly in the doorway and looked

down. In the dim glare of big old bulbs she watched a metal spider thing jittering across the dirty concrete floor. It had big curved blades that snapped and whirled when it moved, but there was nobody in there moving, and the thing just went like a broken toy, back and forth in front of the twisted wreck of the little bridge she'd crossed with Angie and Cherry.

Cherry had gotten up from the floor, pale and slackfaced, and peeled the derm from her neck. "Tha's maj' muscle relax'nt," she managed, and Mona felt bad because she knew she'd done something stupid when she'd thought she was trying to help, but wiz always did that, and how come she couldn't stop doing it?

Because you're wired, stupid, she heard Lanette say, but she hadn't wanted to remember that.

So they all just stood there, looking down at the metal spider twitching and running itself down. All except Gentry, who was unscrewing the gray box from its frame over the stretcher, his black boots beside Angie's red fur.

"Listen," Molly said, "that's a copter. Big one."

She was the last one down the rope, except for Gentry, and he just said he wasn't coming, didn't care, he'd stay.

The rope was fat and dirty gray and had knots tied in it to hang on to, like a swing she remembered from a long time ago. Slick and Molly had lowered the gray box first, down to a platform where the metal stairs weren't wrecked. Then Molly went down it like a squirrel, seeming barely to hang on at all, and tied it tight to a railing. Slick went down slowly, because he had Cherry over his shoulder and she was still too relaxed to make it down herself. Mona still felt bad about that and wondered if that was why they'd decided to leave her there.

It was Molly who'd decided, though, standing there by that window, watching people pop out of the long black helicopter and spread out across the snow.

"Look at that," Molly'd said. "They know. Just come to pick up the pieces. Sense/Net. My ass is out of here."

Cherry slurred that they were leaving too, she and Slick. And Slick shrugged, then grinned and put his arm around her.

"What about me?"

Molly looked at her. Or seemed to. Couldn't really tell, with the glasses. White tooth showed against her lower lip, for just a second, then she said, "You stay, my advice. Let them sort it out.

You haven't really done anything. None of it was your idea. Think they'll probably do right by you, or try to. Yeah, you stay."

It didn't make any sense to Mona, but now she felt so dead, so crash-sick, she couldn't argue.

And then they were just gone, down the rope and gone, and it was just like that, how people left and you didn't ever see them anymore. She looked back into the room and saw Gentry pacing back and forth in front of his books, running the tip of his finger along them like he was looking for a special one. He'd thrown a blanket over the stretcher.

So she just left, and she wouldn't know if Gentry ever found his book or not, but that was how it was, so she climbed down the rope herself, which wasn't as easy as Molly and Slick had made it look, particularly if you felt like Mona did, because Mona felt close to blacking out and her arms and legs didn't seem to be working real good anyway, she had to sort of concentrate on making them move, and her nose and throat were swelling inside, so she didn't notice the black guy until she was all the way down.

He was standing down there looking at the big spider thing, which wasn't moving at all. Looked up when the heel of her shoe grated across the steel platform. And something so sad about his face, when he saw her, but then it was gone and he was climbing the metal stairs, slow and easy, and as he got closer she began to wonder if he really was black. Not just the color, which he definitely was, but there was something about the shape of his bald skull, the angles of his face, not quite like anybody she'd seen before. He was tall, real tall. Wore a long black coat, leather so thin it moved like silk.

"Hello, missy," he said, when he stood in front of her, reached out to raise her chin so she was looking straight into gold-flecked agate eyes like nobody in the world ever had. Long fingers so light against her chin. "Missy," he said, "how old are you?"

"Sixteen . . ."

"You need a haircut," he said, and there was something so serious about how he said it.

"Angie's up there," she said, pointing, when she found her voice again. "She's—"

"Hush."

She heard metal noises far away in the big old building, and then a motor starting up. The hover, she thought, the one Molly'd driven here.

The black man raised his eyebrows, except he didn't have any eyebrows. "Friends?" He lowered his hand.

She nodded.

"Good enough," he said, and took her hand to help her down the stairs. At the bottom, still holding her hand, he led her around the wreck of the catwalk thing. Somebody was dead there, camo material and one of those big-voice things like cops have.

"Swift," the black man called, out across that whole tall hollow space, between the black grids of windows without any glass, black lines against a white sky, winter morning, "get your ass over here. I found her."

"But I'm not her. . . ."

And over there where the big doors stood open, against the sky and snow and rust, she saw this suit come walking, with his coat open and his tie flapping in the wind, and Molly's hover swung past him, out those same doors, and he wasn't even looking, because he was looking at Mona.

"I'm not Angie," she said, and wondered if she ought to tell him what she'd seen, Angie and the young guy together on that little screen, just before it faded.

"I know," the black man said, "but it grows on you."

*Rapture. Rapture's coming.*

# FORTY-THREE

# JUDGE

The woman led them to a hovercraft parked inside Factory, if you could call it parking when the front end was mashed up around a concrete tool mount. It was a white cargo job with CATHODE CATHAY lettered across the rear doors, and Slick wondered when she'd managed to get it in there without him hearing it. Maybe while Bobby the Count was pulling his diversion with the blimp.

The aleph was heavy, like trying to carry a small engine block.

He didn't want to look at the Witch, because there was blood on her blades and he hadn't made her for that. There were a couple of bodies around, or parts of them; he didn't look at that either.

He looked down at the block of biosoft and its battery pack and wondered if all that was still in there, the gray house and Mexico and 3Jane's eyes.

"Wait," the woman said. They were passing the ramp to the room where he kept his machines; the Judge was still there, the Corpsegrinder . . .

She still had her gun in her hand. Slick put his hand on Cherry's shoulder. "She said wait."

"That thing I saw, last night," the woman said. "One-armed robot. That work?"

"Yeah . . ."

"Strong? Carry a load? Over rough ground?"

"Yeah."

"Get it."

"Huh?"

"Get it into the back of the hover. Now. Move."

Cherry clung to him, weak-kneed from whatever it was that girl had given her.

"You," Molly gestured toward her with the gun, "into the hover."

"Go on," Slick said.

He set the aleph down and walked up the ramp and into the room where the Judge was waiting in the shadows, the arm beside it on the tarp, where Slick had left it. Now he wouldn't ever get it right, how the saw was supposed to work. There was a control unit there, on a row of dusty metal shelves. He picked it up and let the Judge power up, the brown carapace trembling slightly.

He moved the Judge forward, down the ramp, the broad feet coming down one-two, one-two, the gyros compensating, perfecting for the missing arm. The woman had the rear doors of the hover open, ready, and Slick marched the Judge straight over to her. She fell back slightly as the Judge towered over her, her silver glasses reflecting polished rust. Slick came up behind the Judge and started figuring the angles, how to get him in there. It didn't make sense, but at least she seemed to have some idea of what they were doing, and anything was better than hanging around Factory now, with dead people all over. He thought about Gentry, up there with his books and those bodies. There'd been two girls up there, and they'd both looked like Angie Mitchell. Now one of them was dead, he didn't know how or why, and the woman with the gun had told the other one to wait. . . .

"Come on, come on, get the fucking thing in, we gotta go. . . ."

When he'd managed to work the Judge into the back of the hover, legs bent, on its side, he slammed the doors, ran around, and climbed in on the passenger side. The aleph was between the front seats. Cherry was curled in the backseat, under a big orange parka with the Sense/Net logo on the sleeve, shivering.

The woman fired up the turbine and inflated the bag. Slick thought they might be hung on the tool mount, but when she reversed, it tore away a strip of chrome and they were free. She swung the hover around and headed for the gates.

On the way out they passed a guy in a suit and tie and a tweed overcoat, who didn't seem to see them. "Who's that?"

She shrugged.

"You want this hover?" she asked. They were maybe ten kilos from Factory now and he hadn't looked back.

"You steal it?"

"Sure."

"I'll pass."

"Yeah?"

"I did time, car theft."

"So how's your girlfriend?"

"Asleep. She's not my girlfriend."

"No?"

"I get to ask who you are?"

"A businesswoman."

"What business?"

"Hard to say."

The sky above the Solitude was bright and white.

"You come for this?" He tapped the aleph.

"Sort of."

"What now?"

"I made a deal. I got Mitchell together with the box."

"That was her, the one who fell over?"

"Yeah, that was her."

"But she died. . . ."

"There's dying, then there's dying."

"Like 3Jane?"

Her head moved, like she'd glanced at him. "What do you know about that?"

"I saw her, once. In there."

"Well, she's still in there, but so's Angie."

"And Bobby."

"Newmark? Yeah."

"So what'll you do with it?"

"You built those things, right? One in the back, the others?"

Slick glanced back over his shoulder to where the Judge was folded in the hover's cargo space, like a big rusty headless doll. "Yeah."

"So you're good with tools."

"Guess so."

"Okay. I got a job for you." She slowed the hover beside a ragged crest of snow-covered scrap and coasted to a halt. "There'll be an emergency kit in here, somewhere. Get it, get up on the roof, get me the solar cells and some wire. I want you to rig the cells so they'll recharge this thing's battery. Can you do that?"

"Probably. Why?"

She sank back in the seat and Slick saw that she was older than he'd thought, and tired. "Mitchell's in there now. They want her to have some time, is all. . . ."

"They?"

"I dunno. Something. Whatever I cut my deal with. How long you figure the battery'll hold out, if the cells work?"

"Couple months. Year, maybe."

"Okay. I'll hide it somewhere, where the cells can get the sun."

"What happens if you just cut the power?"

She reached down and ran the tip of her index finger along the thin cable that connected the aleph to the battery. Slick saw her fingernails in the morning light; they looked artificial. "Hey, 3Jane," she said, her finger poised above the cable, "I gotcha." Then her hand was a fist, which opened, as though she were letting something go.

Cherry wanted to tell Slick everything they were going to do when they got to Cleveland. He was lashing two of the flat cells to the Judge's broad chest with silver tape. The gray aleph was already fastened to the machine's back with a harness of tape. Cherry said she knew where she could get him a job fixing rides in an arcade. He wasn't really listening.

When he'd gotten it all together, he handed the control unit to the woman.

"Guess we wait for you now."

"No," she said. "You go to Cleveland. Cherry just told you."

"What about you?"

"I'm going for a walk."

"You wanna freeze? Maybe wanna starve?"

"Wanna be by my fucking self for a change." She tried the controls and the Judge trembled, took a step forward, another.

"Good luck in Cleveland." They watched her walk out across the Solitude, the Judge clumping along behind her. Then she turned and yelled back, "Hey, Cherry! Get that guy to take a bath!"

Cherry waved, the zippers of her leather jackets jingling.

# FORTY-FOUR

## RED LEATHER

Petal said that her bags were waiting in the Jaguar. "You won't want to be coming back to Notting Hill," he said, "so we've arranged something for you in Camden Town."

"Petal," she said, "I have to know what has happened to Sally."

He started the engine.

"Swain was blackmailing her. Forcing her to kidnap—"

"Ah. Well then," he interrupted, "I see. Shouldn't worry, if I were you."

"I am worried."

"Sally, I would say, has managed to extricate herself from that little matter. She's also, according to certain official friends of ours, managed to cause all record of herself to evaporate, apparently, except for a controlling interest in a German casino. And if anything's happened to Angela Mitchell, Sense/Net hasn't gone public with it. All of that is done with, now."

"Will I see her again?"

"Not on *my* parish. Please."

They pulled away from the curb.

"Petal," she said, as they drove through London, "my father told me that Swain—"

"Fool. Bloody fool. Rather not talk about it now."

"I'm sorry."

The heater was working. It was warm in the Jaguar, and Kumiko was very tired now. She settled back against red leather and closed her eyes. Somehow, she thought, her meeting with 3Jane had freed her of her shame, and her father's answer of her anger. 3Jane had been very cruel. Now she saw her mother's cruelty as well. But all must be forgiven, one day, she thought, and fell asleep on the way to a place called Camden Town.

# FORTY-FIVE

# SMOOTH STONE
# BEYOND

They have come to live in this house: walls of gray stone, roof of slate, in a season of early summer. The grounds are bright and wild, though the long grass does not grow and the wildflowers do not fade.

Behind the house are outbuildings, unopened, unexplored, and a field where tethered gliders strain against the wind.

Once, walking alone among the oaks at the edge of that field, she saw three strangers, astride something approximately resembling a horse. Horses are extinct, their line terminated years before Angie's birth. A slim, tweed-coated figure was in the saddle, a boy like a groom from some old painting. In front of him, a young girl, Japanese, straddled the horse thing, while behind him sat a pale, greasy-looking little man in a gray suit, pink socks and white ankles showing above his brown shoes. Had the girl seen her, returned her gaze?

She has forgotten to mention this to Bobby.

Their most frequent visitors arrive in dawn dreams, though once a grinning little kobold of a man announced himself by thumping repeatedly on the heavy oak door, demanding, when she ran to open it, "that little shit Newmark." Bobby introduced this creature as the Finn, and seemed delighted to see him. The Finn's decrepit jacket exuded a complex odor of stale smoke, ancient solder, and pickled herring. Bobby explained that the Finn was always welcome. "Might as well be. No way to keep him out, once he wants in."

3Jane comes as well, one of the dawn visitors, her presence sad and tentative. Bobby seems scarcely aware of her, but Angie, the repository of so many of her memories, resonates to that particular mingling of longing, jealousy, frustration, and rage. Angie has come to understand 3Jane's motives, and to forgive her—though what, exactly, wandering amid these oaks in sunlight, is there to forgive?

But dreams of 3Jane sometimes weary Angie; she prefers other dreams, particularly those of her young protégé. These often come as the lace curtains billow, as a first bird calls. She rolls closer to Bobby, closes her eyes, forms the name *Continuity* in her mind, and waits for the small bright images.

She sees that they have taken the girl to a clinic in Jamaica, to treat her addiction to crude stimulants. Her metabolism fine-tuned by a patient army of Net medics, she emerges at last, radiant with health. With her sensorium expertly modulated by Piper Hill, her first stims are greeted with unprecedented enthusiasm. Her global audience is entranced by her freshness, her vigor, the delightfully ingenuous way in which she seems to discover her glamorous life as if for the first time.

A shadow sometimes crosses the distant screen, but only for an instant: Robin Lanier has been found strangled, frozen, on the mountainscaped facade of the New Suzuki Envoy; both Angie and Continuity know whose long strong hands throttled the star and threw him there.

But a certain thing eludes her, one special fragment of the puzzle that is history.

At the edge of oak shadow, beneath a steel and salmon sunset, in this France that isn't France, she asks Bobby for the answer to her final question.

They waited in the drive at midnight, because Bobby had promised her an answer.

As the clocks in the house struck twelve, she heard the hiss of tires over gravel. The car was long, low and gray.

Its driver was the Finn.

Bobby opened the door and helped her in.

In the backseat sat the young man she recalled from her glimpse of the impossible horse and its three mismatched riders. He smiled at her, but said nothing.

"This is Colin," Bobby said, climbing in beside her. "And you know the Finn."

"She never guessed, huh?" the Finn asked, putting the car in gear.

"No," Bobby said, "I don't think so."

The young man named Colin was smiling at her. "The aleph is an approximation of the matrix," he said, "a sort of model of cyberspace. . . ."

"Yes, I know." She turned to Bobby. "Well? You promised you'd tell me the *why* of When It Changed."

The Finn laughed, a very strange sound. "Ain't a why, lady. More like it's a what. Remember one time Brigitte told you there was this other? Yeah? Well, that's the what, and the what's the why."

"I do remember. She said that when the matrix finally knew itself, there was 'the other.'. . ."

"That's where we're going tonight," Bobby began, putting his arm around her. "It isn't far, but it's—"

"Different," the Finn said, "it's real different."

"But what is it?"

"You see,' Colin said, brushing aside his brown forelock, a gesture like a schoolboy's in some antique play, "when the matrix attained sentience, it simultaneously became aware of *another* matrix, another sentience."

"I don't understand," she said. "If cyberspace consists of the sum total of data in the human system . . ."

"Yeah," the Finn said, turning out onto the long straight empty highway, "but nobody's talkin' *human*, see?"

"The other one was somewhere else," Bobby said.

"Centauri," Colin said.

Can they be teasing her? Is this some joke of Bobby's?

"So it's kinda hard to explain why the matrix split up into all those hoodoos 'n' shit, when it met this other one," the Finn said, "but when we get there, you'll sorta get the idea. . . ."

"My own feeling," Colin said, "is that it's all so much more amusing, this way. . . ."

"Are you telling me the truth?"

"Be there in a New York minute," said the Finn, "no shit."